"I am sorry for any inconvenience I have caused you in coming here, but I promise you my scheming days have ended."

Peter drew in a breath, hesitant to acknowledge her former feelings.

"It's over and done with now," he said. "I have made my position clear. If you will accept it, then we will speak no more of it."

Accept that he never wanted a family, that he didn't want her? Trudy would be lying to herself to say his rejection didn't still sting, but yes, she had accepted it. "Very well," she said.

He offered her a curt nod. With no further business, Trudy turned and left.

Give her marks for candor, Peter thought as he watched her walk away. *And for grit.* She was fast becoming his right-hand man—or woman, rather. She was definitely staff material—efficient, freethinking… *But it comes at a price.* He stopped that thought, reminding himself then that the matter had been settled.

Still, his thoughts betrayed him. *In another time, in another place…*

Shannon Farrington and her husband have been married for over twenty years, have two children, and are active members in their local church and community. When she isn't researching or writing, you can find Shannon visiting national parks and historical sites or at home herding her small flock of chickens through the backyard. She and her family live in Maryland.

Books by Shannon Farrington

Love Inspired Historical

Her Rebel Heart
An Unlikely Union
Second Chance Love
The Reluctant Bridegroom
Frontier Agreement
Handpicked Family

SHANNON FARRINGTON

Handpicked Family

⬦H HARLEQUIN® LOVE INSPIRED® HISTORICAL

Recycling programs
for this product may
not exist in your area.

 LOVE INSPIRED BOOKS

ISBN-13: 978-1-335-36973-4

Handpicked Family

Copyright © 2018 by Shannon Farrington

All rights reserved. Except for use in any review, the reproduction or utilization of this work in whole or in part in any form by any electronic, mechanical or other means, now known or hereafter invented, including xerography, photocopying and recording, or in any information storage or retrieval system, is forbidden without the written permission of the editorial office, Love Inspired Books, 195 Broadway, New York, NY 10007 U.S.A.

This is a work of fiction. Names, characters, places and incidents are either the product of the author's imagination or are used fictitiously, and any resemblance to actual persons, living or dead, business establishments, events or locales is entirely coincidental.

This edition published by arrangement with Love Inspired Books.

® and TM are trademarks of Love Inspired Books, used under license. Trademarks indicated with ® are registered in the United States Patent and Trademark Office, the Canadian Intellectual Property Office and in other countries.

www.Harlequin.com

Printed in U.S.A.

Two are better than one;
because they have a good reward for their labour.
For if they fall, the one will lift up his fellow...
and a threefold cord is not quickly broken.
—*Ecclesiastes* 4:9–12

For Erin

A modern-day, mission-minded angel of mercy

Chapter One

Shenandoah Valley, Virginia
July 1865

Trudy Martin took one look at the ragtag collection
of men blocking the road and pulled the wagon to an
abrupt stop. She had not had much experience handling
buckboards before. In fact, this was a first, and she had
only learned to do so today out of necessity. Her friend
Emily Mackay was teaching her because the teamster
scheduled to drive had not showed. Neither had their
armed Federal escorts, intended to protect this party
from any thieves or malcontents they might meet along
their journey.

How I wish for their presence now, Trudy thought.

Fear snaked up her spine, for even though the approaching crowd consisted mostly of gaunt-faced, frail-
looking war veterans, some missing arms and hobbling
on crutches, she saw the expression of determination
on their faces.

They are just hungry people, she tried to tell herself, but Trudy knew full well that desperation often bred trouble.

Beside her Emily drew in a nervous breath. "They know we have food," she whispered, "and I fear they intend to claim it."

Emily's husband, Dr. Evan Mackay, pulled a matching buckboard alongside them and paused. His lanky, rib-boned mare gave a snort as if to say she, too, was wary of the approaching men. *With good reason*, Trudy couldn't help but think. *Meat is meat no matter how poor the quality.*

She scolded herself for the dark thought, but she knew from what the Mackays had told her, as well as from the articles she'd been proofreading for her employer's newspaper, that here in western Virginia, food was scarce. The country had just endured four years of war and the Confederacy a humiliating surrender—but not before the land they had claimed as an independent nation had been ravaged by Federal forces. Families had been destroyed, and unemployment was widespread. Any soldier fortunate enough to return with his mind and body still intact was hard-pressed to find gainful work, but here, the devastation was particularly acute.

Desperation doesn't even begin to describe this, she thought. *How can the people expect to move forward when all they once had is in ruins?* Nine months after the Federal army had scorched this land it was still as desolate as the moors of Scotland.

Trudy glanced heavenward, noting the angry gray sky. *Rain is on its way*, she thought, *perhaps even a thunderstorm.* She shivered, half because of the changing weather, half because of the still approaching men.

"Just keep on with the plan," Dr. Mackay said calmly.

The plan had been to offer what help they could to a little community that had seen more than its share of hardship and horror. How exactly the town of Forest Glade had been chosen, Trudy could not say, but when she had learned this was to be the team's destination, she'd jumped at the chance to be part of it. Her brother, George, had repeatedly marched and fought through this valley in his service to the Confederacy. He had also been wounded here. But for the grace of God and a kind minister named James Webb, he might not have survived.

George had been treated for his wounds at the church in Forest Glade. Her brother, who had told her about the events in subsequent letters, was currently in a Federal prison, still awaiting release. He could not come and express his thanks to Reverend Webb, but she could.

Also, as a former volunteer nurse from the Baltimore military hospital, Trudy had been confident that she could offer assistance. Dr. Mackay and Emily had thought so, as well. And yet while they had organized this relief mission, they had not initiated this trip. The original invitation had come by way of Trudy's employer, Peter Allen Carpenter. As publisher and editor of *The Free American*, a Baltimore-based newspaper, Mr. Carpenter had taken it upon himself to report firsthand on the devastation leveled upon this once beautiful valley, and had sought to bring others who could provide different kinds of assistance.

He had asked for the Mackays' help.

Mr. Carpenter had *not* asked for Trudy.

He *had* asked for assistance from Trudy's brother-in-law, David Wainwright, wanting an additional writer to help with his coverage. *What will he say when he sees that David has not come?* she wondered. *And worse, that I am here in his place?*

David was a top-notch reporter with a nose for sniffing out corruption. He was as committed to justice and truth as Mr. Carpenter, but unlike their employer, he was also a family man. Elizabeth was now expecting her first child and suffering severe sickness. David, the anxious father-to-be, had been hesitant to leave his wife behind. For reasons not entirely concerning Elizabeth's welfare, Trudy had persuaded David to remain in Baltimore and let her go to Virginia in his stead. Though she wasn't a reporter, she should still be able to assist Mr. Carpenter in his work. She'd been doing so for quite a while, working for him at the paper.

She had boasted of her nursing and editorial skills as well as her ability to take orders and deal with privations. She had insisted Dr. Mackay and Mr. Carpenter would well protect her. She had assured her brother-in-law that she was the best person for the job. However, it wasn't until Mr. Collins, the acting editor in Mr. Carpenter's absence, contracted influenza that David finally agreed to remain in Baltimore. He would look after the newspaper, and all other concerns at home.

"This is best for everyone," Trudy had told him, but now, admittedly, she was having second thoughts. Her brother-in-law had been a soldier. He knew how to marshal and manage unruly men. Her desire to help the people here was genuine, but her reason for wanting to come on this mission had not been entirely humanitarian. A romantic interest had initially played a part.

Her employer, Mr. Carpenter, was a sizable man with a commanding voice and a confident air. He was brave, honorable and wholly committed to the ideals of justice and truth. Never mind that he walked with a limp, an injury of birth. Never mind he was ten years her senior. She'd been smitten the moment she met him—right up until he had told her in no uncertain terms that he would never marry.

She had learned that the day before he had departed for Virginia, the day it had also become public knowledge that Elizabeth was with child.

"Isn't it wonderful?" Trudy had said to him when sharing the news.

"Wonderful?" he repeated. "Hardly. Unfortunate, I would say."

Unfortunate? What kind of response was that? Trudy, though had tried to give him the benefit of the doubt. Mr. Carpenter was a master with words when he put them on paper, not so always when addressing others. "You mean it's unfortunate that your best sketch artist will now be limited in her newspaper duties?" Elizabeth and David made a formidable team, with him writing engaging stories and her sketching the images that brought them to life.

"No," he said. "I was referring to the other matter. Only a foolish man would bring a child into this world."

Trudy had gasped. "You can't be serious?"

"I assure you, I am completely serious. This world is a dangerous, deadly place, Miss Martin. Apparently you've yet to realize that."

Call her naive, for she knew she had a tendency to lean in that direction, but she'd seen her share of suffering. She told him so. Her father had died when she was but a child. Her brother had gone to war and then was left to rot in a Federal prison. She knew life had its struggles, but not all of it was bad. Families, children were the *hope* of the future, the promise of a better tomorrow.

Mr. Carpenter, however, thought just the opposite. "I'll never bring children into this world."

Pain, disappointment raked her heart, for she had felt all her aspirations concerning him going up in smoke. "Then you'll never wed?"

"I'm wed to my paper," he explained. "I'm committed to justice and reform. If you are going to work for me then you had better be likewise committed and put any other ideas you have out of your mind."

Her sister, Beth, had teased her by insisting that Trudy's interest in her employer had been written all over her face as clearly as a typeset page—a charge Trudy had denied. Apparently Mr. Carpenter, though, had read that news. Why else would he have spoken so adamantly about remaining an unmarried man?

Her embarrassment in revealing her feelings as well as her disappointment had been overwhelming. She wanted children. She wanted a home. As handsome, as courageous and committed to the truth as Peter Carpenter was, he was not the man for her.

By the time Trudy had learned this news, however, she had already convinced David to stay in Baltimore, and had promised the Mackays that she would assist them in his place. Whatever discomfort she felt concerning Mr. Carpenter and he her, they would simply have to overlook. She would not go back on her word. The Mackays were counting on her but admittedly, in this moment, she wondered how much help she could actually be to them.

The men were drawing closer. "We heard yun's got food," one of them shouted. "That true?"

"Aye, 'tis so," Dr. Mackay called back. "Meet us at the church in Forest Glade at one o'clock and we will assist you there."

"But we're hungry now."

"I realize that," Dr. Mackay said as the raindrops began to fall, "but we've had some difficulty getting here and we must take stock of our supplies."

Some difficulty indeed, Trudy thought sadly.

An entire wagon load of supplies had gone missing somewhere between Winchester, where they had previously counted a full shipment of goods, and the last rail stop in Mount Jackson. How that had happened Trudy couldn't say. Her heart was grieved at the thought of what they had lost. Several Ladies Aid societies and Baltimore churches had raised the funds and supplies necessary for this journey. Trudy could only hope that whoever had commandeered their supplies had done so because they were in even more desperate need than the people in front of her.

"How do we know you'll be there at one o'clock?" A tall man asked. "Don't trust no Yankees."

"Actually, we're from Maryland," Trudy said. Her announcement did not have the effect she had hoped.

"Even worse," the man sneered. "Yun's talk outta both sides of your mouth. You promise help and then don't deliver."

At that comment Trudy couldn't help but take offense. She knew there was suspicion in the South toward the border states like Maryland—slave states that had not seceded from the Union. But she couldn't help thinking it was unfair, especially when so many Maryland men had left to enlist in the Confederacy. *My brother certainly delivered*, she wanted to say. A knowing nudge from Emily, though, and a sharp, albeit well-meaning glance from Dr. Mackay kept her quiet. Obviously they thought the less she said right now the better.

Trudy reckoned that was wise advice, for as the group approached she studied the tall man who appeared to be the leader. Although his frock coat was full of holes and his boots had nearly just as many, Trudy recognized he was not to be tangled with. The look in his eyes scared her. She had seen it before in the faces of wounded soldiers at the hospital, the ones who had been through the worst of battle and were unable to forget. *The ones who are haunted by hate*, she thought.

Emily recognized it, too. "Perhaps it's a good thing our planned military escorts did not arrive," she whispered. "Their blue uniforms would only add fuel to the fire."

Trudy swallowed back the lump in her throat. Had she already done so by announcing they had come from Maryland? The man with the vengeful eyes was studying her intently.

"Gentlemen," Dr. Mackay said, "I understand your frustration."

"You don't know nothin'," the leader retorted. "You're a Yankee. You're used to hot meals and warm beds."

"Aye. 'tis true that I'm from the North," Dr. Mackay admitted. "Pennsylvania. Before that, Scotland, but I'm not here as a soldier. I'm here as a Christian offering aid."

"Well, we'll see about that."

The rain had stopped but still Trudy shivered. The other two able-bodied men in the group were carrying pitchforks. As for the ones hobbling on crutches, no one knew what they concealed in their clothing.

And here I sit helpless beside Emily. If David were here, he could help protect her. What real use am I? If something happens to her, to her husband, what about poor little baby Andrew?

Emily had sacrificed time with her precious seven-month-old son to come to Virginia. Andrew was home in Baltimore with Emily's parents.

Determined to do her best by the baby and his mother, Trudy stole a glance to her right, then her left. The road on which they were presently parked was sunken, with high banks on both sides. Even the most skilled teamster would find escape impossible. She looked again at Dr. Mackay. Trudy knew he would do his best to defend them both, but he was severely outnumbered.

It was then that a pair of riders crested the knoll. One was dressed in the black garb of a parson. At sight of the other, Trudy's heart skipped a beat. She would have recognized those broad shoulders anywhere. Peter Carpenter was riding toward them.

Oh Lord. Thank you!

"Gentlemen," Peter called in his typical commanding voice as he approached. "It was determined that you should come to the church this afternoon to receive assistance."

"We don't want to wait," the tall leader retorted.

"I realize that, Mr. Zimmer, Mr. O'Neil, Mr. Jones," he said, addressing the two with the pitchforks, as well, "but it's only fair to the other folks in the area to wait. Come to the church at one and we will see to your needs."

Trudy felt her anxiety slipping away. *They will listen to him*, she thought.

The parson had caught up to him. The poor man looked as weathered and threadbare as his parishioners. While he continued the conversation with the disgruntled men, Mr. Carpenter urged his horse toward Dr. Mackay's wagon.

"Where's the other buckboard?" he asked.

"Part of our shipment was mislaid," Dr. Mackay said.

"Stolen?" Mr. Carpenter clarified.

"It looks that way." Dr. Mackay then explained how the Federal escorts had never arrived. "I thought it more foolish to remain idle at the station, so we started for our destination."

Mr. Carpenter grumbled in agreement. Then he noticed her. His left eyebrow arched. "What are you doing here?"

She was used to his curt tone and unpolished manners. *But this is not surprise speaking*, she thought. It was obvious disapproval. It wasn't as though she had expected open arms, but still…did he think she had followed him here purposefully, relentlessly intent on claiming him as a husband? That certainly wasn't the case now.

But will he believe that? "David couldn't come," she said with all the steadiness of voice she could muster.

"So I see."

She started to tell him why but he clearly didn't care to hear it now. "I've already plenty of responsibility, Miss Martin," he said. "I've no need for more." And at that he whipped his horse back in the direction of the men.

Irritated couldn't even begin to describe what Peter was feeling in that moment. *Furious* perhaps was more like it. No doubt Miss Martin had some plausible excuse for deliberately inserting herself into these events, but he didn't have time for it now, not when a pack of unruly, hungry men were pressing their grievances.

Reverend James Webb, the underfed and overwhelmed parson of these parts, was still trying to assuage the fears of those gathered. "I assure you, Jack, Tom, Arthur, there will be food for all, if you'll only let these people get it organized."

"How d' we know if you'll still have food by one o'clock?" Jack Zimmer yelled.

"How do we know ya won't give it to someone else?" Tom O'Neil added.

As the men continued to pepper the parson with questions, Peter stealthily felt for the derringer tucked discreetly inside his frock coat pocket. Yes, this was a mission of mercy but he was not about to be *at the mercy* of a riotous mob. He'd seen what desperate men could do before. Back in 1861, an unruly pack in Baltimore had rioted and brought about the opening bloodshed of four years of war.

And for what good? Peter thought. The result was that a generation of America's brightest and best were dead and the country was reunified in name only. Southerners hated Northerners and vice versa, and the freedmen who'd once been controlled by slave masters were now victims of an ineffective Federal bureaucracy. The promise of a more perfect union for all had yet to be fulfilled and Peter took that offense personally. He'd had two brothers give their lives in the hope of a better tomorrow and he was determined not to let their sacrifices be in vain.

Sadly he wasn't surprised by Dr. Mackay's report

that the Federal escorts had deserted the wagon convoy, nor that a shipment of supplies had been stolen. Who'd taken it…well, of that he couldn't be sure. He'd met more than one US soldier who'd rather see Southerners starve, and just as many Southerners who would steal or kill to prevent that from happening.

Clutching the derringer, he cast a quick glance at Miss Martin. *And she has no idea what she has stepped into. This is no place for a lady. Mrs. Mackay has a husband to look after her.* Peter knew that because Miss Martin was his employee, her welfare would now fall to him. *And that's the last thing I need.* He already had a woman for whom he needed to claim responsibility— as soon as he could find her. *Caroline.* Caroline Carpenter. His brother's widow.

His thoughts quickly returned to the Baltimore belle before him. *Foolish woman,* he thought. *I never should have hired her.* He told himself he should have known from the beginning that her naive boldness would be trouble. He remembered vividly the day she had stepped into his office. "My sister tells me you are in need of workers for your newspaper," she had said. "I'm here to apply."

He'd stared at her for a moment, half in shock, half in admiration over her straightforward approach. Most women seemed somewhat intimidated by him. Even now her sister Elizabeth still had a tendency to call him "sir."

"What can you do?" he'd asked.

Miss Martin had confessed that, unlike her sister, she had no artistic talents, but that she had a good grasp of grammar and had won numerous spelling medals in school. "I thought you might be in need of a proofreader."

In actuality, he had been, and he had offered her a position on a trial basis. She had excelled in her tasks, and soon Peter had offered her the position permanently. Truth be told, she had been a great help to him. *Up until the point she pegged me for a husband. I thought I had put a stop to that. Evidently she did not take the hint.*

In that instant Jack Zimmer rightfully reclaimed his attention. His voice was growing more emphatic with each word he spoke. "Look, preacher, we aren't leaving here till you give us some food."

Jones and O'Neil were armed with pitchforks. The others were lame, but taken collectively, they could still be a considerable force. Peter assessed his own strength. If he stayed on his horse he'd have the upper hand, *but Zimmer knows my weakness. If he forces me to the ground I'll be useless.* He glanced at Reverend Webb. *Preacher won't fight. He's a man of peace. And Dr. MacKay is closest to the women...*

The derringer was his only safeguard. Although he despised the thought of firing it, he would do so if it came to that. Miss Martin had left him little other choice. Hopefully just showing it would be enough.

"We can give you all a little something now," she suddenly announced.

Everyone, including Peter, immediately turned in her direction. That naive, hopeful look was on her face. *Have mercy*, he grumbled to himself.

"We packed small sacks of cornmeal," she said. "We can give you some of that. They are at the back of Dr. Mackay's wagon."

Don't tell them what you have! Peter thought. *Let alone where it is!* But much to his surprise, her offer seemed to defuse the tension.

"It be real flour?" Mr. Jones asked. "None a that ground-up chalk the carpetbaggers bring through?"

"Yes, sir," she said. "Real food. Real cornmeal."

While Jones and O'Neil were pleased enough to drop their pitchforks, Zimmer still didn't look happy. Wheat had been the primary staple before the war. The cattle and the slaves ate the corn. But these people would have to settle for anything they could swallow.

Jones pressed his way to the front of the group. "Well, word or not, I'm not going to pass up the chance for some meal right now. I'll take what's offered."

O'Neil stepped toward the wagons also. Reverend Webb encouraged the others to form a queue. On the principle that some food was better than none, Zimmer joined it, as well.

"What about medicines?" he asked. "People around here are sick."

"Aye," Dr. Mackay said, "but first we must reorganize our supplies. Come to the church. We will do our best by you there."

The situation had been remedied, at least for now. Still Peter kept his guard. With one eye he watched the men. With the other he studied Miss Martin. She was smiling, no doubt pleased with herself and hoping he would be pleased with her. Well, he wasn't, and at the risk of being ungentlemanly, he was going to let her know that.

The cornmeal had been distributed without further incident and the men were now returning to what remained of their homes. Emily was helping her husband resecure the oilcloth cover over their wagon while Trudy held the second one in check. Mr. Carpenter was still on his horse, his back ramrod straight as if poised for battle. Since there had been no skirmish with the hungry men, was he now about to engage her in one? Apparently so, for when the last local man disappeared over the knoll, her employer slid from his horse and lumbered toward her.

He had that look in his eye, the one he showed in the newsroom whenever a reporter missed a deadline or the proof sheets weren't to his liking. Trudy's thoughts tumbled nervously over one another. Inadvertently she tightened her reins. Her horse threw his head in protest. Quickly she tried to correct her mistake but only made matters worse. Now the horse seemed determined to back up.

"No… No… Don't do that! Please, no."

"Loosen the reins, Miss Martin!" Mr. Carpenter commanded as he muscled his way, albeit somewhat awkwardly, into the driver's box. His ink-stained hands reached for hers. Forcefully he commandeered the reins.

"Stand!" he called to the beast.

The horse promptly obeyed. Trudy had no doubt that it would. Even she felt the sudden urge to sit bolt upright at attention.

"You must be more careful."

"Y-yes…" She replied. For a split second she was tempted to call him "sir" but she knew he did not like that title.

"It's Mr. Carpenter or Peter," he'd always said, and although she had wanted to call him by his Christian name, she certainly would not do so now. He might think more of the familiarity than she actually meant.

"Miss Martin," he said as he put on the brake and then turned to her. His probing brown eyes seemed to bore right into her soul. "Why exactly are you here in your brother-in-law's place?"

Trudy swallowed hard. "Exactly?"

"Yes, Miss Martin."

"Well… Mr. Collins is ill and cannot oversee the paper…"

Still the look… Elizabeth called it frightening, like standing before a judge who was eagerly awaiting confession so he might pronounce sentence. Trudy was beginning to understand. *He uses this tactic to assert his authority, to intimidate.* Why hadn't she noticed this about him before?

Do not worry. I've no longer any interest in you whatsoever, she wanted to say, but she had been raised to be a lady. Even if at times she failed to live up to the standard, she was determined now to salvage some shred of dignity. *And a lady wouldn't dare broach the subject of romance with a man.* So she was committed to explain in as few words as possible. After all, she *had* come here for other reasons—ones totally unrelated to him.

"Elizabeth is feeling very poorly—"

"And you thought it best to leave her and come here?"

Guilt threatened to creep back in but she lifted her chin. Elizabeth was fine. She didn't need her help, but according to Emily, the people here did. "David was worried and Mr. Collins is now ill, so he will be caring for his wife and overseeing the paper in your absence."

Mr. Carpenter rolled his eyes at that. She did not stop to ask why. Trudy then explained that her brother had been wounded here. "I wanted to express my thanks to Reverend Webb."

"This is no sightseeing expedition, Miss Martin."

The look he gave her then made her wanted to leap from the wagon, run all the way back to Mount Jackson and climb aboard the first train to Baltimore, but Trudy steeled her resolve.

I have injected myself into his cause, wrongly, perhaps, but it is done and I will see this mission through. "I realize that, Mr. Carpenter," she said firmly, "I am here to render aid, not play the role of a tourist."

"Good," he said in that commanding voice of his. "As a representative of my newspaper I expect you to do your job."

"I shan't do anything else."

"Good," he said once more. "Make certain of that."

I will, she thought as she continued to hold his look. *Believe me, the subject of romance is firmly closed.* He had read her motives once before. Trudy trusted he had read between the lines now, for without further word, her employer disengaged the brake and urged the horse forward.

Chapter Two

It wasn't the encounter with Zimmer and the rest of his rough-looking compatriots that had left Miss Martin silent. It was Peter's remarks that kept her stone still beside him. He felt bad for speaking harshly to her, especially when he accused her of sightseeing, but he told himself it had to be done. She said she had come because of her brother, a desire to help him and the reverend who had tended him. He just wanted to be certain that was her *only* reason.

If she had put the idea of marriage to him out of her mind, then he had been successful. If he had made her reconsider marriage in general, then even better. *If only Caroline had more carefully considered such things before my brother came along.*

The wagon jolted and Miss Martin's arm brushed his. Peter's thoughts returned to her.

Romantic notions aside, he was genuinely concerned for her welfare. *She does not belong here.* Ideally they'd soon go their separate ways. Just as they'd resumed their trek to the church, Dr. Mackay had mentioned the possibility of sending for more supplies. Hopefully Miss

Martin would be the one to return to Baltimore to do so. *It's the best place for her.*

Miss Martin's innocent, open nature was refreshing, but it was also unnerving. *She believes the best about everyone she meets and thinks that love, faith and hope are enough to set the world right.*

His brothers had thought the same.

But hope can't reverse time or raise the dead, Peter thought. *This world is no longer a Garden of Eden, not since jealousy, greed and murder entered it. And in this desolate place, there are too many who would take advantage of that innocence rather than protect it. Better by far for her to be on her way.* He cast Miss Martin a glance as the wagon lurched forward. Silence still reigned.

Presently she was taking in the scenery, but it was not the majestic Blue Ridge Mountains or the rock-dotted Shenandoah River that held her attention. It was the imprint of war. For miles she had viewed charred remains of barns and stables, empty homesteads now covered with vines, but the nearer they came to the town of Forest Glade, the more evident the destruction.

The once prosperous little hamlet on the north fork of the river was now only a shell of its former glory. The flour mill had been destroyed. The sawmill was much the same. Remnants of warped and twisted machinery sat rusting into oblivion. Of the workers' houses opposite the sites, not a structure remained intact.

"This makes me angry," Miss Martin said suddenly.

"It should," Peter replied.

After the space of a heartbeat she then said, "I can't help but wonder what has happened to the people who lived here, who worked here? Are the men we met just now on the road the most desperate of the lot or are there others worse off than they?"

He could hear the emotion in her voice, the compassion. That was another thing he admired about her. At her age most Baltimore belles would be focused on replacing their outdated wardrobes as soon as possible. He gave her a quick once-over. Here she sat in homespun, protected from the rain by only a plain knitted gray shawl and an unembellished straw hat. She looked damp and uncomfortable but she was not complaining.

Again his conscience was pricked. *I did speak harshly to her. Perhaps more harshly than necessary.* "That's what I'm here to find out," he said, "and to hold those responsible who promised to make reparations."

She looked at him with those wide, innocent green eyes. "I'll help you in any way I can," she promised.

Great. He sighed under his breath, for in his opinion she was still a little too eager to help him. Making quite the effort to keep his irritation from coming through in his voice, he then said, "Well, I'm not all that certain how much help you can be. I can't have you going off investigating, gathering information on your own."

She took no offense at that. Thankfully, she realized he didn't doubt her research abilities but her physical safety. "That's why you wanted David," she said.

"Yes," he said simply.

She turned her attention back to the road. So did he. The wagon rocked and bounced over the uneven ground. About a half mile beyond the crossroads stood the church. Its faded white steeple still pointed faithfully toward the rolling gray sky, but vines and thistles were fast consuming its foundation. Boards had been nailed across several broken windows to protect the panes from further damage. Peter couldn't help but wonder what it had looked like when Daniel first saw it, or when Miss Martin's brother had, for that matter.

Were they both here at the same time? Knowing that detail had no bearing on his personal mission, Peter pushed the thought from his mind. As they pulled into the churchyard, Reverend Webb's wife, Sarah, met them. "Thank the Lord for your safe arrival," she said. "I'm so pleased to see all is well."

But not without incident, Peter thought.

Her husband, James, explained what had happened on the road. Peter then reported the lost cargo. The woman's tired face fell even further. "What exactly remains of your supplies?" she asked.

"We'll need to take inventory to be certain of that," Dr. Mackay said.

"Never fear," Miss Martin added, her optimism apparently rebounding. "We can still assist many with what remains."

The Mackays introduced themselves, and then Miss Martin. Mrs. Webb offered her a smile. Eager to converse with the woman, Miss Martin climbed down from the other side of the wagon and hurried to where the reverend's wife stood.

Having secured the reins, Peter gingerly made his way to the ground, listening as Miss Martin explained that her brother had lodged at the church facilities.

"Oh?" Mrs. Webb said.

"Yes, and I was eager to come and thank you and help you in any way I can."

Her enthusiasm was obvious. Peter didn't doubt it was sincere but he couldn't help but think, *You won't*

*be so optimistic when you see the inside of the church.
I'm certain it's a far cry different from your own.*

Half of the pews were missing. According to Reverend Webb, they had been used for firewood, stretch-
ers and crutches following the battle of New Market
when the church had served as a field hospital. Looking
closely at the floor, one could still make out the blood-
stains that had seeped into the wood planks.

Miss Martin noticed them at once. Peter saw the
look of horror wash over her face. However, it quickly
passed. Apparently she was determined to soldier on,
but still in her naive way.

"Are you in need of further seating for your congregation?" she asked the reverend. "Perhaps we can find
someone to craft more pews."

Peter couldn't help but roll his eyes at that. Crafting
pews would not be high on anyone's list around here,
not when homes needed to be rebuilt first.

"Thank you, miss," Reverend Webb said with all
the gentleness of a seasoned saint, "but we have all we
need, at least for those who attend now. Many of our
church members are no more."

"No more?"

"Deceased, miss. The fortunate ones have relocated,
reunited with family elsewhere."

"Oh," she said slowly. "I see."

Do you? Peter wondered. *Do you now see the real
world? For I don't have time to enlighten you.*

There were articles to write on the local provisional
authorities and missing supplies to locate. He also
wanted to assist in the reunion of displaced family members, but there was one particular family member he
was most desperate to find—his brother Daniel's bride.

Caroline. The bride Daniel had no business taking.

Peter drew in a breath. How did one even begin to locate such a woman when no one around here, not even the reverend, seemed to know who she was?

Trudy couldn't help but feel sorry for this poor country preacher. He obviously cared for his community, and the fact that he could no longer account for much of it weighed heavily upon his heart. She laid a hand on the parson's arm, and his dark mustache lifted with a smile.

"We will do all we can to help those people who remain," she said.

"Thank you, miss," he said. "I am most grateful to you and the others. Your coming is such an encouragement."

At least it is to someone, she couldn't help but think, for despite what she had hoped had been a closing conversation, Mr. Carpenter still looked irritated with her. *Or is it simply the circumstances in which we find ourselves?* If that were the case, then she could understand a little of what he was feeling.

Trudy had promised Reverend Webb they would do all they could to serve this community but knew their ability to do so had been diminished severely. The crates that had disappeared en route were the most valuable they carried. The wheat, dried meat and medicines were lost. So was the seed they had brought for planting fall vegetables. Mr. Carpenter had ruefully noted that not only were these items the most valuable in aid but they would also fetch the greatest price on the black market.

"Whoever took them knew exactly what would bring the most profit," he'd said.

Those and his previous words taunted her. *"Only a foolish man would bring a child into this world."*

Whatever his opinion, it doesn't negate the fact that there are children in this world, she thought, *children who require assistance.* In fact, Reverend Webb had already mentioned needy youngsters in his congregation, specifically a six-year-old boy named Charlie, and a baby named Kate. Both were now fatherless because of the war, and their mother was desperate for relief. *Will we be able to provide such?*

"We can wire for more supplies," Emily said, as if reading Trudy's thoughts.

"Yes," she agreed, for Trudy knew the churches and aid societies back in Baltimore would again be generous. *My dearest friends, Julia, Rebekah and Sally will spend long hours gathering and packing what they can.* For four years now they, along with Trudy and Elizabeth, had knitted socks and sewed shirts and other items for those in need. She was confident they would again rise to the occasion.

"We *will* wire back to Baltimore," Dr. Mackay said. "And we will do so straightaway. Reverend Webb says the telegraph office in Larkinsville is still in order."

"It is indeed," Mr. Carpenter said. "The question is, though, will the shipments arrive here intact and in time to help this community? Some of these people will not see August if they do not get regular, proper nourishment soon. If a second shipment goes missing…" He paused as if to let them consider that for a moment. "It won't do us any good to order more supplies while someone out there is stealing them for their own profit."

"We don't know for certain that's what happened," Reverend Webb said.

"Shipments loaded on a train don't just vanish between one rail station and another," Mr. Carpenter insisted.

Trudy's heart squeezed. She knew her employer had a tendency to lean toward cynicism, but she had never seen him quite like this before. His frustration over the lost supplies was now bordering on despair.

"Well, that's where you come in," Dr. Mackay said to him. "I trust you will discover this person or these persons responsible for the missing supplies." He then gestured to Trudy. "And now you even have your experienced newspaper assistant to help you."

She could feel the color rising to her cheeks. Although she had promised to help Mr. Carpenter in whatever way she could, she remembered what he had said earlier, *"I can't have you going off investigating, gathering information on your own."* Based on the irritated look he was still giving her, he obviously didn't want to work alongside her. His words confirmed that.

"From what I have seen of the people in this community, I believe Miss Martin's efforts will be better served in medical endeavors rather than journalism," he said. "She was, after all, a nurse."

"Oh?" Reverend Webb said as Mr. Carpenter left the circle of conversation. "Wonderful. Then I trust you and Mrs. Mackay will work well together."

"We always have," Emily said.

"Indeed," Trudy replied.

Emily then looked to her husband. "Your orders, love?"

The barest hint of a smile tugged at Dr. Mackay's lips. *They are so much in love*, Trudy couldn't help but think. She couldn't help but wonder if someday a man would look at her that way. *It certainly won't be Mr. Carpenter.*

A self-pitying lump threatened to form in Trudy's throat, but she swallowed it back.

"When the people arrive we will need to first assess their conditions outside," Dr. Mackay said. "If there is even the slightest indication of typhus or smallpox, we must immediately isolate them."

Trudy understood. She knew from experience that they could not bring patients bearing such illnesses into close contact with others. They must be quarantined. "Where shall we put them?" she asked.

"My house," Reverend Webb said.

Trudy could tell Dr. Mackay did not like the preacher's sacrifice any more than she, but if typhus or smallpox patients came to them, they had to be treated somewhere. Trepidation wiggled its way up her spine. What would happen if the reverend and his wife took ill? Who would nurse them? What would happen if the entire relief staff took ill?

She pushed those fears from her mind. Dr. Mackay was still speaking.

"We will need to prepare a treatment area for the noninfectious patients here inside the church," he said. "I expect many cases of malnutrition, unhealed wounds and the like."

Under the physician's guidance, Trudy and Emily prepared a medical area for detailed assessment of complaints and treatment. Trudy hoped whatever they encountered would not be serious, given their minimal supplies. They had been left with plenty of soap and bandages, as well as basic surgical instruments, but the case of morphine and ether was gone.

After organizing the treatment area. Trudy helped Sarah Webb sort through what remained of the dry goods and fresh vegetables. They set allotments of equal portions for each potential visitor. Sacrificially, Mrs. Webb had also raided the last of what remained of her own supplies and prepared a soup.

"I'm sorry it isn't more," she lamented, "but between the Confederate requisition armies and then the Yankees, this was all I could hide."

"You must have had a secret compartment in your larder to save as much as this," Trudy said, trying to inject a little lightheartedness into the heavy situation, "or was it the root cellar?"

"Neither," Mrs. Webb admitted, a hint of mirth in her face. "I reburied last year's potatoes and rutabagas in sacks in the garden." The smile then faded. "But I'm afraid this is the end of my resourcefulness."

"You are out of food, as well?"

"Yes. Just about. I managed to save a few of our smallest potatoes for seed this year, but the harvest was very poor. I did come across a patch of ramps the day before you came, though."

Trudy had never heard of ramps before, except for those used in the place of stairs. "What is that?" she asked.

Mrs. Webb again smiled. "It's like a leek. You eat the bulb."

"Oh?"

"They are excellent in soups."

Trudy leaned over the pot. Even as thin as the mixture was, it certainly smelled *excellent*.

Across the way, Mr. Carpenter had set up a desk of sorts, one made out of a piece of salvaged wood and two sawhorses. According to Reverend Webb, he had been collecting names and basic information to locate missing family members, including reconnecting former slaves with loved ones who'd been separated during the war. Apparently he planned to publish notices about the missing in his paper, and convince fellow publishers in other cities to do the same.

It was hard not to admire a man who used his press in such a way. Trudy eyed him stealthily for a moment. Mr. Carpenter's hair was as black as coffee. He had dark eyebrows, a slight cleft in his chin and a strong, handsome jaw. He could have passed for a rich statesman were it not for the crumpled collars and askew cravats he always wore. He had a tendency to tug at them when he worked. He disliked the confinement of frock coats as well, always preferring to roll up his sleeves. He had done so today. Trudy couldn't help but notice once again his muscular forearms.

Catching herself, she shook off such thoughts, remembering that Peter Carpenter had proven he was not the man for her. Yes, he was handsome. Yes, they shared a belief in helping others, but he was not interested in marriage. He didn't want a family.

And he isn't exactly a churchgoing man, she reminded herself. Oh, she knew that he believed in God, but for some reason "organized religion," as he put it, had "no practical use." *So how exactly has he come to know and be on such good terms with the Webbs?* she wondered. Had it been some connection before the war? Her curiosity getting the better of her, she asked Mrs. Webb.

"My husband, James, nursed his brother Daniel after the battle of New Market."

"Oh," Trudy said, her eyes inadvertently going to

the still stained floor. "Mr. Carpenter has never really spoken of him." Although Trudy knew he had a brother. She had learned that detail during the time that she, her mother and her sister had taken shelter in Mr. Carpenter's parents' home outside Baltimore when the city had been threatened by Confederate attack. *He has two, if I remember correctly. Daniel and Matthew.*

"I suppose he wouldn't speak much of him," the preacher's wife said. "It must be very painful."

"Painful?"

"Daniel survived the battle, but wound fever took him and several other Virginia soldiers a week later."

"I see," Trudy said. A cold chill passed through her, but her feeling was not limited to her employer's loss alone. Trudy knew very well that fever could have just as easily taken her own brother.

Mrs. Webb must have recognized it, as well, for she looked at Trudy sympathetically. "I thank the Good Lord that he spared your own brother."

"Indeed," Trudy replied. "And I shall be even more grateful when he is released from prison."

Mrs. Webb patted Trudy's arm. "I pray for him daily, and all those like him. May God grant them the courage and grace to return to peaceful society."

"Amen," Trudy said.

Mrs. Webb then continued with her previous story. "James wrote a letter to your Mr. Carpenter with the terrible news that his brother had passed away. Daniel wanted it that way. I remember him saying he didn't want his parents to learn about the death of their youngest son by letter."

Leaving Mr. Carpenter to deliver the dreadful story.

"And Matthew?" Trudy then asked. "His other brother? Did he survive?"

Sarah Webb shook her head sadly. "I'm afraid I don't know anything about him, except that he was a Yankee."

With that the woman walked away. Trudy resisted the urge to follow after her even if by eyes only. Mrs. Webb had been headed in the direction of Mr. Carpenter's table. Instead Trudy picked up the nearby water pail and marched outside to the pump.

After collecting a bucketful, she took it to the fire to heat. They'd need plenty of wash water to clean and reuse the dishes once people began arriving. While waiting for it to boil, she again glanced heavenward. The sky that had previously been so threatening was beginning to brighten, but an eerie dampness lingered. Trudy remained at the fire for a few minutes more. Even though it was summer, the chill from her wet clothing had reached all the way into her bones.

Or is it my heart? She wondered. She told herself she must be careful with any display of compassion toward her employer, lest he assume she was still infatuated with him. Still, she couldn't help but want to comfort a man she knew must be grieving.

And is he grieving for one brother or two? Trudy, along with most of her friends, had known divided loyalties. Why, her sister, Beth, had married a Boston man who'd served in the Federal army while her brother was being held in a Yankee prison. *But George will gain his freedom and David and Elizabeth are blissfully happy.* What had happened to Mr. Carpenter's family? Was his brother Daniel a husband? A father? Was Matthew? Had he been killed, as well? *Is that why Mr. Carpenter is so against having children of his own?*

Trudy desperately wanted to know. Even though she knew it would be better for her to put the man and his troubles far from her mind. *He wouldn't appreciate sympathy or tenderness.* Showing such would only further irritate him.

I must concentrate on my tasks at hand. I must be prepared. Reverend and Mrs. Webb had given all they had to help her brother in his time of need, and now their little community was facing malnutrition, disease, maybe even starvation. Trudy was determined to spend every ounce of strength she had helping them and their community in return.

Chapter Three

"It is almost one o'clock," Dr. Mackay said as he glanced at his watch. "Our guests will be here soon."

Peter looked up from the article he had been crafting about the need for the army to take a more serious role in protecting food shipments, just long enough to see Mrs. Mackay move to the front window. "They are already here," she said, "and by the looks of things they have formed a line that wraps all the way around the building."

Peter laid aside his pencil and pushed to his feet. He'd finish the piece tonight. Now was the time to be on alert. If the number of people looking for help was that large, there could be trouble.

He had already spoken to Reverend Webb about making certain the men from the road didn't try to claim a second helping of cornmeal. The preacher agreed. As softhearted as he was, he realized better than anyone the necessity for stretching what they had to help as many people as possible.

A story from childhood scripture readings suddenly flashed through Peter's mind, the one about how the

Lord fed five thousand with only five loaves of bread and two small fish. *Daniel's favorite story.* He quickly shoved the memory away. *Reminiscing won't help now.*

"Before we open our doors," Reverend Webb said, "let's pray."

Peter no longer believed in divine intervention, but he wouldn't disrespect the reverend's request. In his mind, God had created the world, then sat back and let it run unimpeded. Evil men had and would continue to have their way. The only thing a decent man could do was try to stem the tide of injustice and look after the people caught in its wake. *People like Caroline and her child.*

Fending off the despair that threatened to wash over him, he moved toward the center of the room, where the rest of the group had already converged, stepping up to the parson and his wife. Mrs. Webb shifted her position at the last second to make more room in the circle. Inadvertently she placed Peter between herself and Miss Martin. He saw the flush come over the young woman's face when the reverend then requested that they all join hands.

What words the preacher actually prayed Peter couldn't say. He was much too conscious of the slenderness and softness of Miss Martin's fingers, testaments again of her sheltered life. She had no idea what heartbreak was waiting for her outside.

She will soon find out. Not that he wished to deliberately hurt her, but someone needed to educate her on the realities of the world today. Peace had been declared and the reconstruction of the Union had begun, but the people outside had been impoverished by their own country. Of the Confederate veterans who had managed to return, few were able-bodied. Arriving home, they found their lands in ruins, and no longer their own, for they had been confiscated by the Federal government.

The only thing taking root around here is the seed of resentment. What will they do if they are given the opportunity to avenge themselves? An angry man may be all too willing to lash out at anyone he can find— even someone as harmless and well-intentioned as Miss Martin.

Of course, not every man out there was a danger or a threat. Many were well-intentioned themselves, simply seeking a way to get on with their lives, but lacking the resources to move forward. The slaves were free, but the freedmen Peter had talked to had been told by Federal authorities to remain on the plantations, let their masters feed and clothe them until the end of this year. *What kind of freedom is that? Their masters have no food to give them. The slaves had been promised forty acres and a mule of their own.* Taking their chances, many were migrating north, seeking work in any form, desperate to be reunited with loved ones.

Peter couldn't help but then think of the ordinary family farms, and the people on them who had simply disappeared. *Who will gain their land? In time enormous profit will be made from these derelict farms, but it isn't going to be claimed by the ones who had once labored on them.*

The world was a cheap mess. Someone was going to profit, of that Peter was certain. Someone always did.

His lame leg was aching. It always bothered him when the weather was damp or he had stood on it for too long. He would have to remember to use his cane. Presently, though, he couldn't remember where he had left it. He shifted his weight just as the reverend offered prayers for the regional garrison commander.

"Bless him, Lord. Give him the wisdom to look after those in his care…"

Peter couldn't help but think that that request, if heard at all, would be better presented on behalf of Reverend Webb himself. In Peter's time here, no leadership, save one overworked preacher trying to shepherd what remained of his refugee flock and protect it from encircling wolves, was doing anything to help.

But for so many, there is nothing to be done. Too many men had gone into battle never to return. Reverend Webb had told him there were at least a dozen surnames in this community that were destined to die out upon the widow's death. Either her sons had perished, leaving her childless, or daughters alone would struggle to carry on a father's legacy.

As for the children Peter had come upon, some weren't even old enough to attend school, meaning they had been born since the start of the war. What had those men been thinking, fathering children while knowing hostilities were on the horizon? Deep down he knew he shouldn't be angry with Daniel, let alone his brother Matthew, for being among them, but he couldn't help it.

Inadvertently, he cast a glance at Miss Martin. Her head was bowed. Her feathery auburn eyelashes rested against her creamy skin. She was the picture of youthful innocence. *The sooner she learns that romance breeds nothing but trouble, the better off she will be.*

Peter released her hand the moment Reverend Webb pronounced his amen. He turned at once, bound for the front door. The preacher had already asked him to greet and give those outside their instructions. Dr. Mackay, however, stopped him.

"Take Miss Martin with you," he said. "She can assess their medical conditions, then direct patients to either me or Emily." He turned to her before Peter had a chance to object. "Remember, no typhus or smallpox inside the church building."

"Yes, sir," she said.

Peter drew in a deep breath. He knew the effects of those two epidemics and didn't like the idea of Miss Martin being the doctor's first line of defense.

"Perhaps you should do the assessing, Doctor," he said.

This time Miss Martin took immediate offense. "I've dealt with infectious diseases before," she said before Mackay could speak.

"Indeed," the doctor then said. He looked back at Peter. "And I've not time to explain to you how to assess patients." He went on to deliver instructions to his brave little nurse. "Make them aware of our stations and send any with acute needs to me, the lesser ones to Emily. You know what to look for. Just like our days in the hospital."

"Yes, of course."

He then handed her several sheets of paper and a pen. "Take down their names, and the location and number in their household if they will divulge such information. It will be helpful to know for future ventures."

"Certainly."

Clearly the matter had been firmly decided. Peter wanted to press that point, but Miss Martin was already headed for the door.

* * *

The chill Trudy had felt previously evaporated the moment Mr. Carpenter had taken hold of her hand. She scolded herself for such a reaction, even though it was only a fleeting feeling. The moment Reverend Webb pronounced the amen, Mr. Carpenter gave her a look as if to tell her he thought the whole arrangement of the circle had been her idea. He then gave Dr. Mackay an almost icy stare when the physician suggested she accompany him outside.

He clearly does not want me here. Evidently he thinks I am unsuited for the task.

Trudy blew out a breath. Determined to prove him wrong, she marched to the front door before her employer could say or do anything else. Stepping outside, however, she gasped. Emily had been correct in saying that line wrapped all the way around the church building. It wasn't the number of people, though, that disturbed Trudy. It was their condition. They were even more desperately downtrodden than the men on the road. Most of them were young women and children. The women were presumably now widows because no man was beside them, *and by the looks of them, no man has taken care of them for quite some time.*

The woman at the head of the line was so thin, so frail in appearance that Trudy wondered how she had remained standing. In her arms she carried a small baby. A little dark-haired boy, five or six years old, was standing beside her. The boy was wearing shoes but his clothing was tattered and full of holes. Through one particular spot Trudy could view his ribs.

Is this Charlie and baby Kate? Trudy wondered. *Is this the family of which Reverend Webb spoke?*

Her heart broke afresh, for there were many others just like them. Looking upon them, her confidence faltered. She had tended frail and malnourished bodies before, but this was quite different! These women and children hadn't volunteered for the cause, yet they had been forced to suffer its cost. *The reverend said there would be children, but somehow I suppose I was still expecting soldiers. I had no idea it would be like this!*

Grief washed over her in waves and she could feel the tears gathering in her eyes. She was so overwhelmed that she didn't know where to start.

"Hold firm, Miss Martin," Mr. Carpenter commanded behind her, but in a voice only she could hear. "These are proud people. They need your assistance, not your pity."

Knowing he was right, and determined to prove she could handle what was expected of her, Trudy drew in a deep breath, steeled her resolve. Just as she moved to descend the porch steps, he caught her arm.

"Let me go first," he said.

"But I must assess—"

"What are the most prominent symptoms of typhus?"

Feeling her own irritation growing, she spouted off the list. "Severe headache, high fever, sensitivity to light, rash on chest and back…although if they have that, they probably won't be standing."

He nodded. "And smallpox?"

"Much the same, but the red spots will first appear on the face."

"That's what I thought," he said. "Now, give me your list. I'll take down their names and assess for those diseases."

"But—"

"Don't argue with me. Go see to that little boy right there. He looks well enough."

He didn't wait for her to respond. He simply took the pen and paper from her. Then he announced to those gathered who they were and what they were about to do.

Trudy knew full well she should not waste time feeling angry over his forceful, take-charge behavior, but she couldn't help herself. *Yes, I faltered for a few seconds, but I am fully capable of discharging my duties.* Then the idea struck her, *Is he trying to protect me?*

Shaking off the thought before her mind could go further with it, she moved to the first mother and children in line. She offered her best smile. "My name is Miss Trudy," she said, bending toward the boy. "What is your name?"

"Charles T. Jackson," he said proudly. "The T is for Thomas, but Ma just calls me Charlie." He gestured to the woman beside him. "This is Ma…and Kate."

Trudy looked then to the woman who said that her name was Opal. Apparently she and the children had walked six miles this morning to come to the church. The distance had taken its toll on Opal's feet. She was wearing makeshift shoes, a slice of hickory bark for each sole, secured by strips of cloth to her ankles. Her stockings, having been darned many times, were now threadbare. Trudy could tell her feet were bruised and blistered. Emily would need to tend them.

"If you'll go just inside and see Mrs. Mackay," she told Opal. "She's the one with the white apron. She'll see to your feet. Mrs. Webb will bring you some soup and I'll see if I can't find a pair of shoes for you."

"Not me," Opal said, "but for Charlie. His shoes are much too small."

Trudy had seen the effects ill-fitting footwear had on the infantry, and if this boy had similar injuries... She pushed the thought away and smiled again at Charlie. "Better let Mrs. Mackay take a peek at your toes, too."

He nodded obediently, but then his attention was stolen by Mr. Carpenter, who was working his way up from the line. Trudy's was, as well.

"No smallpox or typhus," he whispered as he bent his head toward her ear.

Trudy breathed a sigh of relief, then watched as Mr. Carpenter turned and started working his way back down the line. He was leaning heavily on his good leg. She knew his other must be hurting. Presently Mr. Carpenter was taking names and asking questions concerning the local authorities and the missing food.

"That lieutenant over there at the garrison don't concern himself with our matters," Trudy heard one man tell him.

"Wouldn't want no help from him even if he was," another said.

"That man a Yankee?" Charlie asked her, his eyes apparently still focused on Mr. Carpenter. Trudy quickly turned her attention back to the boy. She wasn't certain of the best way to answer his question, given what had happened on the road. "He's not a soldier," she said. "He's a newspaperman. He is trying to find fathers and brothers who are missing."

"Oh," Charlie said. "I wanna be a newspaperman when I git big."

At that, Trudy couldn't help but smile. She gave the boy's dark hair a loving tousle, then moved to the next family in line.

Blisters and minor skin infections were common

sights, but there were plenty of coughs, bleeding gums and bruising, as well. The people's lack of nourishment was manifesting itself in ways beyond thin faces and prominent ribs. Despite the blessed lack of a potential epidemic, her hope was low by the time she reached the end of the line.

A few sacks of cornmeal and Mrs. Webb's soup, generous as it was, aren't going to stem the tide. These people need meat and a regular diet of good nutrition, but she knew full well there wasn't a chicken to be found in all of Virginia, and as for fresh vegetables, there were few now to offer. Still, faith compelled her to remain positive.

If God by his grace will sustain them a few more weeks, Dr. Mackay will send for more seed, more food, more medical supplies. We just have to do the best we can until they arrive.

Lifting her skirt, Trudy marched up the porch steps, intent on helping Sarah Webb distribute the soup and rations. It did not take long. When the last of those in need had been fed, Mrs. Webb offered her and the others a cup. Trudy was most grateful for the meager meal, as were her friends. They eagerly ate what was given—all, that is, except one of them. Mr. Carpenter had accepted his portion, although Trudy noticed he discreetly gave his cup to little Charlie when he thought no one was looking.

By the time darkness had fallen, most of the people had been tended. Miss Martin had efficiently assessed and directed those in need. Peter was relieved. There had been no trouble, socially speaking—no attempt by Zimmer, O'Neil or Jones to collect more food than al-

lotted to them. Reverend Webb had insisted Zimmer
was a bit of a bully but not one of serious action. Blus-
tering was about all he would do.

*What man with a hungry family in these conditions
wouldn't do the same?* he thought. As for Zimmer's
family, Peter had not met them. The distance across the
mountain was too far for them to travel and, apparently
having no pressing medical needs, they had remained
at home. Peter would have liked to have spoken to Zimmer's wife, but he had through his conversations today
learned one important detail. Mrs. Zimmer's name was
not Caroline. Unfortunately, Peter hadn't met any other
Carolines today and no one he had talked to had ever
heard of anyone by the surname Carpenter.

His leg was aching and his belly rumbling. Peter
found a quiet spot in the corner of the room and sat
down. The most serious medical cases, coughs and rein-
fected wounds, remained. Those patients were destined
to sleep on the floor or pews softened by what blankets
Mrs. Webb could spare. He glanced about. The place
looked as pitiful as any wartime field hospital, except
the majority of those in distress were not soldiers. They
were women and children.

Two of the widows in relatively good health had remained for the night rather than risk walking home in
the dark with their small children. Peter wondered if
the real incentive wasn't the opportunity to share in the
church's store of lamp oil and the hope that the reverend's wife might produce more food come morning. If
that was the case, he couldn't blame them. Remembering his frock coat on the back of his chair, he picked it
up, rolled it into a ball and gave it to a particular dark-
haired little boy. He had seen the child eyeing him a

time or two today. Earlier he had given him his cup of
soup because he knew that more than likely, the boy
was still hungry after eating his own share.

"Here, young man, this will serve as a pillow. The
floor can get hard."

The child offered him a crooked, albeit appreciative,
smile. His mother, sitting beside him and cradling a
small baby, looked up at Peter with a measure of surprise and thankfulness. "Bless you, sir," she said.

Ignoring the "sir," Peter crossed back to his makeshift desk, inadvertently casting a glance in Miss Martin's direction. Despite his doubts about her abilities,
particularly after her initial shock, she had done well organizing the people. It had made the day less confusing.
After directing each person where they needed to be,
she had served as a general steward, floating from station to station, serving food, washing cups and bowls,
fetching bandage rolls and emptying basins.

Presently she was seated on the floor, her skirts
spread out around her, tearing a piece of faded fabric into bandage strips. She was studying *him*, with a
somewhat puzzled expression on her face, almost as if
she were trying to decipher his actions.

No doubt she saw what I did with my coat. Peter offered her a look in return. One that said, *No, I have not
changed my mind on bringing children into this world.*
It had the effect he had hoped, for Miss Martin then
quickly returned her attention to the bandage rolls.

He went back to his unfinished article, which he was
certain would not remain unfinished for long. *I have
plenty to say and plenty of fire to fuel it.*

He planned to work on it through the evening and
then, as soon as it was light, ride to Larkinsville. From

there he would wire the article back to his staff in Baltimore, and give notice of the missing supplies so that a new shipment could be arranged. Afterward he planned to have a chat with the local garrison commander. From that he hoped to discover what had happened to the Federal escorts that were supposed to protect the wagon convoy.

He settled himself at his desk and picked up his pencil. Words, however, would not come. His thoughts were in a tangle. Peter had expected his sister-in-law to be heavy on his mind, but for some reason Caroline's image, the face he had tried so desperately to properly assemble based on his brother's written descriptions, was hopelessly crowded out by the very real, very near and very maternal image of Miss Martin. She was now bending over the little boy he had just visited and she was kissing him good-night.

Chapter Four

Peter did finish the article, although it took much longer than he had anticipated. His thoughts didn't clear until Miss Martin left the church building. She and Mrs. Webb went to the parsonage to gain a few hours of much needed sleep.

With the medical supervision squarely in the hands of Dr. Mackay and the night watch falling to Reverend Webb, Peter completed his article, then claimed the empty corner behind his makeshift desk. Curling up on the floor, he closed his eyes. Sleep however, came only in snatches. Thoughts of Daniel, of Caroline stole most of the night.

Daylight was just beginning to break over the Blue Ridge Mountains when Peter saddled his horse and prepared to mount. A polite greeting, however, kept him from doing so.

"Beggin' your pardon, sir. This be the place to git some help?"

Peter blinked, trying his best to focus on the figure emerging from the darkness. It was a freedman. The man was tall and lean with clothes as ragged and ill-fitting as those of the local white men.

"Yes, this is the place for help," Peter replied. "Go on inside and the reverend will see that you get a hot meal."

The freedman nodded. "That's awfully kind of ya, sir, but I was most lookin' for the newspaperman."

"You've found him."

The man stepped closer. He removed his slouch hat and laid it across his chest. "Name's Robert, sir—"

Peter stopped him with an upturned hand. "Enough of this 'sir' business. I'm no army officer. The name's Carpenter. What can I do for you?"

Brilliant white teeth shone in a smile for a fraction of a second. Then Robert looked down and fingered his hat before saying, "I'm looking for my wife, Mr. Carpenter. She went north some years back. I been to see the bureau agent over in Larkinsville but he weren't much help. Then I heard about you."

Peter wondered exactly what the man had heard. He waited to learn for himself.

"Folks say that you're puttin' notices in your paper. That you help find people."

"That's true." Or at least, that was what he was attempting to do. "If you'll give me your information, I'll place the notice."

The man nodded but then hesitated. "Thing is…well, I can't pay."

"If you could, you'd be the first," Peter said.

"I can work, though," Robert said. "You need somethin' fixed? I can do that."

"I'm sure you can," Peter replied. "And believe me, there is plenty to do around here. Go on inside and see the reverend. Get yourself something to eat and we will talk when I get back."

He mounted his horse, then clicked his tongue. The old mare reluctantly lifted her hooves. Peter didn't look back to see with his own eyes, but he knew for certain that the freedman had entered the church. He'd heard the hinges on the front door groan, and then the soft, polite greeting from inside.

Miss Martin. Knowing her, she had probably been watching from the window and came to fetch the man the moment Peter started away. He shook his head but admitted to himself that if the world was different he would be flattered by her attention. She had a comely face in a fresh, pure sort of way. She wasn't a woman taken by powders and rouge. *And she isn't vain enough to try to hide her freckles. She's content with the looks the Creator granted her.* Peter allowed his thoughts to linger there a moment or two longer. Her eyes were green. Her hair was red, not screaming with the intensity of an out-of-control fire but warm, rich, like a slow August sunset.

His brother's description of Caroline's hair then came to mind. *"Like Virginia soil when it is first turned...that rich reddish brown..."*

His jaw inadvertently tightened. If Daniel had paid less attention to the woman standing beside that freshly turned Virginia soil and simply marched through it, Peter wouldn't be looking for a widow and a child. Daniel had written that her father and younger brother had both died early on in the war and her mother had been taken by typhus some years before that.

Peter wondered if Caroline and her child had been able to survive the hardship of war, the sicknesses, the privations. Had she found a family elsewhere? Had she married quickly and passed Daniel's child off as the offspring of another?

A child should know his own father, Peter thought as he broodingly plodded along. *And he will if I have anything to say about it.* He planned to move Caroline and the child in with his parents back in Baltimore, provide for them personally. *And if she has remarried?* Then he would see to it that she and the child were properly cared for and he would keep in contact to make certain it remained that way. *I owe that to my brother's child.* It was hard, however, not to be discouraged. His printed notices in the local area papers concerning Daniel's wife had generated no information. Was he only fooling himself that he could find her?

He thought then of the freedman who had approached him earlier. *Am I only fooling him as well? Can I really hope to find anyone?*

Peter urged the mare to hurry along, although she continued to step gingerly. Where the ground wasn't rocky it was spongy from yesterday's rain. It seemed a metaphor for his state of mind. *Hard facts and muddy uncertainty. Such is life.*

After two hours navigating roots and ruts, he saw the town of Larkinsville ahead. This tiny hamlet had fared better than the others in the surrounding area. The buildings were still standing. The telegraph office was operational. Any damage the town had suffered during the war was being quickly repaired. The smell of fresh lumber was everywhere.

I suppose the presence of a Federal garrison has something to do with that, Peter thought.

He went straight to the telegraph office to dispatch

his article to Baltimore. Then he wired David Wainwright personally concerning the lost supplies. "Don't wire yet with delivery plans," Peter telegraphed. "More information to follow." He knew the charitable citizens of Baltimore would act quickly to fill the present need, but it would take them several days at least to collect another shipment of supplies. In the meantime, Peter hoped to discover what had gone wrong with the first.

Having finished with the telegraph office, Peter then rode to the garrison. A scar-faced sentry forced him to dismount at the gate. After securing the mare, another Bluecoat directed him to the officer in charge, Lieutenant Glassman. The lieutenant was a fresh-faced lad who more than likely had ridden out the war in the comfort of a senior officer's shadow, perhaps a father or uncle. *He probably sheltered in a command post while other men of his age were dying in ditches.*

Still, Peter did his best to cultivate a respectful relationship with the young lieutenant. Not everyone had been able to do his *proper* duty. He knew that better than anyone. *And Glassman is, after all, the local man in charge. Animosity won't serve me or Reverend Webb's community well.*

"Ah, Carpenter," Glassman said as he laid aside the cigar he'd been puffing and leaned back in his desk chair. "I see you are back. Trouble?"

It was only then that Peter noticed the well-dressed man in the corner of the room. The stranger was wearing a silk vest and a brushed cutaway coat. His cravat was adorned with a jeweled pin. Peter sized up the man at once. The clothes and that superior lift of the chin told him he was either a politician or a carpetbagger. *No doubt I'll determine which in a matter of minutes.*

"I hope not," Peter said, in reference to Glassman's remark concerning trouble.

The officer smiled, then cordially gestured toward the guest in the corner. "This is Mr. Johnson."

Peter offered him a nod. Glassman then asked, "So what brings you to see me?"

"Questions," Peter said.

Glassman chuckled softly. "I'd expect nothing less from a newspaperman." He then gave Johnson a toothy grin. "Mr. Carpenter runs a nice little press up in Baltimore."

The word "little" irked Peter, as did the shared laugh between Johnson and the lieutenant. His business here was no laughing matter, and as for his paper, he had churned out more news than many of the big Eastern papers combined. *At least, real news…not war propaganda or plays on public fears.*

"My question…" he said slowly, doing his best to constrain his irritation as he drew the men's attention back to real discussion.

"Yes, yes," Glassman said.

"I've come to find out what happened to the escorts that were supposed to meet the food shipment in Mount Jackson."

Glassman blinked. "Escorts?"

"Yes. I arranged for them here in this office just last week. They did not arrive at the station, and as a result my party had to travel unaccompanied." He then added for emphasis, "There were ladies in the party."

"Egad!" Glassman exclaimed, looking positively chagrined. "Did they arrive safely?"

At least his concern for the ladies does him credit, Peter thought. "They did, but not without several tense moments along the road." He explained what had happened, but he did not give any of the men's names. The lieutenant might decide to arrest the men for unlawful assembly or worse, trying to incite a riot. Peter did not want that. Zimmer and the men of the valley had suffered enough already. What Peter *did* want was to know what had happened to the escorts and, more importantly, the missing supplies.

"Rebel thieves," Johnson said sneeringly when Peter told Glassman about the lost crates.

The lieutenant held his judgment in reserve for now. "I am sorry to hear of your loss," he said. "If you'll see the sergeant out front, he will help you file the proper paperwork for registering complaints."

Peter would do that, of course, if for nothing more than for the sake of proving to Glassman that he operated within the law, but he placed no faith in the army finding the missing supplies. He was certain they had already been eaten or sold. "Thank you, lieutenant, but at this point the escorts are more my priority. If," he said, choosing purposefully to be vague, "I wire for another shipment of supplies, I must be assured of your men's protection."

"Of course. Of course," Glassman said. He shuffled the stack of papers in front of him. "Date of delivery?"

"For the first shipment?"

"Yes."

"Yesterday."

"Yesterday?" Glassman said, eyebrows raised. "Well, that explains it."

"Explains what, exactly?"

"The detail detachment was transferred to guard Mr.

Johnson's shipment of lumber and dry goods." The lieutenant then added, "It was, of course, larger than yours."

Peter could feel his anger brewing. "And that made mine less important?"

"No, not at all," Glassman insisted, "but we are limited in numbers. We must prioritize. Mr. Johnson has important government contracts—ones which will grow the economy."

And I am trying to feed homeless war veterans and their families. Confederate veterans. Is that the issue here? "And are his supplies for sale?" Peter asked. Although he already knew the answer.

"I'm afraid not. They have been promised to others. But if you need more supplies, you might try the stores here in Larkinsville in a day or two."

So I may pay even higher prices for less, Peter thought, his anger rising. He cast Johnson a furtive glance, knowing he had read him right. The carpetbagger aimed to be rich, *if he isn't already.*

"I do apologize for any inconvenience this has caused you," Johnson said.

"It isn't my inconvenience," Peter said, "but it is a great inconvenience to the people of Forest Glade." He turned his eyes back to the young officer. "They are under your authority, lieutenant, and they are hungry."

"As is most of our defeated foe," Glassman conceded. "However, it is government policy, in the spirit of late President Lincoln's wishes, that the rebels be welcomed back into the fold. As you say, they *are* my responsibility. Let me know when your next shipment is due to arrive. I'll make certain the escorts are in place."

For now, it was all Peter could do. He'd made his point, but he wasn't certain how helpful it would be.

Glassman could promise all the assistance he wanted but he saw where the man's heart lay—with his pocketbook. Peter wouldn't be surprised if Johnson and the lieutenant already had some sort of deal going, but what exactly and why? Was Johnson simply paying for assured protection of his own supplies or was he actively trying to sabotage any form of competition so he may hold the monopoly and charge higher prices?

Either way people will starve. Peter however kept his disgust hidden. There was no point in playing his hand now, even if all he got out of his silence was an eventual story on government corruption.

So he thanked the lieutenant for his time, offered a conciliatory nod to Johnson. He filed his formal complaint with the sergeant, then mounted his horse and rode back to Forest Glade.

Once the dampness from the previous day's rain had evaporated, the weather grew quite warm. Trudy didn't think anywhere could be warmer than Baltimore City during the summertime, but evidently July in rural Virginia could be just as fierce. Even with the church windows thrown open wide, the sanctuary had been stifling. Still, she and everyone else soldiered on.

Today Trudy had collected names for Mr. Carpenter's list in addition to washing cups, fetching clean, cool water and washing and bandaging blistered feet. Now that the evening sun was sinking toward its mountainous horizon, she paused to glance out the window. She was feeling worried in spite of herself. Mr. Carpenter had left early this morning and there was still no sign of him.

She told herself she simply wanted to share with him

the information she had gathered today, that her eagerness was a desire to help the freedman who had found his way here this morning.

Robert Smith had walked into the church anxious to find his wife. She had been separated from him almost twenty years ago.

"The war is over and slavery's done away with now," he'd said hopefully. "I thought…well, I hoped…"

Reason told Trudy that the odds of locating his beloved Hannah after so much time were slim to none, but hope in God and a determined belief that true love conquered all compelled her to take down his information.

"Mr. Carpenter said you could use workers," Robert had also said. "I can do almost anything with my hands."

"I'm sure you can," Trudy said. "Let me fetch you something to eat first, and afterward you can speak with Reverend Webb."

The big man eagerly accepted the small allotment of cornbread and tea even though it would hardly be enough to assuage the hunger he must surely be feeling. "I'm sorry I haven't more to give you," she said. "We haven't the supplies we had hoped."

"That's alright, miss. I'm much obliged." He didn't seem that eager to be left on his own, so Trudy continued to engage him in conversation.

"Have you walked a long way?" she asked.

"From South Carolina, Miss."

So far… "And you are headed for…?"

"Not really sure yet, ma'am. Figured I stay here a while, see if I git word. If'n that's alright."

"Of course it is," she said.

Sadly there were a few disapproving looks from

some of the townsfolk, but no one dared to argue why a man of color was getting food. Apparently deep down they either sympathized with him or they knew it would do no good to argue supremacy to Reverend Webb. The preacher had welcomed the freedman heartily.

The two of them were now repairing the church roof. Despite the valley's scorching by General Sheridan's men, red cedar trees still abounded and apparently the ex-slave was an expert in crafting singles. Trudy could hear him singing while he worked.

"I looked over Jordan and what did I see... A band of angels comin' after me, comin' for to carry me home..."

Trudy listened to the unfamiliar but stirring words while she continued to stare toward Larkinsville, eyes straining for the first glimpse of an approaching rider. Realizing, though, she shouldn't be lingering at the window, Trudy whispered a quick prayer for Mr. Carpenter's safety, then turned from the glass. As she did, she nearly tripped over little Charlie.

He, his mother and his baby sister had remained here at the church because Dr. Mackay wanted to keep watch on Opal's cough.

"See my shoes?" Charlie said, proudly showing off a pair of ankle boots, slightly scuffed but of proper size. "Mrs. Webb found 'um for me."

"Very nice," Trudy said, kneeling down to his level. "I suspect your toes are much more comfortable now."

He grinned. His poor teeth were crooked and misshapen, but the smile was heartfelt and happy. "Yes, ma'am. I can wiggle 'um now."

"Very good," Trudy said. "Then they'll have lots of room to grow."

Charlie's cheerful expression shifted to a somewhat uncertain one. "Were you lookin' for that man?"

She could feel the heat rising to her cheeks. "Which man?" Trudy asked, hoping he wasn't wise to her actions. After all, men had been coming and going for the last two days, gathering supplies and seeking treatment for their families.

"The one who makes the newspapers," Charlie clarified.

Oh dear. When am I going to realize that—

"Will he be back?" he asked.

That question eased her guilt a little, knowing she wasn't the only one anxiously awaiting Mr. Carpenter's return. Obviously the newspaper publisher had made an impression on Charlie. *No doubt giving up his soup and frock coat are part of it.*

She offered the boy a smile. "Yes. Mr. Carpenter went over to Larkinsville today but he will be back."

The uncertain expression only grew. Trudy didn't know why until Charlie then said, "My pa went to Larkinsville to 'nlist."

She could almost hear the rest of the sentence, though it remained unspoken…*and he didn't come back*. Her heart ached for the little boy. Tenderly she stroked his dark hair. It was the color of coffee, just like her employer's. "The war is over now, Charlie," she said gently. "No one is enlisting anymore."

The sound of approaching hoofbeats drew both their attention back to the window. "Well, here's Mr. Carpenter now," she said.

Charlie stretched to the glass, pressed his nose against the pane. "He looks hungry," he said.

No, she thought, *he looks frustrated. His visit to the Federal garrison must have been less than satisfactory.*

"I'll get him some tea!" Charlie proclaimed.

Trudy was touched by his eagerness but thought it wise to rein it in. "Let's give Mr. Carpenter a moment to settle." The last thing she wanted was for him to think they had been waiting by the door, eager for his return. The boy, however, waited just long enough for her employer to dismount. Then he tore away from the window.

"Charlie!" Trudy moved to catch him but it was no use. Mr. Carpenter hadn't even time to step completely into the building before Charlie had commandeered a cup of hot tea, raced back and held it up to the man.

His left eye brow arched. He looked at the boy, then at her. A frown came over his face. Trudy's heart withered inside, partly for Charlie's sake, the rest for her own. *Does he think I prompted the boy's actions? That somehow I'm trying to soften up his stance on children?*

He looked back at Charlie. "No, thank you," he said.

Trudy noted the heartbreaking expression on the boy's face as he lowered the cup. Even though she knew it would only increase Mr. Carpenter's perturbation, she stepped in.

"I think what Mr. Carpenter means is that he appreciates your tea, Charlie, but would rather you give it to your mother instead."

She looked back to her employer. His hard expression softened. Apparently he realized how his words had come across to the little lad. "Yes," he said quickly as he leaned forward on his cane. "You see, I had a meal in Larkinsville. In fact..." He reached into his pocket, drew out a biscuit. "Here. I couldn't finish this. You take it." He then offered Charlie an awkward smile.

The boy was thrilled and quickly accepted the biscuit. With a smile of his own he tottered back to his mother. Mr. Carpenter then returned his look to her. His eyes were dark and probing. Trudy couldn't quite decipher the emotions she saw in them but she could read a storm brewing, not one of anger necessarily, but something...

"I didn't put him up to that," she said bluntly.

The man blinked. Given the confused expression now on his face, Trudy decided it best to be completely forthright. "I am sorry for any inconvenience I have caused you in coming here, but I promise you my scheming days have ended."

He drew in a breath, hesitant to acknowledge the former feelings to which she was referring. She knew, however, he understood. She *could* read that in his eyes.

"It's over and done with now," he said. "I have made my position clear. If you will accept it then we will speak no more of it."

Accept that he never wanted a family, that he didn't want her? She would be lying to herself to say his rejection didn't still sting, but yes, she had accepted it. "Very well," she said.

He offered her a curt nod in return.

Remembering Robert, Trudy then told him about the information she had taken down for the paper. "I laid it on your desk," she said.

"Excellent," he said. "I'll wire the notice next time I return to Larkinsville."

She wanted to ask him how today's venture had gone, but she knew him well enough to know that if he had received good news from the garrison commander, he would've proclaimed it. If the news was discouraging, he'd stew on it for a while, until he figured out a way to remedy the situation. So with no further business pressing, Trudy turned and went to check on Charlie and his family.

Chapter Five

*G*ive *her marks for candor*, Peter thought as he watched Miss Martin walk away. *And for grit.* There was no doubt she had put in a long, hard day. Her face showed it, as well as her clothing. Her stained cotton skirt was sweeping the floor. The back of her apron was tied in a lopsided bow. It was stained, too. No doubt it had come loose on her more than once and she'd stopped whatever she was in the middle of in order to secure it. He wondered then why he noticed such details.

I'm a journalist, he told himself, *and in truth, I admire her work ethic.*

She was fast becoming his right-hand man—*or woman, rather.* The paper currently in his hand, the one she had given him, bore testimony to that. Not only had she gathered Robert Smith's physical description and basic information for publication but she had also thought to include a personal note, something only Smith and his wife would have known—his pet name for her, Chickadee.

Peter would have thought to ask something of that sort but it surprised him that Miss Martin had. She was definitely staff material—efficient, free-thinking…*but it comes at a price*. He stopped that thought, reminding himself then that the matter had been settled.

Still his mind betrayed him. *In another time, in another place*, he told himself. He was nearing forty. A man at his age with his physical limitation and lack of gentlemanly polish didn't get that many looks.

Shoving the thought away, he went in search of Reverend Webb. Unfortunately he'd have to tell him how futile his efforts with Lieutenant Glassman had been today and prepare him for the unlikelihood of any real help from the man or his soldiers in the future.

He found the preacher at the well, a bucket of water at his feet. Jack Zimmer was with him. This time so was his wife. Darkness was falling but Peter could see how awkwardly the woman's clothing hung on her frame. Mrs. Zimmer wasn't dangerously thin like some of the other women he had come across in these parts, but he wondered what her shape had been before Philip Sheridan's army had set fire to the land.

Peter nodded to her and her husband.

"Ah, Peter," the reverend said, releasing the pump handle. "How was your venture into Larkinsville? Have you returned with good news?"

Peter blew out a breath. "I'm afraid not. The lieutenant has no idea as to the whereabouts of the rest of our supplies."

The reverend's dark mustache drooped. Beside him, Zimmer kicked the dirt beneath his worn-out shoes. "I told you, you ain't gonna get no help from him."

"What about another shipment?" the reverend asked, as usual doing his best to look ahead to possibilities. Peter hated to dash his hopes but he had to be frank.

"Wiring for supplies isn't the problem," he said. "In fact, I did that today. Getting them here without having them…intercepted…is."

Zimmer nodded affirmatively. "That lieutenant is too busy protecting the carpetbaggers to care about the real citizens of Virginia."

The reverend sighed. "That may be, but we will just have to keep praying." He picked up bucket and turned for the church. Peter watched him go. He wouldn't discourage the man from praying—that, of course, was his job.

But more is needed than prayer, he thought. *Zimmer's right. Lieutenant Glassman isn't going to be much help. I'll have to concoct some sort of scheme of my own to make certain this second delivery arrives safely.*

He'd leave that, though, for tomorrow. He was too tired to think tonight and his leg was hurting. But before heading inside he wanted to take advantage of Mrs. Zimmer's presence and ask her a few questions.

"I wonder, ma'am, if I may speak with you for a moment."

"Yes. Of course," she said.

"It concerns a relative of mine," Peter explained. "A woman named Caroline Carpenter. She lived somewhere in this valley. She married a soldier in General Early's command sometime about—"

Mrs. Zimmer didn't let him finish. "I'm afraid I don't know any Carpenters," she said.

Peter was unwilling to give up just yet. "Well, that would be her married name. Unfortunately, I don't know her maiden one. Do you know of anyone in these parts named Caroline?"

She shook her head. "I'm sorry. I'm afraid not…but I'll ask about."

At least that was something. "Thank you," Peter said. "I'd appreciate that."

He turned and lumbered back into the church. By now his foot and leg were aching. *Too much riding, too much standing, too much walking.* He needed real rest but knew he'd not find it until he located his brother's widow and child.

The sunlight crept slowly across the valley floor and filled the church with warmth the following morning. Trudy could tell it was going to be another heated day. Apparently so could baby Kate. Opal's little girl was fussy and with Emily busy tending to Opal, the baby was relegated to Trudy's care. Not that she minded. She loved children. She always had.

I always will.

The thought that Peter Carpenter never wanted any children of his own suddenly stung her afresh, but Trudy was determined not to think about what might have been. She had promised him she would accept his position. Determined to do her duty, she focused her attention on the little one in her arms. *This baby needs love and I can provide it.*

Not that her mother didn't adore the child. Clearly, she did, but her health would not allow her to properly care for the baby right now. Blistered feet and malnutrition hadn't been Opal's only ailments. Her seemingly benign cough had taken hold of her lungs. Although Dr. Mackay had said at first that it was not serious, Trudy could tell it was becoming so. When the doctor had listened to the woman's lungs this morning he had frowned. Emily was presently boiling herbs and preparing a plaster to nurse the now rattling cough.

In the food department, Mrs. Webb was making the most of what remained. Thanks in part to Robert Smith, she was stretching the supplies yet again. He had shown her a way to bake corn cakes with only a little meal and oil.

"We call 'um hoe cakes," he said, "cause we bake 'um in the fields on the end of a hoe over a small fire." According to him they hadn't much taste "but they'll fill a belly."

"Filling bellies is my goal," Mrs. Webb said. "I'll leave James to fill their souls." And the married pair attempted to do just that for every person who came through the church doors.

Of those in their care, Charlie and his baby sister seemed the healthiest of the lot. Trudy suspected Opal had given whatever food she'd had to her children.

Charlie was short and small-waisted for his age but otherwise no worse for wear. The baby readily devoured her daily allotment of pap—water and meal or a bread-and-milk mixture when it could be found. Today, however, she wouldn't let a spoon near her mouth at all. Trudy wondered if a tooth was festering.

"Rub some raspberry cordial on it," Trudy knew her own mother would say.

The only problem was there wasn't any cordial to be found. What the Federal army hadn't looted, the Confederates had requisitioned for their own men. So without a remedy, Trudy walked the floor, bouncing the baby lightly in her arms while humming the tune she'd heard Robert singing previously. It took much repetition but eventually Kate became enamored by the sound of the music and with Trudy's face. The baby stared up at her with her dark eyes, her festering tooth forgotten at least temporarily. Trudy kept walking, kept humming to ensure continued peace.

Beside her, Charlie kept pace, watching wide-eyed, until suddenly he stopped in his tracks and asked, "Miss Trudy, where did this baby come from?"

She froze. *Oh dear. What a question!* Knowing by the look on his face that the little boy wasn't going to allow her to ignore it, she scrambled for a suitable answer. "Uh, well, Charlie...the same place from which all babies come. God sends them."

"Why?" he asked.

"Uh, well, because He thought it best."

"Why?"

Oh dear! Trudy could feel herself reddening. Clearly this was no longer a discussion for the center of the room. Well within earshot, Dr. Mackay had looked up from his nearby work and grinned sympathetically. And Mr. Carpenter...while opposite her and the good Doctor, he was just as capable of hearing.

Thankfully it appeared he hadn't noticed the turn their conversation had taken—at least, not yet. He was busy scribbling away at his desk, oblivious to her presence. For once, Trudy wanted to keep it that way. She quietly drew Charlie to the far side of the church, well away from the men. Finding an open spot against the wall, she sat down. Baby Kate, as if sensing she was being discussed, was now wiggling. Trudy shifted her from one arm to the other, bouncing her still as she looked toward her brother.

"You see, Charlie," Trudy began, "God sent your sister because He wanted to bless you and your mother."

She didn't say a word about Charlie's father. After the comment about him enlisting in Larkinsville, she didn't want to further upset the child.

The boy's thoughts went there anyway. "If God wanted us to be happy, then why didn't He just keep the baby and let my Pa come home to us?"

As if sensing she were unwanted, Kate grimaced, then looked as if she were about to wail. Trudy kissed her cheek, bounced her again and hummed a few more measures of the song. All the while she was praying, *Lord, help me.*

She looked again to Charlie. "I don't know, love. I'm sorry. I wish I did. My papa is in Heaven, too."

Charlie's face brightened ever so slightly with a look of curiosity. "He is?"

"Yes."

"What does he look like?"

Ah, the innocent faith of a child. He speaks of my father in present tense. Trudy smiled while she shifted the baby again, this time to the center of her lap. The little girl reached over to grasp her brother's shirt sleeve. "My papa looks a lot like me," Trudy said, "or at least, he did when he was here on Earth. He had red hair and freckles on his face."

"My pa looks like me," Charlie said proudly, "only much bigger."

Dark hair, dark eyes and much bigger. Trudy couldn't help but wonder if that wasn't another reason why he'd taken to Mr. Carpenter. For a child his age, those simple similarities were probably enough to link him to the man he loved.

She put her arm around the little boy and drew him

close. "Then your pa must have been a very handsome man."

Looking up at her, Charlie grinned, for he realized that Trudy was declaring him handsome, as well.

In the grand scheme of things, it was only a minor victory over sickness and poverty but Trudy took pleasure in the smile and in the fact that God had allowed her to coax it. Even Kate now seemed content.

"Here comes the doc," Charlie then said.

Trudy turned her head in the direction Charlie was pointing to see that Dr. Mackay was indeed making his way toward them.

"I have need of each of your help," he said.

Charlie snapped to attention. "Yes, sir," he said eagerly.

Dr. Mackay smiled. "There's a fine lad." He then looked at Trudy. "Em tells me you are familiar with botany."

Botany? "Elizabeth and I have a flower garden at home," Trudy said, "but I am hardly an expert."

"Do you know wild onion?"

"Yes." Wild or not, that particular plant made its appearance in city gardens from time to time.

"Good," Dr. Mackay said. "I'd like you and Charlie to see if you can locate some."

The boy stood a little taller. "You mean, we're gonna go foraging?"

"Aye, lad, and I would like for you to bring back as much wild onion as you can find."

"Is it for my ma?" Charlie then asked.

"Indeed it is," Dr. Mackay said, although his tone lost some of its brightness. Trudy understood why. Charlie had known almost instinctively what they were going to do with the onions. "I'm going to make a plaster to help her breath better."

The little boy lifted his chin. "Then I'll bring back lots," he promised.

Dr. Mackay patted his shoulder, then looked again at Trudy. "See if you can locate some fever root, as well."

She bit her lip momentarily. "I'm afraid I don't know what that looks like."

"The flowers are similar to a gentian," Dr. Mackay said, "only smaller. I'll sketch it out for you."

"Thank you. That would be most helpful." Trudy's eagerness to do her duty was only tempered by the knowledge of why Dr. Mackay wanted these particular plants. Evidently the herb poultice Emily had used previously to treat Opal had been ineffective. *She's growing worse*, Trudy thought, and she couldn't help but wonder if that wasn't the primary reason Dr. Mackay wanted her to take Charlie with her. He did not want the boy worrying about his mother.

And if we don't locate what he needs? She shoved the dark thought away, focusing instead on the present. "What about the baby?" she asked.

Mrs. Webb walked by just as she said that. "I can take her now." The preacher's wife held out her arms and smiled at the child. Kate lunged toward her. "And if you run across any chicory," Mrs. Webb then added, "bring it back for coffee."

Trudy had learned back in the hospital by way of a wounded Virginia soldier that chicory root could be roasted, ground and brewed like coffee.

"It doesn't taste nearly as good as the real kind," the soldier who'd told her had said, "but it will warm a belly."

Keeping warm wasn't the issue. The July heat was taking care of that just fine, but filling bellies was necessary, and who here wouldn't enjoy a cup of coffee? She knew for a fact her employer would. Back home in the office he drank it by the gallon. Trudy promised to keep her eyes peeled for the plant.

While Dr. Mackay sketched her a picture of fever root, Trudy assisted Charlie with tying his shoes. She noticed he was now sporting a fine pair of socks, ones she didn't recognize. "Where did you get these?" she asked.

He looked down at his ankles. "Them's my good ones. I only wear 'um for special 'casions."

She felt honored that he considered foraging for plants with her a special occasion. "I see," she said, "but you would do better to wear these more often. Where have you been hiding these?"

"In my pockets."

At that Trudy couldn't help but chuckle. "That's a very handsome stitch," she then commented, knowing a bit of it from her own efforts at sock knitting. "Did your mother make them for you?"

"No. Her friend did."

"Oh? Which friend?"

"Miss Agnes. She made 'um for me and she made a blanket for Kate before she died."

Trudy's heart wretched. He spoke so matter-of-factly about death. *It has become so commonplace for him.* "She must have thought very highly of you and your baby sister," Trudy said.

Mr. Carpenter cast her a questioning look as he moved past them.

"I'm taking Charlie out to forage," for some reason she felt compelled to explain.

Charlie, innocent of her inner turmoil, bless his heart, then promised, "We'll bring you back some coffee!"

Coffee? How does he know I was thinking of that? Trudy knew she was blushing. Did Mr. Carpenter think she'd told Charlie that the chicory would be especially for him? Apparently he did, for after a split-second look of incredulity, the man then replied, "Happy hunting, then." He promptly turned on his heel and headed for the front door. Where he was going he did not say and she did not dare ask.

With shoes properly tied and armed with a sketch of the mysterious fever root, she and Charlie started off. The sun was already climbing toward the center of the sky but a gentle breeze made the going pleasant. The birds were singing.

"Let's go this way," Charlie said, pointing toward the river.

"We will on the way back," Trudy said, for she knew they were more likely to find wild onion in the dryer woodlands or meadows than along the riverside. As for the chicory or anything else edible, she realized acquiring it would take patience and a keen eye. People had been foraging in this valley long before she arrived and the fires set by the Federal army had destroyed much of the landscape. The plants and berry bushes were slowly returning but it would be quite some time before the valley boasted the natural abundance it had before the war. She and Charlie would probably have to cover some distance before they found any of what they hoped.

He seemed up for the challenge, however. He hurried

along ahead of her with a spring in his step. "Maybe we can find some nuts!" he said.

"It's a little early in the season for them," she said, but Trudy hadn't the heart to discourage him totally. "We'll keep our eyes open, though. Perhaps we will come across some hazelnuts."

They marched along. She carried a basket. He carried a stick, which he was presently using as a sword, waving around at Yankees. "Back you, Bluecoats!" Charlie commanded.

Trudy saw no one in blue, but halfway up a partially wooded hillside, she spied something pink. Her heart skipped a beat. Was it the wild onion? "This way, Charlie!"

They hurried to the spot. Sure enough, the sleepy-looking, bent over pastel flower heads were nodding in the breeze.

"Yep," Charlie confirmed. "That's onions. I can smell 'um."

Trudy giggled. She could, too. Knowing she'd smell just like them before the day was through, she dutifully fell to her knees and gave each plant a tug. The bulbs were small and shallow. The earth easily surrendered to her hands. With Charlie helping, they soon had all they needed. "Dr. Mackay will be pleased," she said.

"So will my mama," he replied.

"Yes," Trudy said, giving him a loving stroke of the chin. "She will be pleased, indeed."

Wiping his hands on his trousers, Charlie then stood. "Now we can find the chicory for Mr. Carpenter."

"Well, first the fever root," Trudy gently corrected him, "and yes, then the chicory."

They continued on their way. All of their walking

had made Trudy warm, and she could feel the sweat trickling down the back of her neck. She took off her bonnet. The sun was high but she preferred to have the air dry her neck.

They trekked further, up one hill and down another. Much to Trudy's dismay, fever root was nowhere to be found—and much to Charlie's, neither was chicory. Coming into a small undisturbed meadow, however, she did locate a bit of wild bergamot. Trudy rubbed her fingers against a few of the leaves and inhaled the pleasant citrusy-mint aroma.

"Smell this, Charlie."

He took an exaggerated sniff. "What's that for?"

"We can make tea from this."

"That's nice," he said, but his tone made it clear tea certainly wasn't coffee.

Still Trudy picked the bergamot leaves carefully. Not wanting it to end up smelling like onions, she didn't put them in the basket. Instead she carefully wrapped them in her handkerchief, then slid them inside her pocket.

Charlie was now busy dragging his stick through the dirt. She could tell he was getting tired. She was, too, but when she asked him if he was ready to head back, he said no. "I promised Mr. Carpenter I'd bring him some coffee."

"Oh, love, he won't be upset with you if you can't find it."

Charlie, however, did not yet wish to return to the church. "Let's go just a little further up this hill," he said. "See what we can find."

"Very well," Trudy conceded, for she was still searching, too. In addition to Dr. Mackay's fever root, she had hoped to find something edible. No one knew for certain when the next shipment of supplies would arrive, and their current stores were quite low.

In a partial clearing with a small trickling stream, Charlie stopped for a drink. While he was busy splashing water in and about his mouth, Trudy spied some daylilies. She happened to remember, thanks again to that soldier in the hospital, that the tubers could be baked like potatoes.

"Oh, Charlie, look! Mrs. Webb will be quite pleased that we have come across these."

He looked in the direction of the lilies. Evidently he'd had some experience with the flower. "Mama says them roots is hard to git outta the ground. Did you bring a hatchet?"

"No, but Dr. Mackay loaned me his knife and Mrs. Webb gave me a small trowel." She retrieved them both from the bottom of the basket.

His eyes widened. "Can I use it?"

"The trowel?"

"The knife."

She knew better than to surrender such an item to a six-year-old boy. "You'd better let me," she said.

His lower lip pushed forward with a pout, but he came and knelt down beside her.

Trudy began digging, then tugging, but to no avail. "They are all tangled together," she said.

Taking Dr. Mackay's knife, she slid it in and out of the tubers, loosened more dirt, and tried again. Three small ones popped out. She handed those to Charlie, then again took the knife in hand. She knew as small as it was, it would never go entirely through the hard tubers. Besides, she wanted as much of them as she could garner. *If I can just make a deeper cut between them and then around the edges...*

Determinedly she worked, but the larger roots refused to surrender. *Come on! Come on!* And then it happened. Slice! Only it wasn't the tubers that had given way. It was her own flesh. The knife had slipped and cut her hand.

The shock was so great that the pain didn't register for a moment or two, but when it did it, was excruciating. Charlie gasped when he saw what had happened. His face was pained as if the injury had happened to him.

"It's alright," Trudy tried to reassure him. She pressed her other hand to the spot to stem the flow. "It's not that deep." A closer look, however, revealed that it was quite deep after all. A wave of nausea swept over her. She was an accomplished nurse and had dealt with blood numerous times before, but her own, she supposed, was a different story. Her stomach rolled and her heart raced as she pressed her hands harder together.

"We had better start back," she said as calmly as possible. "Can you put the roots we have in the basket?"

"Yes, ma'am." He worked quickly, and when he had finished, Trudy clenched her injured hand tightly, then picked up the basket with the other. It was far too heavy now for Charlie to handle.

They started down the hill, yet she could only manage a few yards before she had to sit down upon the ground. She was feeling dizzy and chilled, even as she sweated.

"You don't look so good," Charlie said.

She knew she was pale for she could feel the blood draining from her face. *What am I going to do? I can't walk and I can't send Charlie on his way by himself.*

If something happened to him she would never forgive herself.

But if I faint right here upon the spot he will still be on his own and he will be scared!

The blood was trickling from the sides of her fist. She held the hand above her heart and squeezed tighter. It helped to stem the flow, but the dizziness was only getting worse. Keeping her hand aloft as best as she could, she put her head between her knees.

"Miss Trudy?" Charlie said. She could hear the fear in his voice.

"Don't fret, love. Just let me rest a moment or two. Everything will be alright."

But everything was not alright. The pain was getting worse by the second and so was the nausea. How would they ever get back to the church? They had walked such a long way.

Her eyesight was getting fuzzy. She knew she was in danger of swooning. *Oh Lord, please*, she prayed. *Please give me strength. Pease help me...*

Chapter Six

Peter heard the boy's frantic voice as he urged the horse up the hillside. "Miss Trudy! Miss Trudy? Should I go git help?"

That coupled then with the sight of Miss Martin sitting on the ground, her head bent toward her skirts, set Peter's heart racing. Something was terribly wrong.

"That don't look good," Robert Smith also observed.

Peter had asked the man to accompany him to Larkinsville today to wire off the notice for locating his wife. He had also planned to telegraph officials over in Augusta County to see if they had any information of Caroline there. *There has to be a marriage license on file somewhere*, Peter had thought. *If the records haven't been burned.*

Leaning forward in his saddle, Peter hurried the mare up the hill. The boy spotted him first. "Mr. Carpenter, help!"

Miss Martin lifted her head. She was as pale as a fresh ream of paper. Peter then saw the overturned basket of wild onions, the crimson stains on her dress. With his own blood coursing loudly in his ears, he quickly dismounted the horse. Robert collected the animal while he hurried for Miss Martin.

"The knife…" she tried to explain. Her voice was thready and breathless. "It slipped… My hand…"

Yes, he saw her hand. She was clutching it tightly, but not enough to block the slow red trickle. There was blood about the hem of her skirt, as well.

"Are you hurt elsewhere?" he asked.

She didn't answer.

"Your legs?"

"I tried to bandage…my underslip…wouldn't tear…"

He tried to make sense of what she had said. "So the blood on your skirt is from your hand?"

"Y-yes. I was trying to cut the lily tubers…so we could roast—"

"Hush," he commanded. Talking was only making things worse. She was growing more pale by the moment. "Now let me see…"

Taking her hand in his, Peter carefully opened her palm. As he did the bleeding grew much worse. Fetching his own handkerchief from his breast pocket, he pressed it into the wound and then closed her fist around it.

"Keep it up across your chest," he said. He knew he had to get her back to the church. She needed much more assistance than he could render here. *She needs Dr. Mackay.* "Can you stand?" He asked.

"I… I'm a bit l-light-headed."

As she was one who had tended battle wounds and assisted surgeons, he knew it wasn't the mere sight of blood that had weakened her. He could guess what it really was. "You didn't eat anything this morning, did you?"

She shook her head slightly, her eyes unwilling to meet his.

He knew she had been trying to be noble by saving her allotment for the others, but her sacrifice would in reality only inconvenience everyone else. *She was probably already light-headed when she cut herself,* he mentally grumbled, *and now she won't be of much use to Dr. Mackay with nursing or Mrs. Webb with preparing the food, at least for a while.*

The editor in him read through the sequence of events once again and sized up the present situation. He was reminded of another inconvenience she had caused. If Miss Martin hadn't convinced David Wainwright to remain at home then he could be the one telegraphing notices from Larkinsville and dealing with the missing food shipments. *Leaving me to find Caroline and the child.*

Clearly his search could not be furthered today. Miss Martin needed to be helped back to the church. Peter cast a glance at his other compatriots. By now poor Charlie was almost as pale as Miss Martin.

"Is she gonna be alright?" he asked.

"She'll be fine," he said, but even he heard the irritation in his voice. He tried to offer a smile. "Don't fret."

"The basket," she said.

"I'll git it," Charlie assured her.

"Fever root," she then said.

"What?" Peter asked.

"Dr. Mackay w-wanted us to f-find it and Ch-Charlie wanted chicory…"

"For coffee," the boy explained.

The latter was a frivolous concern at the moment but Peter couldn't help but be touched by her commitment to the child. It was hard to remain angry with her when she had such a heart for helping others. "We'll see to that later," he told her.

While Robert helped Charlie with the basket, Peter helped her to her feet. "Slowly..."

She obeyed his command but her legs were so wobbly that she swayed and nearly knocked him off balance when he steadied her. *We'll both be on the ground here in a moment.*

She had dropped her hand. "Keep it elevated," he reminded her. "Come now, slowly, that's it. I've got you."

She pressed closer to him. Peter couldn't help but notice she smelled of bergamot and onion, an odd combination for a lady. He carefully steered her to the mare. Getting her on it would prove a challenge. She could grasp the horse's mane but hadn't the strength to pull herself up and over. *And with my wretched leg, especially on this uneven ground, I won't be able to lift her.* He looked back at Robert. "Mr. Smith, would you kindly...?"

As the freedman came forward to assist, Peter climbed into the saddle. With one hand he grasped the reins tightly. With the other he reached for Mrs. Martin's good hand. "Steady now," he said to her.

Her complexion had gone scarlet. *No wonder.* They had agreed to put the idea of romance behind them, but this close contact made the conversation difficult to forget. He didn't want her to see him now as some knight in shining armor. *Surely, though, my difficulty walking will cure that. After all, I am a cripple.*

Robert hoisted her up and over, settling her just in front of the saddle horn. Peter was thankful she wasn't wearing one of those frivolous hoops and that she didn't hesitate to ride astride. Still very much a lady, however, she tugged self-consciously at her skirts, trying to hide her petticoats and ankles from him.

I'm not looking, Miss Martin, he wanted to say, but he didn't want to embarrass her. Her efforts left her even further depleted. She sagged toward the horse's neck.

"Lean back against me," he insisted. He slid one arm around her waist. "It's important that you do, especially as we move downhill."

"Yes, s-sir," she muttered.

He decided to let that go. Peter glanced back to see about the boy. Robert had him securely in place as well, along with the basket of onions and lily tubers. Peter clicked his tongue at the mare. "Walk on…"

They started gingerly down the hill. Her head was resting against his shoulder. The smell of bergamot was now stronger than the onions and the former was quite pleasing. Peter did his best, however, to ignore it, just as he was trying to ignore the warmth she was generating. It was different than what he felt under the sun.

He shifted his position ever so slightly. When he did, so did she—in the opposite direction. Was she trying to grant him a measure of distance, knowing he wished for it? He respected that but he couldn't very well have her riding off balance. It wasn't good for her or the mare.

"Lean back, Miss Martin."

At his gentle tug, she silently surrendered. The warmth returned. Reaching level ground, Peter picked up the pace. Robert rode up beside him.

"She don't look so good," he said. "Her hand is still bleeding."

Peter looked around her. Her hand was once again in her lap. Another crimson stain was taking shape on her skirt. He reached out, placed her hand high on her shoulder. "You must keep it elevated, Miss Martin."

He cast a glance at the boy, whose eyes were full of fear. "Don't worry, young man," he told him. "She'll be just fine."

Peter had said the words with more confidence than he actually felt. He could feel her sagging deeper against him. Fearing she was going into shock, he told Robert, "Ride on ahead and tell Dr. Mackay what has happened. That way he will be prepared when we arrive."

The freedman nodded and snapped his reins. He and the boy hurried off.

Her hand was sliding downward again. Once more, Peter reached for it.

"Elevated, Miss Martin."

"Yes, s-sir…"

"Peter," he said firmly, in effort to keep her talking.

"Y-yes. Peter…"

"Good," he said, "and your name is Gertrude." He knew she didn't like to be called that, so he said it just to provoke her. It achieved the effect he had hoped.

"No," she said with more strength than previously.

"No?" he said in mock innocence. "Then what, pray tell, do you prefer to be called?"

"T-trudy."

"Trudy," he repeated. "Trudy what? Trudy Sue?"

"N-no… Not Sue."

"Trudy Margaret?"

"No."

"Penelope?"

She heaved a frustrated sigh. "Anne," she said.

"Anne?" Peter repeated. "Is that what you said?"

"Y-yes…" Her voice was fading again.

"Very well. Stay with me, Trudy Anne. We will be back to the church soon."

Her slender shoulders rose and fell once more.

"I'm s-sorry."

"Sorry for what?"

"S-sorry to inconvenience you…"

"We've already been through that, Trudy Anne. There is no need to discuss it again." Yes, he *had* been irritated by his change of plans today, but her situation, her distress and at the same time her obvious concern for Charlie's feelings had softened his heart. "You are no inconvenience," he told her. No matter what the circumstances, he would never forgo an opportunity to help a woman in need.

"…stitches." Trudy clearly heard Emily say. Although what words preceded that she did not know. Trudy opened her eyes to find her friend hovering over her, holding a tin cup.

"Drink this," Emily commanded in that forcefully sweet way of hers. "It's willow bark. It will help with the pain."

Trudy took a slow sip, then returned her head to her pillow. She felt groggy, disjointed. *Where am I? What happened?*

"I'm sorry I haven't anything stronger to give you," Emily said.

Something stronger to give me? She splayed her fingers beneath the blanket that was presently covering her. Sharp pain from her palm brought her to full awareness.

Now she remembered. She was at the church in Virginia. The medication had been stolen. Dr. Mackay had sent her foraging and she had sliced her hand trying to dig up daylilies. "Is Charlie alright?" she asked, immediately trying to sit upright.

Emily pressed her back. "Easy, now. He's fine, but you have swooned twice already and I'll not have it happen again."

She had? *I thought I was made of sterner stuff than that.* "Sorry," Trudy replied sheepishly. "I suppose I am not as accustomed to dealing with injuries as I thought."

"I think it was more your empty stomach that was to blame. You didn't faint on me until *after* I finished stitching."

Trudy swallowed another helping of tea. "And the second time?"

"That actually *was* the second time. The first took place in Mr. Carpenter's arms. Evan had to come and carry you from his horse."

Trudy felt the color fly to her cheeks at the memory. Despite her pain and fogginess, she vividly recalled Peter Carpenter's arm around her waist, recalled leaning her head against his broad chest. His breath had been warm and gentle in her ear.

Emily offered her a knowing grin. "A pleasant memory?" she teased.

Trudy's embarrassment intensified as Evan came to check on her.

"And how's the patient?" he asked.

"I think she will live," Emily said slyly.

"Aye," he said, "provided that in the future she eats her fair share." He bent closer and stuck his finger in her face in that fatherly, former military physician sort of way. "Now you hear this, lassie. You forgoing your rations will not be helpful to us. It will only cause more trouble."

"Yes, sir," she said, and with that another memory came to mind. She had called her employer "sir" and he had corrected her. *"It's Peter,"* he had said.

Peter, Trudy thought. The name meant rock, strength. He had indeed been that for her today, but after mentally reliving those moments of rescue, Trudy felt the guilt come calling. Hadn't she promised herself, hadn't she promised *him* that she would put aside any romantic thoughts concerning him?

He is not the man for me, she again reminded herself. *He is an arrogant, cynical man and he does not want children.*

Dr. Mackay had moved to check on Charlie's mother. Opal was sleeping just a few feet away. Trudy could smell the onion poultice from here.

"Where are the children?" she asked Emily.

"Mrs. Webb took the baby over to her house for a while." Emily then craned her neck, glanced about the room. "And I believe Charlie is still out with Mr. Carpenter. They are hunting for fever root and chicory."

As Emily moved to assist her husband, Trudy allowed herself to indulge in a grin. *So he kept his word*, she thought. Peter had promised he would look out for the boy.

Her hand involuntarily twitched, sending a bolt of pain up her arm. The temptation to feel sorry for herself in that moment was strong, but one glance at the woman lying on the pallet next to her was enough to quell it. Opal had suffered and was still suffering much more than she. She had claimed a husband but he had become a casualty of war and now her own health was frail.

When Emily returned to her, Trudy then asked, "How is she?"

"Opal? I believe the poultice is helping."

Trudy breathed a sigh. At least some good was coming from her misadventure today.

Emily then leaned forward. Evidently she couldn't resist teasing Trudy a bit further. "My dear, are you aware that you smell of men's shaving balm?"

Shaving balm? Peter—that is, *Mr. Carpenter* hadn't been wearing any of that. At least, none she could detect. Then she remembered the bergamot. She had forgotten all about the leaves wrapped inside her handkerchief. She told Emily about them. "I had hoped to bring back something for tea," she said as she reached for her pocket with her good hand.

Out came a very wrinkled handkerchief. Trudy was certain her find would now be useless, but much to her relief, most of the leaves were still intact. Only a few had been crushed, their oil seeping into the handkerchief. "Well, it's better than I hoped, but still less than I wished," Trudy said to Emily.

Her friend took the cloth from her. "It's enough for a pot or two. Well done."

Brewing tea, however, would have to wait. A rail-thin, one-armed man had just stepped through the front door. Dr. Mackay motioned for his wife to help as he assessed the man's condition.

Trudy watched them for a few moments, then looked again at Opal. Now awake herself, she offered Trudy a small smile.

"Thank you for looking after my Charlie," the woman whispered. "He has taken so well to you and Mr. Carpenter. I've not seen him this content since before the baby arrived."

Trudy offered her a smile in return. It cheered her to

know she had been helpful to the woman and her family. "I suppose Charlie misses having all of your attention," she said.

"And his father's," Opal said sadly. "He used to take him for walks in the woods. They used to forage for nuts and chicory even before the war."

Nuts, she couldn't help but think. *Yes, he had hoped to find those as well as his coffee.* She commanded herself not to think of Peter Carpenter at that last part. *He is not the subject of this conversation. Charlie is.* "I'm sorry that the outing today was marred by my accident."

"Don't be. Although I am sorry for your injury, it proved a valuable lesson to him."

"How so?" Trudy wondered.

"I've told him repeatedly to stay away from knives but he doesn't listen."

Trudy remembered his eagerness to help her today. She shuddered to think what would have happened today if *he* had been the one holding the knife. "Perhaps now he will heed your words."

"I do hope." Opal chuckled until a fit of coughing seized her.

Trudy pushed herself upright with her good hand, then reached for the nearby cup of water. Emily however, beat her to it.

"Let me, love," she insisted. "You need to rest."

Relenting, Trudy watched as Emily carefully lifted Opal's head and placed the cup to her lips.

"I feel so guilty for lying about," Trudy lamented when Emily returned the cup to the table.

"Why?" her friend asked.

"There is so much work to be done."

Emily offered her a knowing look. Trudy knew she

understood all too well. Emily couldn't stand to be idle, either. "If you'll lie still for the rest of this afternoon, then I'll let you keep the night watch."

"Tonight?" Trudy asked.

"Yes." Emily grinned. "Will that do?"

Trudy nodded slowly, but in actuality she felt mixed emotions at the offer. For the last three nights she had slept in the Webbs' parsonage while Emily or Mrs. Webb had filled the role of night nurse. She was eager to take her turn, but Trudy also knew whose turn it was tonight to patrol the churchyard.

Although there was no reason for them to speak to one another or even be in the same room, after all that had transpired today, their close contact and her swooning, she did not think Peter Carpenter would appreciate her continued company.

They had managed to find one sprig of fever root. After that Charlie wished to resume his search for chicory.

"Let's look down by the river," he said.

Knowing that the likelihood of finding the plant there was just as high as it was in the meadows he and Miss Martin had already trekked, Peter allowed him to lead the way. The boy simply couldn't conceive that his once abundant valley was running out of bounty.

By now his leg was aching, but Peter refused to turn back just yet. The boy was having an amusing time, and he needed more outings like this. *His father would have done such, if he had survived the war.*

Once again Peter couldn't help but think of Daniel. He knew full well he might not be able to find his brother's family. If that was indeed the case, then he wanted to make a difference in the life of the little boy in front of him. Admittedly, he was taken with the lad—even if he was constantly asking questions.

"What happened to your leg?" Charlie had wanted to know the moment they left the church building.

"Nothing happened to it," Peter had said. "I was born this way."

"Why?"

"Why?" Peter shrugged. "Your guess is as good as mine."

"Can you run?"

"*Run?* No."

"Does that make you sad?"

"No." At least, most of the time it didn't. "You don't need to be able to run to print a newspaper."

Apparently Charlie had liked that answer. He looked up at Peter and grinned. He was still grinning now. The sight of that innocent, gap-toothed smile produced a lump in the no-nonsense newspaperman's throat. The boy reminded him of his little brother. Daniel was ten years younger and when he was a child, he thought the sun rose and set on Peter.

Whether it be a broken toy or misunderstanding concerning some other boy, Daniel looked to his big brother to fix all his problems. Peter always did. *But I wasn't able to keep him from war and I couldn't go with him.*

Even if he had found a regiment that would have accepted him, made him a quartermaster or an adjutant, Peter knew he still would have been a liability. Daniel would have worried about him and that would have been a distraction. Being distracted on the battlefield got you killed.

He'd gotten killed anyway. Had he been thinking of

his bride the moment he engaged the enemy? *A family is a liability in times like these. As is any attachment.*

Still, Peter couldn't help but feel sympathy for the boy beside him—a boy who no longer had a father, a teacher, someone to guide him. Peter wasn't an expert in the woods, but he'd share what information he did have. He pointed to a nearby birch tree.

"Has any one ever told you about the many uses of that tree?" he asked.

Charlie spun about. "What tree?" Finally he turned in the direction Peter was looking. "That'n?"

"Yes," Peter said. "See this?" He pulled off a piece of peeling bark. "This is everything a man could need."

Charlie's dark eyes squinted cynically. "It's just bark."

"Ah, that's where you are wrong. The Indians used this to start fires. Some even made articles of clothing from it."

"How?" Charlie asked, his interest now piqued.

Peter scratched his head. "Well, that, I don't quite remember. I just know I read somewhere that they did." He handed Charlie the bark. "People also used to peel it very thinly and use it for paper."

"To make newspapers?"

"Well, this was before printing presses, but yes, newspapers of a sort. They made notices and they would tack them on to the trees so others could read them."

"What if they couldn't read?"

"Then they would draw pictures."

Charlie immediately began peeling off pieces of the bark and shoving it into the small haversack he was carrying. Clearly he had some project in mind, although what, exactly, Peter did not know. The boy only slowed when he let out a yawn.

"Alright now," Peter said. "I think that's enough foraging for today. You need a nap."

Charlie quickly closed his mouth. "No, I don't. Besides, we gotta find the chicory."

Ugh. That again. This child is relentless. "Do you drink coffee?" Peter asked.

"No."

"Well then, if it's for me, I'll tell you… I appreciate your efforts, but I need rest more than I need the coffee." Unlike Charlie, Peter viewed sleep as a luxury, not a punishment. *I suppose that makes me even more of an old man.*

He hadn't felt like one earlier, though, especially when Miss Martin was nestled against him. His heart had been beating as quickly as a schoolboy's. Peter certainly felt like one right up until the point when she'd fainted and he hadn't had the physical strength to get her down from the horse. *Dr. Mackay had to assist me. I couldn't help her any more than I could help Daniel.*

Pushing both of them from his mind, Peter focused his attention again on the boy in front of him. "Besides," he told him, "we don't need the chicory now. We can use this bark to make tea."

"What kind of tea?"

"The kind that will settle your stomach when you've had too much coffee," Peter said. "Come on. Walk this way with me and I'll tell you all about it."

With that, Peter managed to return Charlie to the church.

Chapter Seven

By late that afternoon, following an extra helping of vegetable and lily tuber soup that Emily insisted she eat, Trudy was back to work. Two more freedmen came to the church that day in search of their families. She took down their names and particulars, thankful that the injury had not occurred to her right hand.

The soreness lingered in her left, but the tightness of the skin testified that already the wound was beginning to heal. She had God and the Mackays to thank for that. *And Mr. Carpenter.* When that last thought came unbidden, Trudy tried to push it far from her mind. Collecting information for notices to be printed in his newspaper, however, coupled with her own guilt, made that task impossible.

Once again I have hindered his work, she thought, for according to Emily he and Robert had planned to be traveling today back to Larkinsville.

"Have they some lead on our missing supplies?" Trudy had asked.

"Not to my knowledge," Emily had said. "Mr. Carpenter told Evan that he was looking for his brother's wife and child."

Trudy blinked. "His brother's wife? Do you mean Daniel?"

Emily had nodded. "I believe that was his name. He died sometime back."

"But his wife is still living? And there's a child?"

"Mr. Carpenter seemed to think so."

Pondering that bit of information made Trudy feel even guiltier than she already did. *No wonder he has been so gruff with me. He has so much on his mind. No wonder he wanted my brother-in-law to come to come. David could be the one writing about the local concerns and investigating the missing shipment, leaving Mr. Carpenter more time to search for his relatives!*

Then she thought of another task that he was now undertaking thanks to her. *He's out foraging with Charlie because I cannot! If only I had not been so intent on impressing him and everyone else by bringing back those lily tubers!* She sighed, thoroughly disgusted with herself. *Why do I still feel the need to prove myself to him?*

She continued to take down the information from the two freedmen in front of her. The poor men's faces looked as haggard as their clothing.

Who knows when they have last had a decent meal? she thought. Yet they were not bitter. In fact, they were willing to share what they had in payment for their printed notices.

"Don't reckon you could use these, could ya?" The tallest man held forth a sack. Trudy peeked inside. In it were two skinned squirrels.

Every bit of food was appreciated, and meat was better than plant roots. By cutting back on the food they had brought for themselves, mostly hardtack biscuits and dried fruit, Trudy and her friends would be able to stretch the meager rations a few more days. Thankfully, Dr. Mackay had had the foresight to carry those rations in his personal carpetbag on the train. If he hadn't, Trudy wondered just what they would be eating. "We can indeed," Trudy said. "Wherever did you find them?"

"Back down a ways," the first man said.

Where that was exactly, Trudy did not know, but it must have been far from here. She had not seen a squirrel or a rabbit or any other edible four-legged creature since she'd been here. They had all been trapped out.

"Well, thank you both." She handed back the bag. She wanted to see to the task herself but knew she would not be able to prepare the squirrels with one hand. "Give them to Mrs. Webb, and then if you gentlemen would like something hot to eat now, she will be happy to serve you along with providing space for overnight lodging."

"Oh no, miss," the second man said. "Though we're much obliged. We be on our way after we sit a spell."

"To Philadelphia?" Trudy asked. That was the destination they had listed in their information.

"Yes, miss."

"But won't you rest for a little while longer? You've still so far to travel."

"Every mile covered tonight is one less for tomorrow," the tallest man said.

She admired their perseverance. "Then may God bless you and your families," she said.

While Mrs. Webb fed them and then convinced them each to accept a brand-new pair of socks, Trudy looked in on Opal. She was again awake, but fitfully so. Dr. Mackay had claimed the baby and was in the corner of the room, listening to her lungs. Opal was studying the doctor and her child intently.

"Don't worry," Trudy said. "Dr. Mackay is just being cautious. See…a smile." The Scotsman pulled the stethoscope from his ears. "He's pleased with what he heard."

Opal coughed, deeply, hoarsely. "I worry about her and Charlie," she then said.

"I know you do, but try not to. The baby is well cared for, and I'm sure Charlie is having a very nice time with Mr. Carpenter." Or at least, that was what she wanted to think. Peter wasn't exactly a nurturing man. *But he is looking after Charlie and he is trying to discover the whereabouts of the rest of his family.*

"You think very highly of him," Opal said. "Don't you?"

"Of Charlie? Of course I do. Everyone around here does. He's the sweetest little thing."

"He is…but that wasn't who I meant."

Trudy's heart began to thud. Since her disastrous attempt at foraging, she had been thinking of him more tenderly than she knew she should. Was that obvious to the others? To him? *I didn't ask for him to rescue me—to hoist me on his horse and whisk me back here to the church.* Although she was very grateful that he had. To be honest, too grateful.

"What kind of man is he?" Opal asked.

Trudy didn't know how to answer that, or rather, she didn't wish to do so. If Opal already guessed that she thought so highly of him, then what was the sense in further praise?

The woman, however, seemed desperate to learn.

Evidently Charlie's safety was weighing heavy on her mind. "Is he an honest man?" she asked.

"Yes. He's honest." *To a fault.*

"Is he given to liquor or gambling?"

"No, of course not!" Trudy insisted. "I wouldn't work for a man who was!"

Opal was halted by another coughing spell. After it passed, her next question was, "Is he churchgoing?"

Uneasiness moved through Trudy. She didn't like speaking of her employer's faults, especially when she was only now perhaps beginning to understand the reason for some of them.

The news of his unknown sister-in-law and niece or nephew was still rattling around in her brain. Was that another reason why he would not marry? Did he feel a sense of obligation to this woman? *Of course he does,* Trudy thought. *He may not be a gentleman, per se, but he is certainly no scoundrel.*

"He believes in God," Trudy assured Opal, but she failed to mention that he made little time for the faithful attendance of worship services. *Is he angry with God because of the war, because of what has happened to his family?* She couldn't help but wonder. *Does he feel pressed to try to fix things himself?*

She knew she had the tendency for the latter herself. Not because she was distrustful of God's dominion—she wasn't—but because she believed it was her Christian duty to help others, and sometimes that got her in to trouble. *Sometimes I overstep and take matters into my own hands. Hence my presence here.*

"You need not worry," Trudy said once again. There was no point stewing over what had already been done or what embarrassment she might have caused herself or her employer. God in His mercy had already brought about some good by her being here. She had found the wild onion for Opal and she had bandaged more blistered feet than she could count. And her time with Charlie was dear to her—a little blessing amidst the despair. "Charlie is being looked after very well. I'm certain he and Mr. Carpenter will return shortly."

Thankfully they did. Not more than five minutes later, Charlie came bounding into the building with a grin as wide as the Shenandoah Valley itself. Trudy stealthily moved to refill Opal's tin cup of water while the boy told his mother all about his adventure.

"We didn't find any chicory but we did find this!" Charlie then reached deep into the haversack hanging across his chest. "Look!" He held forth a handful of grayish-white curls.

"What is that?" Opal asked.

"It's everything a man could need."

The phase sounded suspiciously like a quote from someone else. *My employer, perhaps?* Curious to see what *exactly* a man needed, Trudy leaned forward to take a peek. "That's bark from a river birch, isn't it?"

"Yessum," Charlie said. "Mr. Carpenter said it's good for startin' fires and that people used to make paper out of it. Even books!"

Ah, now she understood the reference to what "every man needs" or at least what *one man* needed. Paper, in any size or form, was a precious commodity to Peter Carpenter.

"That would be a very small book," Opal said.

"Mr. Carpenter says they would carve big pieces." Charlie gestured with his hands to indicate how wide.

"Then they would write on it. Sometimes Indians would even make clothes out of it."

"Well, let's hope we don't have to resort to that," Opal said with a laugh.

Trudy couldn't help but smile. It was good to see the mother and son sharing a happy moment, and it warmed her heart to know her employer, however unknowingly, had orchestrated it. The joy was short-lived, though, for Opal experienced another coughing spasm. This one was so bad it drew Dr. Mackay's attention. After handing the baby to Emily, he looked to Trudy.

"Perhaps…" he said, nodding discreetly toward the boy.

Trudy understood at once. It wasn't good for Charlie to see his mother in such distress. "Come on, young man. You must be very warm. Let's get you something to drink."

"This bark makes tea," he told her.

"Oh?" Well, that would be useful. The bark together with the bergamot leaves she had collected would provide a variety of drink for a few days.

Just as she succeeded in steering Charlie away from his mother's pallet, Mr. Carpenter stepped inside. Trudy could tell by his posture and the strain on his face that his leg was giving him trouble.

"He needs a drink of water, too!" Charlie insisted as he promptly raced to the man's side.

The strained look eased with the barest hint of a smile as Peter looked down at the child. It didn't escape Trudy's notice that he was growing quite fond of the dark-haired, dark-eyed little boy.

Her heart swelled. *Perhaps deep down, beneath that arrogant facade, he truly is a nurturing man.*

"You go with Miss Trudy," Mr. Carpenter said in a tired voice. "I don't want anything to eat or drink right now. I've got night watch and I need to rest a little before taking my post."

The boy's lower lip protruded. Clearly he wanted the man's continued company. "But you said you would tell me more about the newspaper presses."

"And I will," Peter promised, "but we will talk about that later."

The boy's disappointment did not fade. Mr. Carpenter then looked at Trudy. *Help me*, his tired eyes pleaded.

She didn't need to be asked twice. "Come, Charlie. You needn't ask Mr. Carpenter about the presses. I can tell you a bit about them."

His eyes widened. "You can?"

"Of course. I work there, as well."

The little boy put his hand in hers, allowing her to lead him away from the tired newspaperman. Trudy resisted the urge to look back to see whether or not her employer was watching her, although she knew he was. She could feel his eyes upon her. *He has no interest in ever becoming a husband or a father*, she reminded herself. *He has a widowed sister-in-law to find.*

"What would you like to know?" she asked Charlie as she filled him a cup full of water from the bucket on Mrs. Webb's table.

"What do they look like?" he asked.

"The presses?"

Charlie nodded then took a gulp of water.

"Well, I am told they come in all sorts of shapes and sizes," Trudy said. "Ours isn't the biggest but it works quite nicely."

"Pa told me once that he saw a press that looked like a big table. The man put ink on it, then a paper on top, then he pushed a lever an' mashed the paper."

They claimed the corner farthest from Opal's pallet so Charlie's inquisitiveness would not disturb her. He climbed onto her lap and she wrapped an arm around him to hold him steady. "That's a flatbed press," Trudy said. "Our paper has a double cylinder."

"What's that?"

Hmm, how to describe... "Well...imagine two giant logs... Instead of laying a single sheet of paper down upon the ink, the paper rolls through the cylinders, allowing more sheets to be printed at a time."

"Oh. Do you put the ink on it?"

Trudy chuckled to herself. *Thankfully, no.* She'd seen the pressmen's hands. She had also seen Mr. Carpenter's when he stepped in at times. They were black as pitch after the work and the ink took forever to fade. "No. I don't handle the ink, but I do collect the first pages printed. We call them proofs."

"What do you do with 'um?"

"I give them to Mr. Carpenter. He makes certain that they are to his liking before we print the copies to sell."

"I would be good at that," Charlie said proudly.

She smiled at him, wondering exactly to which job he was referring. Before she could inquire, Charlie pushed to his feet.

"Come buy my paper!" he loudly exclaimed. "There's lots of news to read!"

Laughing, Trudy promptly pulled him back to her lap, partly so she could tickle him, partly so his "hawking" wouldn't wake his now sleeping mother. "Perhaps one day you will, young man," Trudy said as he wiggled and giggled in her grasp. In her opinion, there was nothing more precious than the sound of a child's laughter. It was as if everything were right in the world.

Peter didn't like this valley at night. There were too many places for a man to hide. The rocks and trees, not to mention the various mountain caves, were perfect places to camouflage those bent on mischief. He supposed that's why the Federal and Confederate armies had played cat and mouse in it for so long.

Unofficially they were still doing so. Peter had yet to discover exactly who was responsible for the missing supplies—hungry Southerners or greedy Northern opportunists. *But I have to find out before the next batch of food and medicine is shipped. We can't afford to lose another load of supplies. Charlie's mother is growing worse by the hour.*

Just this evening Dr. Mackay had confided to Peter that he was truly worried about Opal's chances for recovery. "She's been without proper nourishment for so long that I fear she hasn't the strength to fight the infection in her lungs."

Peter felt his heart sink at that news. *That will make two more orphans with which to concern myself.*

Not that he was legally responsible for the boy or his baby sister. They were not his blood kin. And yet, he would not turn his back on them. His conscience wouldn't allow it. Unless Reverend Webb and his wife personally planned to take the children in, Peter knew he couldn't leave them here in Forest Glade. *The preacher will never be able to find a home for them here. No one can afford to take them.*

He told himself the children would stand a better

chance of being claimed by an actual family if they went to Baltimore, although he didn't like the idea of them being placed in an orphanage while they waited for that to happen. *Perhaps I could—*

He realized he was letting his mind run much too far ahead. The children's mother *could* still recover. It *was* possible. He thought of lifting a prayer on her behalf but decided against it. Prayer required faith and waiting, and neither suited him. He was a practical man. God knew that when He had made him. He'd take care of what needs he could and leave the praying up to people like the Webbs and Miss Martin.

He cast a glance at the solitary oil lamp glowing in the front church window. She was serving as night nurse tonight. He hoped she would be conscious of her injured hand and not do anything to impede its healing.

A screech owl cried out, and the old mare on which Peter was riding gave a frightened snort. He patted her neck. No wonder she was skittish. There were no stars tonight. No moon to give light. Clouds had rolled in from the west at sunset.

"I know, old girl. I'm sorry," Peter said in his most comforting tone. "I'd rather be resting, as well, but we've got to keep watch."

The snap of a twig made him tug the reins and turn the horse around. Peter looked behind him just in time to see the handle of a pitchfork coming at him. He immediately reached for his derringer, but it was too late.

Thwack!

With a thud, he landed on the hard, unforgiving ground. His breath fled. His horse scurried away, as well. Seeing Peter was still conscious, a shadowy figure then lunged for the fallen derringer.

"No!" Peter shouted and the wrestling began.

Though life was supposed to pass before one's eyes in moments like these, Peter's did not. Instead he saw a litany of things yet to be accomplished. Discovering the location of his brother's wife and child. Seeing to their care. Ensuring little Charlie and his sister's safe-keeping. Telling Miss Martin how much he appreciated her—something he had never done before. Realizing he might never again see her smile.

The shock of the last gave his attacker the upper hand. The unknown man twisted the weapon in the direction of Peter's heart.

Zing!

The sound of metal hitting bone ricocheted in Peter's ears. Suddenly the attacker slumped forward onto Peter's heaving chest.

What on Earth? He lifted his eyes to see Miss Martin standing over him. The pitchfork was in her hands.

Trudy heard the blood thudding through her ears, felt the weight of the weapon in her hands. Wielding it had ripped open her stitches. She could feel the fluid oozing into her bandage, but she held her guard until Mr. Carpenter rolled the attacker off his chest and then crouched over him.

The man lay completely still.

"Who is he?" she asked. Her voice sounded like it was coming through a long tunnel.

"I don't know," Peter said. "Step back."

As she did so, he reclaimed the derringer and promptly fired a shot into the air. Trudy knew it was for a twofold purpose—to alert Dr. Mackay and Reverend Webb and to scare off any other attackers. She tried not to think about what might happen if there were additional aggressors circling in the darkness, and if they didn't heed the shot's warning.

"Are you hurt?" she asked.

Mr. Carpenter shook his head, but when he tried to stand she knew otherwise. Whether the fall from the horse had caused it or the struggle that ensued, she did not know, but his ankle was injured. At once he crumpled back toward the ground. Tossing aside the pitchfork, she tried to steady him, but he was too heavy. She fell to the earth beside him.

"Let me be," he said gruffly, but the tone softened when he said, "Your hand is bleeding again." Reaching into his vest pocket, he handed her another handkerchief. Emily still had his first one soaking to rid it of blood. Trudy pressed this new one to the wound as he pulled away from her.

Her mind was racing and her heart was pounding too frantically for her to feel any sting of rejection. Reality was sinking in and she was only now coming to realize what she had done. Mr. Carpenter was searching for the pulse of the man on the ground.

"Is he d-dead?" Trudy asked.

It took the space of a few tenuous seconds before he answered. "No," he said.

"Oh thank You, God," she said out loud. She would never be able to forgive herself if she had taken a man's life, even the life of a man who had threatened someone she cared for. "What do you think he wanted?" she asked. "Why did he attack you?"

"I don't know why, but my guess is he wanted what they all want these days. Money, medicine, anything to trade for food."

Now Trudy felt even worse. Had she injured a hungry man? "Then he isn't a profiteer?"

"I don't think so," Mr. Carpenter said. He was methodically going through the man's pockets, searching for clues. "Although I can't rule out he isn't working for one. Look at how he is dressed."

Trudy crept closer. "What do you mean?"

"A homespun shirt much too large for his frame. His shoes are obviously not his own. See, the toes are cut out of them so his feet can have enough room."

"God forgive me," Trudy gasped, her emotions still churning. "He must surely be suffering to act in such a way…but when I saw him knock you from your horse…"

Her employer seemed to find her shuddering amusing, for he gave her a grin. "Well, I'm glad you did, or I might be the one lying here in the dirt, and my heart might not be beating."

He chuckled, but the thought of such a thing made her stomach pitch. Trudy turned her face from him. *How can he take the matter so lightheartedly?* she wondered. She feared she was going to be sick.

Dr. Mackay and Reverend Webb came running toward them.

"Gentlemen," Mr. Carpenter said. "I believe Miss Martin is in need of some birch tea. She is a bit overcome." He then very calmly listed his wishes. "I'd appreciate it if one of you would kindly escort her back inside. After that, I could use a length of rope. Also, my horse is missing."

Dr. Mackay promptly went to the unknown, still unconscious man. Reverend Webb came to her.

"Come with me, Miss Trudy. Dr. Mackay will see

to all of this. I'll take you inside." She went, but only so that her employer wouldn't see that she was crying. The thought of the death of the assailant at her hands or Mr. Carpenter at his was simply overwhelming, as it would have been for any God-fearing woman. Given their history, however, she didn't want Peter to mistake her tears for anything more than that.

Chapter Eight

Peter's eyes followed Miss Martin back to the church until Dr. Mackay recaptured his attention. "Who is he?" he asked.

Once again Peter said he did not know. "But I intend to find out as soon as he is awake again." Peter didn't remember seeing this particular man before in these parts. *But just because I didn't see him doesn't mean he hasn't been here.*

The assailant was beginning to stir. Dr. Mackay had already succeeded in giving him a preliminary examination. The injury he had sustained wasn't serious, but the man was likely to have a knot on the back of his head the size of a lemon come morning. The doctor said it was already making itself known.

"And Trudy did this?" The Scotsman asked in disbelief.

Peter felt a grin tugging at his lips. He remembered the wild look in her eyes as she stood over him with pitchfork in hand. *She looked as though she could stand toe-to-toe—or rather, toe-to-claw—with a female bear and come out as the victor.* "She did indeed."

Dr. Mackay shook his head in disbelief. "Remind me never to cross *that* lass."

The reverend returned that moment with his coil of rope. Dr. Mackay set to work at once securing the now moaning assailant. Peter sat looking on, then asked the reverend, "Is Miss Trudy alright?"

The man nodded. "She's a bit shaken but she is well enough. Sarah and Mrs. Mackay are sitting with her."

So the gunfire woke them, as well, Peter thought. He was sorry for that but it couldn't be helped. "She tore open her stitches," he said as Dr. Mackay secured the final rope knot. The physician looked up.

"Badly?"

Peter shrugged. "I didn't look that closely."

"I don't believe it was too bad," Reverend Webb said. "Anyway, your wife is presently tending her."

Good, Peter thought.

"What about you?" Dr. Mackay asked him.

Only then did he let himself remember his own pain. "I believe I have dislocated my ankle."

"Your club foot?"

Peter shook his head.

Dr. Mackay then shook his head with a sympathetic smile. "I'm sorry, lad. Looks like you'll be laid up for a day or two." The physician knelt and placed his hands on Peter's ankle. Without warning he snapped it back into place.

The pain Peter had been experiencing diminished somewhat but his frustration did not. *Why couldn't I have landed on the other foot?* He was used to limping on that one. *I can't afford to be laid up by an injury. It will mean additional delay in locating Caroline.* He glanced again at the man on the ground. *And with scoundrels like this roaming the valley...* He shook off the thought. He didn't want to think about the consequences if a man like that attacked his brother's wife.

His thoughts then shifted to Miss Martin. Yes, she had handled herself impressively tonight, but she'd had the element of surprise in her favor. *What if she had been the one who was surprised?* Peter seriously wondered if he would have been able to rescue her. He wondered also exactly why he had been thinking of her when he hit the ground.

Seeing her standing over him, red hair whipping in the wind, he couldn't help but think how beautiful she was. *But I will never tell her that.* He knew what would happen if he did. *She'd think more of it than she should, that its more than a case of simple attraction.*

The man on the ground was struggling against his bonds. Peter forcefully pushed to his feet despite his pain. He wanted his attacker to see who had been victorious in this fight. For good measure he showed his derringer. Dr. Mackay puffed out his chest and crossed his arms just as the man opened his eyes.

"What do you want?" Peter demanded to know.

"Just food!"

Call it a sixth sense, a newspaperman's intuition, but Peter wasn't buying it. There was something in the man's eyes. "You could have just knocked on the door," he said. "You could have asked. If you were after food, you didn't have to knock me from my horse to get it."

At that the man said nothing. Peter simply let the silence grow. He knew there was a story here.

Dr. Mackay then spoke. "We'll give you some bread."

Peter, who was still watching the man's face carefully, detected the hint of a sneer. *This man doesn't want bread.* "Perhaps you'd prefer the fare at the Federal garrison," he said. "My colleagues and I will be happy to take you there come sunup."

At that, Dr. Mackay raised the man to his feet. Evidently he had seen the sneer, as well. "Reverend, I do believe this man is requesting the shelter of your stable. I hope you will not mind." The physician looked then at Peter. "I'll stand guard."

Reverend Webb didn't object to the doctor's plan, but as the assailant and the Scotsman traipsed toward the small shelter, he said to Peter, "Are you sure about this? The Federal garrison? He could just be a desperate man."

"He's not," Peter insisted. "I've seen the type before, feigning innocence, and apparently so has Dr. Mackay. He's no hungry Confederate veteran, Reverend. Put that out of your mind. The man didn't bat an eye when I told him we'd take him to the Federal authorities. Lawless rebels are punished swiftly nowadays with prison, even hanging, but this man wasn't the least bit frightened."

"I see." Reverend Webb, said although his tone was decidedly sad. "Do you think he has friends?"

"You mean coconspirators?" Peter clarified. "Perhaps even friends at the local garrison?" The well-dressed businessman Johnson immediately came to mind.

The reverend nodded. "Do you think he's involved in our missing supplies?"

"If he isn't, I believe he knows who is."

Reverend Webb drew in a breath.

"Can you manage things around here without me and the doctor tomorrow?" Peter knew he'd need the Scotsman's assistance to guard the prisoner, maybe even Robert Smith's. *Thanks to the fall, I'm even less of a man of strength.* Reverend Webb recognized that, as well.

"Can you ride all the way to Larkinsville with those ankles of yours?"

He had to. There was no way he was going to hand responsibility for this scalawag off to someone else, even a former army physician. *I am going to see this through. I am going to get answers. I am going to find out what happened to our supplies.* His friends needed them. The people of this valley like Opal and Charlie and the baby needed them. *Caroline needs them.* "Yes, but I'm not taking him to Larkinsville," Peter said.

"You aren't?"

"No. I don't trust Lieutenant Glassman."

"Then where *will* you take him?" the reverend asked.

"The next closest garrison is Lexington, correct?"

"Yes, but that's quite a bit further."

"Don't worry about me," Peter said, "but do me a favor…"

"Of course."

"Keep an eye on Miss Trudy while I'm gone." Peter could feel the grin again tugging at his lips. "She has a knack for involving herself where she shouldn't."

Par for the course of this trip so far, Peter's best laid plans had come to naught. Dr. Mackay would not permit him to travel to Lexington at sunrise.

"No," he said firmly. "You must get some real rest. You've not had a decent sleep in days. If you try to leave now with your ankle still so tender, it will pain you the entire journey, and your other foot is not strong enough to compensate. You know that as well as I."

Peter did, of course, but the fact that the man was right gnawed at him almost as much as his limitations. Unfortunately, to get anywhere with the garrison authorities, he had to present a strong front. He could allow Dr. Mackay to escort the man this morning. He offered to do so. The able-bodied, six-foot-four former Federal soldier would certainly be able to impressively press their case, *and do so probably better than I can.*

Peter's pride, however, wouldn't allow it. He'd been the one who had been ambushed. He'd see this through. Besides, he still needed to send his wires. "What about traveling tomorrow?" he asked. "You, me and Robert."

Dr. Mackay huffed. He clearly wasn't happy about that option, either, but he conceded. "Alright," he said, "but you must stay off of your feet today. You must rest."

"Agreed." Peter decided he would put the time to good use. He'd fire off another article for his paper, maybe a straight editorial this time. In it he'd press the need for more law and order in these parts, and more accountability for the soldiers who were supposed to be providing it.

And perhaps another day's confinement in the stable will make my still-unnamed assailant rethink his course. Perhaps he will offer up some piece of information that will be useful. The man had been incredibly tight-lipped. In fact, the only time he had opened his mouth at all was to partake of the small meals Reverend Webb brought him.

Come the following morning, though, even after repeated questioning by each of the men, Peter's attacker still held his tongue. To make matters worse, Dr.

Mackay was now unable to accompany Peter to Lexington. Opal had taken a turn for the worse.

"I can't leave her," he said. "The infection has now spread to both lungs. You'll have to ask the reverend and Robert to go with you."

Reverend Webb was wiry and strong but unsteady with a weapon, and a gun was a must for escorting a man to the Federal garrison. Robert could handle himself, but Peter would rather have the former soldier with him, as well. Once again he lamented the fact that David Wainwright was not here.

Dr. Mackay then said, "I have a request…"

"What's that?"

"Take Trudy with you."

It was all he could do not to roll his eyes at the physician. His request was like adding insult to injury. So Dr. Mackay wanted to send the wild pitchfork-wielding nurse along to look after him? *Yes, that will be quite helpful.* "You can't be serious."

"I am indeed," Dr. Mackay said. "I need her to charm some ether and morphine out of the garrison medical officer."

As much as Peter detested the idea of taking her along with him, he knew Dr. Mackay wouldn't be asking unless it was absolutely necessary.

And it is, he conceded. *I know nothing about medical supplies beyond the fact that ether is used for anesthetizing patients during surgery and morphine for the pain following. Miss Martin, however, is quite familiar with both, and she will be intelligent enough to know if our request is filled with genuine articles or someone is trying to deceive us.* It was a sad commentary on the state of the army these days that someone might actually try to trick them with the wrong supplies, but unfortunately it was how some officers operated. Some couldn't stand the thought of assisting a former enemy.

"So you are planning to operate on Charlie's mother?" Peter then asked.

Dr. Mackay nodded gravely. "I don't wish to, but I may be forced to insert a chest tube to drain the fluid in her lungs. I've done it before without ether, but I'd prefer not to do so in this case."

Peter's heart sank as he felt the weight of the woman's suffering, the suffering of her children. "I see," he said. "Then I will travel as quickly as possible."

"Don't press it," Dr. Mackay warned. "Don't risk further aggravating your own infirmities. I will wait as long as I can on the procedure. I'm still hoping her lungs will clear on their own, but even if I must operate and you don't return with the ether in time, she will still need the morphine."

Which is worth its weight in gold nowadays, he thought. Miss Martin had better be quite the charmer to score that. "Are you sure she'll be able to procure what you wish?" Peter asked.

Again the doctor nodded. "I'll send her with a written request in my name."

"Very well," Peter said.

The man laid a thankful hand on his shoulder, and then grinned. "And don't worry about looking after that lass. She won't be any trouble. After all, she knows how to handle a weapon."

"Tell her to bring that pitchfork with her," Peter said. "She can guard our mysterious friend." He had shared in the man's joke, but truth be told, he really wasn't

looking forward to sharing the bench seat with Miss
Martin all the way to Lexington. She was becoming
a distraction to him. Why exactly, he was not certain.
He'd seen pretty faces before, but the last time he had
been thinking of Miss Martin's particular face, he had
nearly gotten killed.

The events of the previous evening had frightened
everyone except Charlie. Thankfully, he had slept
through the entire episode, gunshot included, and was
blissfully unaware of the danger that had befallen his
beloved newspaperman. Trudy couldn't help but wonder, though, if word had somehow spread through the
surrounding community, for not a visitor had stepped
foot on the church property all day.

Are they now too afraid to come here? Trudy wondered. *Are they fearful they also will be attacked?* She
privately expressed her thoughts to Emily.

"No, love. It's not that," Emily said. "It is just a quiet
day. It happens. Perhaps God is simply trying to bless you."

"Bless me?" Trudy said, not following her friend's
line of thinking. "In what way?"

"With a day of rest." Emily eyed Trudy in a motherly sort of way. "You *are* inclined to do more than you
should. You don't want to reinjure your hand again."

"It seems there is little chance of that now," Trudy
quipped, "even if the church is suddenly filled with
visitors." Following her bout with the unknown man
last night, Emily had resewn her hand and then, after
applying a fresh dressing, she had taken a long strip
of cloth and bound the arm across Trudy's chest. "You
have effectively rendered my hand useless."

Emily grinned. "That was my plan. No more pitch-forks for you."

I'll never live this down, Trudy thought. She couldn't help but wonder how Dr. Mackay would have responded if Emily had been the one with the pitchfork. Her friend was a capable woman, married to a good, but strong-willed, sometimes prideful man. *A man much like Mr. Carpenter.*

Trudy had seen the look on her employer's face when he had realized she had come to his aid—part shock, part admiration, part chagrin. *No man like that wants to think he can't handle a situation on his own*, she mused, *and there I was once again, his lovesick assistant, trying to help.*

He had been avoiding her all day long and she had been doing the same with him. The memory of what had happened still brought tears to her eyes, especially when she thought of what might have been had the assailant gained full control of Mr. Carpenter's derringer.

"I might be the one lying here in the dirt, and my heart might not be beating." She shuddered at the memory of the words he had spoken.

Unable to help herself, she cast a glance in his direction. Mr. Carpenter was presently sitting at his desk with his freshly injured leg propped up on an empty chair. He was reading what appeared to be a letter, presumably an older one given the condition of the wrinkled paper.

A letter from whom? she couldn't help but wonder. *Daniel? Caroline?* He was engrossed in its contents, almost as if he was trying to glean clues. *He looks so tired*, Trudy thought, *so discouraged.* She had to resist the urge to go to him and ask if she could render assistance in some way.

To avoid that temptation, and because of the stifling heat, Trudy spent much of the day with the children outside. Beneath a large shade tree, Charlie peppered her with more questions about the newspaper office. Kate rocked back and forth on her little legs, seriously considering crawling but not quite compelled to do so yet. Trudy tried to encourage her with smiles.

"Come on, love... Come to me..."

The baby grinned, rocked a bit more, but remained where she was.

After numerous repeated attempts, Trudy scooped the little girl up into her arms and kissed her neck. Kate giggled. Trudy took pleasure in the sound, but even so, fear today lingered in the back of her mind.

Mysterious men come calling in the night, bent on trouble, and Opal isn't improving... Lord, please help her. The children need her so... Please help us all...

At sunset Dr. Mackay came to them.

"I want you to go with Peter tomorrow to Lexington," he said.

"Me?" Trudy gasped, jaw dropping in disbelief.

"We need morphine and ether," Dr. Mackay explained. Then she understood. He and Emily needed to stay with Opal. Therefore Trudy was the next best qualified to collect the medical supplies.

"Mrs. Webb will look after the children," Dr. Mackay said, "and the reverend will manage any new visitors."

And Mr. Carpenter? What does he think of all this? As much as she wished to keep her distance from him, she realized their embarrassment was not the issue here.

They had a duty to attend. *Dr. Mackay is counting on us. Charlie's mother needs our help.*

"Very well," she told the physician.

Dr. Mackay offered her a smile. "Thank you," he said. "I'll let Peter know."

The summer sun was beginning to pinken the eastern sky as Trudy made her way the following morning to the wagon. She carefully climbed into the driver's box. Emily had freed Trudy's hand from its confinement but warned her to be careful.

"God will be with you," she then said.

Trudy tried to remember that God truly would be with them. *Lord, I know You have a plan. I know You are still in control. Help me to remember that. Let that fact permeate my thoughts, my heart and my actions today.*

She adjusted her skirts as she settled on the bench seat. Inadvertently she glanced behind her. Robert was seated to her right, his eyes and his weapon on the attacker. A shiver ran down Trudy's spine. The memory of the man wrestling Mr. Carpenter on the ground, ready to take his life from him, once again threatened to bring tears to her eyes, but she kept them in check. Peter Carpenter did not want her tears and he did not want her company. The look on his face when she turned back around confirmed it.

"Do you have Dr. Mackay's letter?" he asked.

"I do." She wanted to ask him about his ankle, but she knew he wouldn't tell her even if it was hurting him. So she said instead, "Mrs. Webb packed us some hoe cakes and the last of the squirrel."

"Let's be off," he said.

He gave the reins a click and the wagon lurched forward.

The Earth was silent this morning, like the dawn of creation. No breeze rustled the treetops. Even the birds seemed still to be abed. Only the creaking of the wagon disturbed the stillness, and its occupants were too tired, too on edge or too lost in thought to speak.

Trudy stared straight ahead, eyes open but her heart and mind drawn away by the desperate need to pray. She prayed for Opal, for her healing. She prayed for Opal's children. She prayed for the man behind her whom Robert so carefully guarded, and of course, she prayed for her employer.

Help him, Lord. He needs answers. More than just answers about his attacker and the missing food. Help him find the woman he is seeking.

"How's your hand?"

His voice startled her. Even more surprising was when she turned to him and saw the look on his face. His eyes weren't narrowed by cynicism. His forehead wasn't furrowed contemplatively. His expression had softened, considerably.

Trudy drew in a shallow breath. Would she ever be able to look at him without feeling butterflies in her stomach? "My hand is much better. Thank you. Emily is a good nurse."

He nodded quietly, eyes returning to the road. "So are you," he said.

I am? She had been told that by others before but *never by him*.

She watched as he drew in a breath. "I apologize for giving you such a hard time for coming here," he then said. "You *have* been a help to…us all."

The *us all* sounded suspiciously like a last-minute substitute for *me*. At least, that was what Trudy wanted to think. The pleasure she felt at his compliment was exhilarating but she made certain not to display too much emotion. "Thank you," she said simply.

"And you are good with the children," he then said.

A wide smile broke Trudy's lips. She couldn't help it. To say she was surprised at the direction of this conversation was putting it mildly, but she was eager for it to continue. "They are easy to love."

"My mother always says that," he replied. "At least, when she is referring to her grandchildren."

"Does she have many?" Trudy asked as the wagon rolled along. "I think I remember her saying that you have a sister out west."

"California," he said. "My sister has three children. And my brother Matthew had a child, but his wife remarried after his death." He paused, then added, "She prefers to keep company now only with her new husband's family. They live in Pittsburg."

How sad. "I'm sorry to hear that. That must be very hard on…your mother."

He offered only the barest of nods, but the expression on his face, at least from what she could see of his profile, still reflected openness. Trudy dared offer her continued sympathy.

"I'm sorry about your brother Daniel, as well,"

He cast her a glance, but it was so fleeting that Trudy was unable to read if he wished to continue on the subject or not.

Apparently he did, for after a few seconds of silence, he said, "It's my duty to look after Daniel's affairs."

Trudy decided to take the chance. "Emily told me about Caroline."

He nodded slowly. "Then you know how important it is that I find her," he said.

"I do."

There was a bump in the road, big enough to toss her in his direction. Her arm brushed his. Trudy drew in a breath when they touched but quickly repositioned herself on the bench seat. He didn't seem to notice any of it.

"She has a child," Peter then said, "or at least she did."

"Born during the war?"

He nodded once again. "At least, *expected* during the war. Daniel didn't share many details and the letters I received from him were few and far between."

Trudy understood that very well. Her own brother's wartime letters had been scarce. For her and her family, the silence had been maddening. They never knew if George had been killed or captured or simply could not get word to them. A Confederate soldier's letters were not easily delivered in a city occupied by the Federal army.

"It shouldn't have been this way," he then said.

There was something in his tone that led Trudy to believe he was speaking of more than just his brother's untimely death and the child he had fathered. It grieved her to hear the pain in his voice. "I'm praying that you'll find Caroline and the baby," she said. "I'm confident you will."

A hint of anger crept into his expression. Trudy didn't know at first if it was directed at her, at God, at Daniel or at the whole chaotic world. "He never thought something would actually happen to him," Peter said. "He never considered the possible consequences of marrying during wartime."

She drew in a breath, choosing her words carefully. This was delicate territory. "Few men do, I suppose." She couldn't help but think of her sister Elizabeth's fiancé. Her *first* fiancé, Jeremiah—David's brother. He had died of pneumonia in the Baltimore military hospital before they could wed. "In dark times we all want a small piece of happiness."

"Happiness isn't possible," he said, "at least not in this world."

"That's not true."

He raised his eyebrow cynically at her but she did not back down. "Don't you feel happy when you put together an edition of your paper? Don't you feel a sense of satisfaction when you see justice achieved for someone who is deserving? Or suffering relieved?" She knew he did or he wouldn't be doing what he was doing.

He knew it, as well, for he conceded with a nod. "Perhaps you should consider a future in the law."

She decided to take his words again as a compliment, although she had no interest in the law. She was happy where she was, especially in this moment. Peter Carpenter had said more to her in the last five minutes, in real conversation, than he had in weeks—ever since he'd let her know in no uncertain terms that he wasn't the marrying kind.

That, of course, was still the case, but at least now he wasn't condemning her for her supposed naivety or accusing her of following him here in some matrimonial scheme. He admired her for her abilities and she respected him for his. They could work together—and Trudy told herself that was all she wanted.

Mr. Carpenter didn't say anything else after that but it didn't matter. She was content to simply travel beside him.

Chapter Nine

Peter's freshly injured ankle was aching after only a couple of miles of driving. He told himself that after they unloaded the prisoner, Robert could drive. He knew Miss Trudy was capable of negotiating the rutted road, but with her injured hand, Peter didn't want to ask her to take the reins. Besides, doing so would convey weakness to the prisoner in the back—and to her. He knew he had good reason to show strength to the man, but why he was so determined to prove himself to *her* was entirely another matter. She already knew his weaknesses. Anyone with observant eyes did.

He hadn't known exactly how she would react to traveling with the stranger who had bushwhacked him. After all, she had been quite upset when she realized her activities with the pitchfork could have had deadly consequences.

Perhaps that is a good thing, Peter thought. *She'll be less likely to involve herself in dangerous situations next time.*

He couldn't help but think again of what might have happened if she hadn't knocked the man out cold. *If the*

scoundrel had suddenly turned on her, harmed her...
His blood chilled in his veins, and he cast a furtive
glance at the back of the wagon just to reassure himself
that the stranger was no threat to her now.

Robert had him fully under control. The man was
still bound and the freedman was keeping Dr. Mackay's
personal derringer well in view. Like always, Peter carried his in his right frock coat pocket, ready if necessary.

Apparently Miss Martin was confident the mysterious man would cause no trouble today. She'd settled
into a relaxed posture beside him. Every now and then
her arm bumped his whenever the ruts in the road jolted
the wagon. He didn't mind, though. *I suppose I am getting used to her.*

She'd smiled when he'd told her she had been helpful on this journey. He knew she desperately wanted to
be useful. He was grateful she had assisted him, even if
his pride didn't want to acknowledge that he had often
needed help. She'd listened patiently when he'd prat-
tled on about his family. *She is a kindhearted woman,
a loyal employee.*

His own thoughts mocked him. *A loyal employee?
Really? Is that really what it is?*

Peter gave the reins a snap, urged the old mare along.
*Maybe it isn't loyalty. And she's not the only one who
feels it. I'll concede I am attracted to her. Any man with
eyes would be.* And as for her temperament, in Peter's
mind she was the exact proportion of sweetness and
tenacity he liked.

*But that doesn't change anything. Taking care of a
penniless war widow—if that's what Caroline still is—
well, that is one thing. Miss Martin is quite a different story.*

He stole a glance at her. Presently she was captivated by the rolling Allegheny Mountains to the west. *His* attention was on *her*, particularly her youthful face and form, even though he knew it shouldn't be. *She should be going to balls and dancing until dawn. At ten years her senior and with a club foot to boot, I'd end up being her patient, not a dependable partner.*

Peter was shocked that his mind had gone that far, but he hadn't time to ponder it further. Puffs of dust rose in the wake of the three approaching riders. Two were soldiers. The third was a well-dressed, middle-aged civilian whom Peter recognized at once. The pompous-looking man sat front and center on his steed.

Johnson. The hair on the back of the newspaper-man's neck stood on end for the road was narrow, and he would be forced to let the riders pass. Peter hoped they would do so without incident.

"Mr. Smith," Peter said over his shoulder, "let's do our best to look like four ordinary travelers, shall we?"

Robert understood the message at once. Removing his slouch hat, he covered the derringer he was holding. "Keep in mind," he told the man under his guard, "that 'though you can't see it, it's still pointed exactly where it needs to be."

"In other words," Peter added without turning around, "continue to keep your mouth shut."

He hadn't time to direct Miss Martin for the trio was now upon them. Peter desperately hoped she would keep silent, as well. The last thing he wanted was for her to reveal any information about the man behind them or where Peter was taking him. *If Johnson is what I think he is, if he is involved with the theft of our supplies, and the man behind me is one of his accomplices...* Peter couldn't help but wonder, even with the presence of two Federal soldiers, if the trouble which had previous befallen him was about to be repeated. *And now with Miss Trudy here beside me...*

Johnson noticed the prisoner at once. The proclaimed businessman offered a quick but telling look at the man in the back of Peter's wagon.

You know him, Peter thought as Johnson reined up alongside him. He held his breath as the carpetbagger's look of surprise was then replaced with one of superiority. "Well, well, Mr. Carpenter. Out and about, are we?"

The man's patronizing tone sickened Peter. "We most certainly are," he replied.

"Searching?"

For answers, yes, and I have a feeling you could provide some.

"If you are still looking for supplies, one of my men will gladly assist you."

One of my men? Peter wondered just how true that statement was. These men were soldiers, supposedly in the employ of the United States Army, but they seemed wholly comfortable following this private citizen's commands. Johnson hadn't asked about the man in the back, and neither had the soldiers. Did that make the latter honest men who were simply providing escort? *Or are they waiting for Johnson's directive to intervene?*

Robert's derringer was holding the silence in the back of the wagon. Beside him Miss Martin was smiling sweetly, but Peter knew she was frightened. She had slid closer to him upon the riders' approach. He wondered again just how much protection he could actually provide if the circumstances warranted it. His heart was pounding beneath his vest but he refused to let his fear show.

"Well, that is very kind of you, Mr. Johnson," Peter replied, doing his best not to gag on the words, "but completely unnecessary. My friends and I are simply on routine newspaper business." It wasn't a lie, for one way or another he was going to get a story out of this.

If we aren't killed first... He was holding the reins casually, knowing any sign of tension from him would agitate the horses, which would alert the soldiers to trouble. Even if they were honest men, there was no way he was going to hand over his assailant to them. *For all I know, Lieutenant Glassman will set him free— and command him to attack us again.*

Up ahead was the turn for Lexington and about a half mile beyond that, the county line, where Glassman's jurisdiction and that of his soldiers ended. *If they aren't honest men, will they pursue us beyond the boundary? Ambush us when they think we aren't expecting it?*

He decided to hand the reins to Miss Martin. Even though he didn't like the idea of her driving, potentially further injuring her hand, he'd been left with little choice. *If I need to reach for my derringer...*

She took them without question. Peter then turned in the bench seat, rubbing his right knee as if it were sore—as if that was why he had handed the driving over.

Johnson was still staring him down. The soldiers just looked bored.

"Thank you again, Mr. Johnson for your offer, but I am certain you and your escorts have pressing business to attend. Don't let us detain you."

Peter saw the flicker of uncertainty in the carpetbagger's eyes, but a questioning glance from the ranking soldier beside him dispersed it immediately.

"Very well," the man said. "A good day to you all." After tipping his hat at Miss Martin, Johnson motioned for the soldiers to continue.

Peter heard her release a pent-up sigh. *We aren't out of this yet.* "Go," he told her. She snapped the reins. The wagon lurched forward as Peter craned his neck to look behind them.

"Now you just continue to keep still," Robert said to their prisoner. "Remember, there's bullets in this gun." He motioned his head toward Peter. "And in his, too."

The assailant held his place and said nothing, but Peter took no comfort in the fact. Johnson and the soldiers had disappeared around the bend, yet the look on the man's face told Peter he *expected* them to return. Peter clutched the cold steel tightly and kept his eyes open.

"Turn here," he told Miss Martin when they reached the Lexington road.

She did so without comment. Sensing his urgency, she encouraged the mare to pick up her pace. The wagon bounced along the uneven road. Peter's nerves were on edge and his ankle was now paining him tremendously. He was making great effort not to let it show on his face, but she knew.

"Are you alright?" she asked.

He ignored the question, not wanting to admit that he wasn't. Not to her and definitely not to the man behind them. "When we reach the garrison, I want you to go straight to the medical officer while Robert and I see to our guest."

She nodded dutifully.

"You'll know if you're being swindled."

"You need not worry," she said.

His words had come out more like a question than a statement. He hadn't meant to imply lack of confidence in her. Actually he had intended just the opposite. She had done well today. She'd read the danger in their previous situation. She'd held her tongue. She had taken charge of the horse without question. *She has been quite helpful*, but he didn't see any point in saying that. She had already returned her eyes to the road. *And that is where mine should remain.*

Ahead the valley was opening up into an even wider space, as if the Blue Ridge and the Alleghenies had grown tired of each other's company and decided to part ways. Peter desired the same with Miss Martin. Try as he might, he couldn't seem to focus on anything except the fact that she was sitting beside him.

Shifting his position on the bench seat, he put a little more distance between them. His ankle was throbbing. Still, he reclaimed the reins. Her hand had to be hurting, though evidently she was as determined as him not to show it.

We're a fine pair, he couldn't help but think. *Each one as stubborn as the other.*

Presently they were entering Lexington. The locals here had fared better than the citizens further north. The town was still standing. Evidently General Sheridan had grown tired of burning.

Peter glanced back. The unknown assailant in the back of the wagon was again getting squirmy. Apparently he hadn't actually believed he was going to be taken to the garrison until he saw the fort coming into view. *I suppose he has no friends here.* Peter's hope of honest dealings with the local commanding officer grew. Maybe, just maybe, this man would help him recover his missing supplies or at least protect the next shipment. *And perhaps someone here may have word on Daniel's wife and child.*

From one situation to another, Trudy thought ruefully. God had carried them safely through one, but would He do so again?

She tried not to be nervous as she entered the army garrison. The country was no longer at war and her brother, the former Confederate soldier, had retaken the oath of loyalty to the Union. Before that, however, she had been discharged from her nursing position at the Baltimore military hospital for refusing to sign that same oath back during the war years. She had taken issue with the line that said she would not "give aid or comfort to the enemy." She was a nurse and a Christian, and her conscience would not allow her to turn away a man sick or in need, no matter what color his uniform.

Trudy couldn't escape the nagging fear that her brother's past actions and her own would hinder today's mission. *Not only did I fail to sign the oath, I knitted socks, scarves and hats for Southern soldiers during the war.* Realistically, she knew there was no way the soldiers here were aware of her past—but it felt as if her so-called disloyalty, resulting from sympathy for those on both sides of the conflict, was written on her forehead.

She drew in a shallow breath. *Now I am currently trying to provide relief for former citizens of the Confederacy. Will the garrison medical officer see my ef-*

fort for the compassion it is or would he label me a malcontent bent on continuing war? What if I am held for questioning?

She drew in another breath, doing her best to steel her nerves. She had told Mr. Carpenter she was capable. She did not wish to disappoint him. She quickly corrected that thought. *I do not wish to disappoint Opal. She needs this medicine, Lord. Help me. I am scared and I am distracted.*

Peter was distracted, as well—not only by his family but by the man on the road. He hadn't said such, but Trudy had been able to tell instantly that he did not trust Mr. Johnson. The fact was, she hadn't either. She had seen the look that came over the man's face when he had first noticed their prisoner. It was more than surprise. She was certain it had been a look of recognition.

And why would he recognize a man who harms others?

Her employer's words drifted though her mind. *"This world is a dangerous place..."* She had wanted to ask Peter what he specifically knew about Mr. Johnson, but she did not think it prudent to do so in front of their still silent travel companion.

Tension made her neck ache and her hand was sore again. She didn't blame Mr. Carpenter for asking her to drive, however. She knew he had done so only because he was trying to protect her. *Protect us.*

At the garrison gate he stated their business, beginning with her. "This young lady has a message for your senior medical officer."

A tall, formidable-looking soldier in blue eyed her up and down. "From who?" he asked.

"From another senior medical officer," Peter said authoritatively.

The soldier apparently was satisfied. He motioned to another man in blue who stepped to her side of the wagon and directed her to the medical ward. She wanted to look behind her to see how Mr. Carpenter was faring—with the soldiers, with the prisoner and with himself. She knew his ankle was hurting him. She could tell by the way he kept shifting his position on the seat. The traveling and the encounter with the men on the road had drained him. They had her, as well.

She didn't turn around but she did again lift a prayer on his behalf. *Protect him, Lord, and please give him the answers he needs.*

As she made her way toward the medical ward, time seemed to move in reverse. Once again she was back in the military hospital, following orders, searching for supplies. Like then, there were Federal soldiers stationed in the halls. The flickering glow of the oil lamps cast their large intimidating shadows across the floor.

Trudy couldn't help but remember the morning she and her friends were unexpectedly rounded up by men in blue, then marched to a room full of Federal officers. *We were accused of helping a Confederate prisoner escape. Lewis Thornton Powell.* The man was later caught. Last week he had been hung for his involvement in President Lincoln's assassination.

She shivered at that thought but continued on her journey, reminding herself that she'd had no involvement in such crimes, no knowledge of the escape of Powell, later known as Paine, *and the commanding officers believed me.* Though they had demanded she sign the oath of loyalty, which had brought her tenure with the hospital to an end.

She came to her destination, an area much smaller

then she had expected—just one small room with six empty beds, one orderly and one gray-headed physician. The latter was organizing his medical cabinet on the far side of the room.

The orderly looked up when he noticed her. "Help you, miss?" he asked.

"Yes, thank you," she said with a smile. "I'd like to speak with your medical officer. I have a letter of request to present to him."

The orderly looked over his shoulder and called out, "Hey, Doc? There's a lady here to see ya."

Trudy was taken slightly aback. Things had obviously changed since the surrender. Most officers wouldn't allow such a casual form of address. But when the officer in question turned around, Trudy understood the lack of formality. She recognized the man at once. The remaining tension drained from her immediately.

"Dr. Turner!" she exclaimed. "Gracious sakes! What a pleasure it is to find you here!"

Jacob Turner was an amiable, kindhearted physician whom she knew from the Baltimore hospital. He had been instrumental in convincing the Federal officers that neither she nor her friends had played any role in Lewis Powell's escape. She knew this man would help her again if he could. Although over two years had passed, he recognized her, as well.

"Miss Trudy?" he said, eyes wide with surprise. "Is that really *you*?"

"Yes, sir. It is."

The old man grinned. He came to meet her where she stood, then wrapped her in a fatherly embrace. "How good it is to see you again. What on Earth brings you here?" His joyful look turned then to one of concern. "Are you well?"

"Yes. Quite. What are you doing here? I'd have thought you would have returned to New England, to your family, when the war ended."

"There was still work to be done," he said, "and when my daughter married and my wife agreed to join me here, I reenlisted. What about your family? You are a far cry from Baltimore."

"Indeed." She explained what had brought her to Virginia, including telling him of Elizabeth and David's coming child. He had known the pair back when Elizabeth was a nurse and David an orderly. "Dr. Mackay and Emily are also here."

The man slapped his leg as he let out a laugh. "So he came to help the people of the South on his own? I knew that Miss Emily would be good for him. He was once a hard-hearted officer, you know."

Trudy nodded. Back in Baltimore, in the early days of the war, Dr. Mackay had borne a terrible grudge against Southerners due to the death of his brother, a soldier in the Federal army. The citizens of Baltimore with their divided loyalties had infuriated him. Back then, she had gone out of her way to avoid him. *Odd, that later I would seek out the employment of a man with such a similar personality.* She wondered now who was more cynical, more stubborn, Dr. Mackay or Peter Carpenter. Pushing that thought from her mind, she came to her real purpose. "I've a written request from Evan," she said.

"Oh?"

She pulled the letter from her pocket and handed it to him. The man stroked his chin while he perused it. "I'm sorry to hear about your stolen supplies," Dr. Turner said. "Sadly, it's a common occurrence nowadays. Did you alert the commander?"

"Of the garrison in Larkinsville? Yes, but we received little satisfaction. That's why we came here." She told him then about the attacker but left out the details concerning her interaction with Mr. Carpenter and the pitchfork. Thankfully Dr. Turner had not noticed her hand. The wonderful thing about wearing a fully pleated day dress without a hoop or corded petticoat was that she could keep her hand casually hidden in the side folds of her skirt.

"Well," Dr. Turner said as he finished the letter, "the commanding officer here takes his job seriously. I'm certain he will look into the matter…and as for Evan's supply list…yes, I can give you some of what you need, at least enough to hold you until your next shipment arrives."

She heaved a thankful sigh of relief. *Opal will receive help! God be praised!* "Thank you, Dr. Turner! Thank you very much!"

He patted her arm. "Come. Help me gather what you need."

She followed him to the cabinet for the ether and morphine. He chatted again about Elizabeth. "Wonderful news about your sister," he said. "A child is truly one of God's greatest blessings."

She nodded in agreement but did so with mixed emotions. Once again thoughts of Peter Carpenter invaded her mind—both his disdain for the idea of becoming a father…and his search for a mother and child. Trudy knew that realistically the odds that Dr. Turner knew anything of the whereabouts of Caroline Carpenter and her baby were almost nil. Still, she felt compelled to ask.

She told him as much of the story as she knew. He listened with great interest and sympathy.

"There's many a tale like that, especially in these parts," he said. "I wish I had good news to offer you, but I'm afraid I don't recollect anyone by that name personally."

She swallowed back her disappointment.

"But," he then added, "you might try the Hassler farm. They are a Mennonite family just a few miles north of here."

"You think they may know of her?"

He shrugged. "I cannot say for certain, but I know they took in several displaced women and children during the war and after. One of them might be your Caroline."

"Might be" wasn't certainty, but coupled with the crate of supplies he was packing for her, it was enough to keep her hopes alive. *And it gives me what every newspaperman wishes for—a new lead.* "Thank you. We will look into that as soon as we deliver the supplies."

"That's right," Dr. Turner said, pensively clasping his chin once more. "You will have to return to Forest Glade at once to deliver the medicine, so Evan can prepare for surgery. I might be able to help you with that."

"How so?"

"I'll take the supplies. That way you and your friends can go to the farm."

Her eyes widened. Mr. Carpenter would be most definitely pleased with that! "But will your commanding officer allow you leave?"

The old doctor grinned. "Look around you, dear. I'm not exactly busy. Besides, mysterious bushwhackers in the night? Stolen supplies? I'll not have you put in harm's way ferrying a crate full of morphine. This requires a military escort."

Trudy wanted to kiss him. In fact, she did, square upon his wrinkled cheek. "God bless you, Dr. Turner!"

He chuckled heartily. "Now, no more of that, young lady. I'm a married man." He then turned serious. "You wait here. I'll go speak to my officer."

He was gone for only a matter of minutes, and when he returned he was smiling. "They are hitching the wagon even as we speak," he said. "You go on and look for your Caroline. I'll see you again in Forest Glade."

"Yes, sir!" Following his instructions, she hurried back to her own wagon. Robert was patiently waiting in the buckboard and Mr. Carpenter was just emerging from the officer's quarters when she met him. He frowned when he saw her hands were empty.

"I've wonderful news!" she said.

"Oh?" he said, his left eyebrow lifting.

When she told him of Dr. Turner's intervention with the supplies and escorts, his cynical expression shifted to a knowing look. "That explains, then, why the lieutenant was called away from our exchange and bid me on my way when he returned. What else?"

The simple fact that he could read that she had further good news fueled her excitement. Trudy was nearly giddy. "Dr. Turner suggested that we visit a nearby farm. He said the family there had taken in several displaced women and that one of them might be your Caroline."

The smile that came over his face was as bright as the

sunlight and Trudy reveled in its warmth. How handsome he was when he smiled.

"Good work, Tru!" he exclaimed. Taking her hand in
his, he pulled her toward the wagon. "Come on! Let's go!"

She hurried along, her thoughts racing as fast as her
feet. *He called me Tru. Not Miss Martin, not Gertrude,
but Tru!*

She tried to tell herself that his enthusiasm was only
in response to the news she'd brought him concerning
Caroline, but she couldn't help herself from hoping he
was pleased with *her* rather than just with her report.
He was still holding her hand by the time they reached
the wagon, and the warmth she felt was so exciting that
she barely had the presence of mind to climb into it.

Chapter Ten

The lieutenant in Lexington hadn't given Peter any answers in terms of his assailant's identity or possible connections to the missing supplies, but Trudy's success in securing Dr. Mackay's items, and a Federal escort to ferry them, more than made up for it.

And the Mennonite farm? He could barely contain his newfound energy.

His ankle scarcely troubled him at all now. Declining Robert's invitation to drive, Peter urged the old mare down the road as fast as she could travel. After stopping briefly at the telegraph office, they continued on. Though the wagon rattled and bounced jarringly, Miss Trudy claimed no discomfort. In fact, she was grinning from ear to ear. She evidently was just as pleased as he for the success they had achieved today.

And what success it is. Medicine will arrive in time for Dr. Mackay to assist Opal. With his treatment, Charlie's mother has a fighting chance of recovery. Peter cast Trudy another glance. Her cheeks were flushed but she was still smiling.

She is a beautiful woman.

Tempted to stare, he forced his eyes back to the road. *Now is not the time for distractions. I need to figure out what I will say to Caroline when I see her.* And yet he had no wish to ignore Trudy completely. He was far too filled with anticipation to be quiet.

"This doctor who gave you the supplies," he said, "you said you knew him previously?"

"Yes!" she said happily. "Oh! It's the most amazing thing! Surely God knew we would need his help and He sent him here ahead of us. And then, how He protected us on the road today…"

Peter was feeling generous, so he allowed himself to entertain her statements. The moments today on the road had been tense, but they had gotten through. *And if Caroline is known by this upcoming Mennonite family… If I can finally locate her…* Then perhaps Peter would believe God did actually intervene in the lives of ordinary men.

Trudy was explaining how she had known Dr. Turner from her time at the military hospital, how Dr. Mackay and his wife had known the man, as well. It struck him then how valuable her presence had been today. Would he have had as much success with the medical officer had she not been here?

No, I would not have, he most assuredly felt.

He turned to her again, only to discover she was looking at him. He smiled at her. He couldn't help himself. She offered him a smile in return. A few strands of her sunset-colored hair had escaped the confines of her bonnet and were caressing her cheek. He wanted to reach over and tuck the stands back into place.

"You have very beautiful hair," he said.

Her spring-green eyes widened in delightful surprise. Her cheeks went completely scarlet. "Oh? Well, thank you."

"Yes. It reminds me… Well…it's similar to the color of Caroline's. Only brighter."

"Oh?"

"Daniel described hers as a reddish brown. Like the color of southern soil."

"Farm ahead," Robert announced.

Peter quickly refocused his attention. The freedman was right. The farm in front of them was exactly how Trudy had said Dr. Turner had described it. The modest house and outbuildings were set in a hollow, or rather what was left of them.

"Oh dear," Trudy said, noticing what he did.

A new barn had been raised, but the house beside it still bore the marks of soot from the fire of the preceding one. The remnants of a fence dotted the pasture. Part of it was charred, part of it simply missing. Peter wondered if it had been burned entirely or if one or both of the armies had confiscated the rails for firewood. Four men were presently at work replacing the missing sections.

"Looks like their boys managed to survive the fighting," Robert said.

"The Mennonites are pacifists," Peter explained. "More than likely they chose not to fight for either side."

Looking at the condition of their farm, however, Peter knew the war had not left them alone. He could feel the doubts creeping up on him. He couldn't help but wonder if this family had truly been able to assist as many displaced neighbors as the old doctor had claimed, with their resources obviously restricted by the damage they had undergone. And even if they had, was his brother's wife one of them?

The Mennonite woman, Mrs. Hassler, welcomed them warmly, but Trudy wasn't quite able to listen. Her mind was pondering the events of the day—not the moments of tension but those of delight.

Peter had been complimenting her all day. *He told me I have been a help to him, that I am good with the children...that I have beautiful hair.*

Reason told her not to make more of it than it was, especially the comment about her hair, for it had been coupled with a comparison. *"It's similar to the color of Caroline's..."*

She realized Mrs. Hassler was saying something to her. Her round face was smiling. Trudy did her best to focus. "I'm sorry," she said. "I didn't... I... What did you say?"

The woman only smiled again. "I said, do come inside..."

Peter was standing beside her. His hand lightly touched the small of her back, encouraging her to move forward. Trudy did so. Robert was also welcomed inside.

"Oh," Miss Hassler then said, suddenly noticing. "You are injured!"

Trudy realized she was looking at the bandage on her hand. "Oh it's nothing, really, just a small cut. It's healing nicely."

The woman then looked to Peter. "But you... Were you recently wounded?"

"Take no concern over me," he said in his typical self-denying way. "My interest is in the hospitality you have given to others. I'm looking for a woman by the name of Caroline—"

"Oh yes!" Mrs. Hassler exclaimed, eyes wide. "She's here."

She's here? Trudy thought, her ears beginning to thud. *Then the quest was over?* She glanced at Peter. He was displaying only cautious optimism but she could tell he was trying hard not to smile. The corner of his mouth was twitching slightly.

"Come," Mrs. Hassler said. "The kitchen is nice. There has been a good breeze through the windows there for the last hour. We will sit there."

Trudy was most grateful for that invitation. The late afternoon sun was terribly strong. It felt like a hot iron against her skin.

Inside the kitchen, she, Peter and Robert sat down at the large farm table. The Mennonite woman retrieved a pitcher from her icebox and then set before each of them a small glass of buttermilk. It was a luxury in these parts, and knowing that, Trudy resisted the urge to drink hers down in one gulp. The men seemed to have more trouble. Finishing his quickly, the freedman grinned at Trudy then thanked his hostess.

Mr. Carpenter thanked her, as well. "Ma'am, we are very grateful for your hospitality."

"Yes," Trudy added. "Thank you."

Mrs. Hassler smiled. "There are wheat biscuits, too. I was able to trade some of our flour for the milk."

"How did you manage to keep the wheat?" Peter asked, inquisitive as always.

"My oldest son had hid a bit of our harvest, without my or his father's knowledge. I was angry with him at first for doing so, but he reminded me that even Joseph stored food away in Egypt when famine was coming. That along with the trading has allowed us to help our neighbors in need."

"I understand you've been able to do much for others," Trudy said.

"Indeed," Mrs. Hassler said. "Because of the wisdom my son showed, we had seed for planting this year."

"Did your land yield well?" Peter asked. He was being polite, but Trudy knew the waiting must be getting to him. It was getting to her.

"The condition of the land is still poor, and this year's harvest was small. Still, it has been enough," Mrs. Hassler said.

A young woman with honey-colored, braided hair, piled high upon her head, stepped into the room. Trudy's heart leaped at the sight of her. Was this Caroline? She turned to look at Peter. He pushed to his feet and respectfully stood.

"This is Susanna," Mrs. Hassler explained with a proud smile.

Oh, Trudy thought. *That's right. Caroline's hair is reddish brown.*

"Susanna was once a guest," Mrs. Hassler explained. "Now she is my oldest son's betrothed." The woman turned to her. "Fetch Caroline, will you?"

Trudy chewed on that word, *betrothed*. She had spied at least four sons out working on a fence. If Susanna was pledged to marry one of the Hassler sons, was Caroline engaged, as well? *If so*, Trudy thought, Peter *would be freed from his obligation to care for her.* She held her breath and waited for the woman's arrival. She dared not look at her employer. By now she was bordering on giddiness.

Susanna hurried off to find the girl. Pregnant silence filled the air. Peter returned to his chair and sat completely still. Trudy's hand was again beginning to ache. Looking down she realized she was clenching her fists. Mrs. Hassler filled the waiting with the woman's story.

"Caroline came to us some months back. She had no family. She didn't even have shoes on her feet."

She hadn't mentioned a child, but Peter didn't let her get that far. "And her husband had been killed in battle?" he asked.

"Yes." Mrs. Hassler shook her head sadly. "War is such a dreadful thing."

Indeed, Trudy thought. She glanced at Robert, who continued to sit silently. His life had changed because of the war. He had been granted his freedom, but would his freedom prove all he hoped it would be? Would he find his beloved Hannah? Trudy prayed he would.

"Do you know in which regiment her late husband served?" Peter asked.

Mrs. Hassler again shook her head. "Only that it was a Confederate one."

The details, though few, were matching. Trudy watched the anticipation build on his face as footsteps approached. Then sadly, she watched it fall. When the young woman in question at last entered the room, his look told Trudy that she was not *his* Caroline.

Are you certain? She wanted to say, but even Trudy knew this was not the woman they were seeking. Her hair was as dark as a starless night sky. Still, the newspaperman asked his questions. However, they were now phrased negatively.

"Your husband's name wasn't Daniel Carpenter, was it?"

"No, sir," the young woman said. "It was Silas. He served in General Mosby's cavalry."

Cavalry, Trudy thought. *Daniel had been infantry.*

The look of pain on Peter's face was obvious. Trudy's heart broke for him. She was desperate to help in some way. "You wouldn't happen to know a Daniel Carpenter, would you?" she asked the woman. "He had also married a young lady named Caroline from somewhere in this area."

"I'm afraid not," she said.

"What about—" Peter reached for her wrist, stopping her words cold. This time his touch lacked warmth. So did his voice.

"Leave her be," he said. "We're only wasting her time." He turned back to the young woman. "I'm sorry to have disturbed you."

"'Tis no inconvenience, sir."

Mrs. Hassler recognized the disappointment, as well, and tried to soothe it. "Let me fetch you some more buttermilk…"

"Thank you, no," Peter replied. "We'll be on our way."

His tone was curt, bordering now on flat-out rudeness. Trudy knew it was a mask for the pain, and she did her best to smooth the situation. "We've a friend in Forest Glade who is ill and we are eager to return to her."

"I see," Mrs. Hassler said. "Then may God be with her." To Peter, who was already lumbering his way to the door, she called, "And may God guide you to the woman you seek."

He didn't answer her, at least not that they heard. Trudy thanked the lady for her hospitality, and then she and Robert hurried to catch Peter. For having a lame leg by birth and a recently injured one, he was moving with incredible speed.

"Quickly, Miss Martin," he called.

Miss Martin? Not Trudy. Not Tru. The formal address cut her to the quick.

"The Webbs and the Mackays will be wondering what has become of us."

She climbed into the wagon. "Opal is in competent hands," she said.

"That may be, but I have work waiting and I'll not have this day come to a total waste."

A total waste? How could he say such a thing? They *had* succeeded in getting supplies. He *had* sent his wires. She was sorry Dr. Turner's information had not led to the true Caroline, but still... "Peter," she said softly, knowing he was surely worried, "just because we didn't find who we were looking for today doesn't mean we won't eventually. God is still at work and—"

"I've no time for religious discussions now, *Miss Martin.* As I said, I've work to return to and so do you."

The emphasis also on "Miss Martin" told her in no uncertain terms that he hadn't liked her addressing him by his Christian name. She could feel the heat of embarrassment growing in her cheeks. *And religious discussions?* Did he believe in God or not? Why was he acting this way, especially when they had gotten on so well earlier?

He called me Tru... He took my hand...

As hurt and confused as she was, when he released the brake and winced while doing so, she compassionately laid her hand on his arm. He shrugged it off. Trudy's chin began to quiver.

"Robert, would you kindly take the reins?"

"Yes, sir."

"Don't call me sir!" he snapped.

If the freedman was offended by Peter's tone, he did not show it, but she most definitely was. She could stand it no longer. All the emotion she had been trying so hard to keep pent up inside came pouring out.

"Stop it!" Trudy cried. "Stop it now!" Both men, who had been in the process of changing places, eyed her incredulously. Neither had ever heard her raise her voice before. Well, they would hear it now. "For pity's sake, Peter! He's only trying to help you! Must you treat him with such contempt?"

Robert very wisely, very quietly returned to his previous seat in the back of the buckboard. Trudy's employer, however, stared at her straight-on. His intuition was sharp. He knew she was referring to more than just his treatment of the freedman.

"I don't want your help," he said, his jaw clenched tightly.

"Oh, that's obvious. You are, after all, the mighty newspaper publisher determined to take on the world all by yourself and pull it down just the same! We all shudder in your presence!"

His eyes narrowed. His nostrils flared. "How dare you speak to me in that tone! I am your employer!"

My employer? The employer she had aided, prayed for, defended to others when his quirks caused offense. Well, no more! An injury, a heavy heart, a missing relative…those things would no longer justify his behavior. *What did I ever see in this man? He's rude, condescending and completely puffed with pride!* "You are my employer no longer!" she shouted. "Effective immediately

I am resigning my position at your paper. You will no longer have any say over me!"

He looked as though he couldn't believe she would say such a thing, let alone actually do it. "Resigning?" he repeated.

"Yes!"

"On what grounds?"

"On the grounds that I will no longer tolerate your sour moods, your bullying, your belittling of my beliefs... your...*manhandling*!"

"Manhandling?" A look of confusion filled his face.

Unwilling to explain, she threw her legs over the side of the buckboard, leaped to the ground.

"Where are you going?" he demanded to know.

"Away from you!"

"Don't be irrational."

"I assure you, *sir*, this is the most rational thing I have done in quite a while."

Peter watched half in anger, half in disbelief as Trudy marched up the Hasslers' front steps. The door opened wide for her before she even had a chance to reach it. No doubt the Mennonite woman had heard every bit of the preceding conversation.

Surely everyone in this hollow heard it, he thought.

Peter looked on angrily as Mrs. Hassler welcomed his former assistant inside, then promptly shut the door behind them.

Now what? he thought. He wouldn't go in after her— he refused to do so—but neither did he relish the idea of sitting here until she decided to return. *By the look on her face when she jumped from the wagon, she has no intention of returning. Ever.*

He didn't know exactly how he felt about that. Part of him wanted to drive back to Forest Glade without her. The other part wanted to beg her for her forgiveness. Like a rotary press churning out editions, her words repeated through his mind. *"I will no longer tolerate your sour moods, your bullying, your belittling of my beliefs..."*

Had he really done that? He certainly hadn't meant to do so, but he simply could not subscribe to her naive way of looking at things.

Her beloved Dr. Turner may have been the medical officer in charge today but that was merely a coincidence. No matter what Miss Martin believed, God did not govern personally in the affairs of men. *If He did He'd have had the good sense to stop Daniel from wedding Caroline in the first place, or at least stop us from wasting our time coming here.* He heaved a disgruntled sigh, for he knew it wasn't Miss Martin's fault that Caroline wasn't here. He knew he had acted like a boor. *But better a boor than a bridegroom in times like these,* he told himself.

His guilt, however, was not assuaged. Her charges continued to slice through his mind like a bayonet, even if he couldn't comprehend them all. *Manhandling? When have I ever manhandled her?*

Then he remembered those final moments at the garrison. When she had given him the lead to the Hassler farm, he had taken her by the hand and led her to the wagon. He hadn't meant it in a bullying way. *I was just eager to investigate, eager to get going...* But if Peter was completely honest with himself, he knew it was more than that. He had *wanted* to touch her, and he had *liked* the feel of her hand in his. Had she realized that?

Does she think I am a cad? I told her I was not the marrying kind, but I spent the entire day complimenting her, holding her hand. I called her Tru because she is the most honest, open person I have ever met, and then I belittle her for being so. What is wrong with me?

Knowing what he needed to do but not knowing exactly how to go about it, Peter continued to stare at the farmhouse front door. After a moment, he turned in his seat. Trudy wasn't the only one who deserved an apology.

The freedman was looking at him.

"I'm sorry, Robert. I shouldn't have spoken to you that way."

"Reckon it's not me you need to worry about," the man said boldly.

Peter offered him a self-deprecating grin, then extended his hand. The freedman grasped it firmly. "I appreciate your candor," he said.

Robert smiled. Apparently all was forgiven.

He slowly turned back and faced the house. *Well, not all,* Peter thought. He blew out a breath, took off his hat and raked his fingers through his damp hair. He was sweating, and the confinement of his frock coat and collar were driving him insane.

After giving both a tug, he looked at the sky. The sun, which had baked him since long before noon, was disappearing before his eyes. Tall clouds were gathering to the west, and on the ridge a long, ominous black line now obscured the highest peaks. A storm was coming and Peter knew he would have to wait for it to pass before they could head back to Forest Glade. It was of no real consequence to him, however. He knew the real storm waiting for him was inside Mrs. Hassler's home.

Chapter Eleven

"I'm terribly sorry!" Trudy gushed the moment Mrs. Hassler shut the door behind her. "I am so terribly sorry!"

The older woman smiled gently. "Oh sweetness, you aren't the first young woman to seek refuge at my door."

Seek refuge? Was that what she was doing? She wasn't destitute or starving. "But I have no real need of refuge," Trudy said.

"Don't you, now?" Mrs. Hassler replied.

Trudy covered her face with her hands, only then to gesture wildly in front of her. She always talked with her hands whenever she was at her wits' end—and she was most definitely there now. "I don't know what came over me," she said, "but I simply could not spend another moment in *that man's* presence!" The next thing she knew her tears were falling and Mrs. Hassler was drawing her into her arms.

"I believe I know what came over you," the woman said softly. "You're in love, sweetness."

Love? Trudy's head snapped up. "Oh no. I assure

you, I am not! I was taken with him...infatuated...but that is all over and done with now."

"Is it?"

Trudy's insides were twisting but she was insistent. "Yes, most assuredly! That is finished. Peter Carpenter is...is..." She burst into tears again. Once more the Mennonite woman pulled her close.

"He is a man in pain," Mrs. Hassler said softly, "of both body and spirit, and like many a mortal man, he has taken it out on those closest to him. I've seen it before. Come..." she said, looking Trudy full in the face, "what you need is another glass of buttermilk."

Trudy didn't wish to empty the woman's precious supplies, but she allowed herself to be led back to the kitchen. Mrs. Hassler set a second glass before her and then tried to give her another biscuit, as well.

"Oh please," Trudy said. "Thank you, but I couldn't eat it even if I was hungry." Her stomach was still in knots. She did manage to sip the buttermilk, but it didn't taste nearly as refreshing as it had previously.

A knock sounded upon the front door. Trudy jolted, but Mrs. Hassler's mouth hitched with a slight grin. "Well, I wonder who that may be?"

Trudy didn't need to wonder. She already knew. Peter—*Mr. Carpenter*—was no doubt eager to be on his way and he had come to fetch her. *Well, I won't go with him*, she told herself. *Ever*. Trudy realized though, *"ever"* wasn't possible. She couldn't stay here. The Hasslers already had enough mouths to feed. *But I can't climb back into that wagon with him. At least not yet.*

"Shall I tell him you will see him?" the woman asked hopefully.

Trudy shook her head. Mrs. Hassler assumed her former employer was coming to apologize. Trudy was certain he'd only come to berate her more. She didn't wish to go against her host's wishes, but she just couldn't speak with him.

"Alright…" Mrs. Hassler said. Slowly she turned for the parlor.

The curtains from the window behind Trudy kicked up with a gust of wind. There was a chill to it, a dampness, and she knew a storm was blowing in from the mountains. *How fitting,* she couldn't help but think. Only moments ago life seemed so promising. Mr. Carpenter had been on the edge of finally meeting Caroline and he was so grateful for Trudy's assistance. Those hopeful moments had given way to turmoil once again.

It is our history, our pattern. And because of that, Trudy had reasoned she could no longer work for him. Every time she thought she had come to terms with their employer/employee relationship, he would do something to make her question it.

She was angry with the way he had spoken to Robert and Mrs. Hassler, but she realized she was most upset for his inconsistent behavior toward her. *How could he speak so rudely to me after being so complimentary? Why did he take my hand in his?* She wondered then if he was even thinking of her at all when he had said and done such kind, flattering things, for an idea had crossed her mind that she had never before considered, and it was not a comforting one. Today when Peter had complimented her hair, he had specifically mentioned Caroline. *Does he have a history with this woman, a history before his brother? Is he so desperate to find her because his own heart is involved?*

A chill again blew through her. Trudy knew how

"4 for 4" MINI-SURVEY

We are prepared to **REWARD** you with 2 FREE books and 2 FREE gifts for completing our MINI SURVEY!

FREE
Value Over
$20!

You'll get...

TWO FREE BOOKS & TWO FREE GIFTS

just for participating in our Mini Survey!

Dear Reader,

IT'S A FACT: if you answer 4 quick questions, we'll send you **4 FREE REWARDS!**

I'm not kidding you. As a leading publisher of women's fiction, we value your opinions… and your time. That's why we are prepared to **reward** you handsomely for completing our mini-survey. In fact, we have 4 Free Rewards for you, including 2 free books and 2 free gifts.

As you may have guessed, that's why our mini-survey is called **"4 for 4"**. Answer 4 questions and get 4 Free Rewards. It's that simple!

Thank you for participating in our survey,

Pam Powers

To get your 4 FREE REWARDS:
Complete the survey below and return the insert today to receive 2 FREE BOOKS and 2 FREE GIFTS guaranteed!

"4 for 4" MINI-SURVEY

1 Is reading one of your favorite hobbies?
☐ YES ☐ NO

2 Do you prefer to read instead of watch TV?
☐ YES ☐ NO

3 Do you read newspapers and magazines?
☐ YES ☐ NO

4 Do you enjoy trying new book series with FREE BOOKS?
☐ YES ☐ NO

YES! I have completed the above Mini-Survey. Please send me my 4 FREE REWARDS (worth over $20 retail). I understand that I am under no obligation to buy anything, as explained on the back of this card.

❏ I prefer the regular-print edition
105/305 IDL GMYL

❏ I prefer the larger-print edition
122/322 IDL GMYL

FIRST NAME	LAST NAME

ADDRESS

APT.#	CITY

STATE/PROV.	ZIP/POSTAL CODE

READER SERVICE—Here's how it works:

BUSINESS REPLY MAIL
FIRST-CLASS MAIL   PERMIT NO. 717   BUFFALO, NY

POSTAGE WILL BE PAID BY ADDRESSEE

READER SERVICE
PO BOX 1341
BUFFALO NY 14240-8571

NO POSTAGE
NECESSARY
IF MAILED
IN THE
UNITED STATES

possible it was for a woman to love two different men, two brothers, even. It had happened to her sister. When Elizabeth's fiancé, Jeremiah, had died of pneumonia in the Baltimore military hospital, no one knew his brother, David, was secretly in love with her, and no one, including Elizabeth, would ever have guessed she would one day be happily wed to him.

Thinking of such made Trudy's stomach twist inside her—not because she begrudged her sister's newfound happiness or judged her for loving two men, but because despite what she had told Mrs. Hassler about her interest in Peter being finished, she couldn't bear the thought of him being claimed by someone else.

Mrs. Hassler's words came back to her. *"You're in love, sweetness."*

No, I am not, she still maintained, but she was definitely jealous, and of a woman she had never met. *And I shouldn't be! Why would I pine over him? I am acting like a fool!*

She could hear her former employer's deep voice coming from the parlor, although admittedly it was not as loud, as commanding as it had been previously. In fact, it was so uncharacteristically soft that, although she tried, Trudy could not make out the words. Angry now with herself, she tried her best to ignore any further sounds from the parlor. She clearly heard the front door close a moment later, though. *Has someone else come in or has he gone out?*

Mrs. Hassler then reentered the kitchen. This time she was carrying a washbasin. "There's a storm blowing in, sweetness. I'm afraid you and your companions will have to remain here a little longer."

Although she was sorry for any inconvenience to

Mrs. Hassler, she was grateful for the delay. Could she continue to shelter in the kitchen for a little while longer? *Away from him?* She realized how cowardly the thought was. After all, this was a working farm and a broken heart was no excuse to remain idle. Still, she was in no hurry to leave the table.

"My husband and your friend Robert are seeing to your mare," Mrs. Hassler said. "She'll be safe from the weather in the barn."

"Thank you," Trudy replied. "I appreciate your kindness." She hadn't mentioned Mr. Carpenter. What was *he* doing?

She watched as Mrs. Hassler went to the icebox, took out a chunk and then put it in the washbasin. She began to chip the ice into small pieces.

"May I help?" Trudy asked.

"Certainly, sweetness." But the woman had finished with the ice by the time Trudy had crossed the kitchen floor. "Will you take this basin to the parlor?"

"Of course. What do you want me to do with it when I get there?"

Mrs. Hassler handed her the basin and then laid a clean towel across her shoulder. "You'll know what to do," she said with a kind smile. Then, without further word, she promptly ascended the back staircase.

Bewildered, Trudy carried the basin of ice toward the front room. The moment she reached its threshold she stopped. She realized why Mrs. Hassler had been so eager to hand her the basin of ice. There on the settee sat a very tired, very flushed-looking Mr. Carpenter. His dark hair was curling in the humidity of the approaching storm. His collar was crumpled. His tie askew.

Trudy knew now what the ice was for and she inwardly seethed, realizing she had been "manhandled" once again. Only this time it was by a matronly Mennonite woman who obviously thought it imperative that she and her former employer make peace. Trudy knew Scripture commanded reconciliation but this—*this is more than I can bear!*

She had half a mind to turn around. After all, he had not noticed her yet. He was too busy trying to unlace his shoes.

Only then did she realize why he looked so flushed. It was not just the heat. He was in pain. His sprained ankle and the fatigue of his other lame leg made the task of removing his shoes nearly impossible. Compassion slowly slaked her anger. Quietly she stepped forward. Reconciliation was not quite her goal. If she never spoke to him again after what had happened, that was still fine by her. But her nurse's heart would not allow his needs to go unattended, no matter how he had treated her previously.

Peter had never felt more humiliated than he did in that moment. He couldn't even remove his shoes. To add to his embarrassment, it wasn't Mrs. Hassler who had returned to tend him, but his former assistant.

It had been humbling enough when, after apologizing to the older woman for his rude behavior, she had insisted on icing his swollen ankle. Peter didn't want her to give up what precious supply of ice she had for him. It would be a long time before she would be able to replace it.

Mrs. Hassler, however, would not take no for an answer. "You remove your shoes," she'd commanded in a tone that could have sent his reporters scurrying to finish their assignments. "I will be back in a moment."

But now Miss Martin was crossing the floor to meet him. Peter had expected a further confrontation with her but not like this. What was he to say to her? What was he to do? She had already come to his rescue once before. He couldn't have her do so again, especially not for something as ridiculous as this.

He bent once more to his feet, managing to undo the last of his laces. Actually removing the shoes was a different story entirely.

"Leave them," she said. "You will only pain your ankle further if you continue to try."

Her tone was purely professional and she did not wait for his response. She simply knelt before him, set the basin on the floor and then gently slid off the shoe.

Peter felt lower than a worm, especially when she proceeded to remove his sock. He didn't want her fussing over him, especially given how he had treated her. "You don't have to do that," he said.

"I know," she said simply, and after removing his sock, she carefully placed his bare foot in the basin of ice. Peter winced, partly from the cold, the rest from mortification.

As a nurse, no doubt she was accustomed to handling sour-smelling extremities, but how could she handle his, especially after the way he'd spoken to her? Her actions were heaping hot coals on his head. *Is this what she has intended?* he wondered, but her face showed no trace of revenge. *No, of course not. She is not the vengeful type.*

"I'm sorry," he said, for he suddenly felt if he didn't apologize to her then and there that he would burst. "I should not have spoken to you in such a manner, and… earlier… I…shouldn't have dragged you to the wagon."

"Dragged you to the wagon"? He wanted to whack himself on the forehead. What kind of sentence was that? For a man who valued candor, why couldn't he bring himself to display it now? *Yes. I wanted to hold your hand. Yes, for all of my protesting, I enjoy being near you. Yes, I think you are beautiful but it can never be anything more than that.*

Apparently, though, he didn't need to elaborate.

"You were disappointed," she said without looking up. "We were all disappointed."

The ice was already melting. She used the cold water to carefully bathe the most swollen areas of his foot with her delicate fingers. Peter wanted to pull back. He knew he didn't deserve her kindness. Yet he didn't do so. Evidently the cold was numbing not only his ankle but his brain, as well. He found himself longing for a look into her eyes. She denied him the opportunity.

"I owe you an apology, as well," she said, still refusing to meet his gaze, "for losing my temper."

"You had every right," he said. "And again, I'm sorry. I just had such hope that we would find Caroline…"

Only then did she lock eyes with him. In them he saw compassion and remorse, but gone was the besotted look that had lingered even after her arrival in Virginia when she'd said those feelings were in the past. *She has seen me now for what I really am. She has put me in my proper place in her mind.* He told himself he should be glad for that, but he wasn't. Peter suddenly felt empty inside.

"You need not explain. I understand. Try not to lose

hope." She bit her lip, then looked down at his ankle. "Keep it soaking for at least another ten minutes."

"I will."

"I'll find you a fresh cloth in which to wrap it."

"Thank you," was all he could think to say, though the words seemed wholly inadequate.

Thunder rumbled as she walked away. Rain was now pelting the roof. Peter hoped Dr. Turner had reached Forest Glade before the weather made the road impassable. He wondered how long they would have to wait before they could resume their travels.

He sat alone in the parlor. When the ten minutes had passed, Trudy returned, a towel draped over her shoulder and a clean wrapping bandage in her hands. He watched as she carefully lifted his foot from the basin, probed his ankle gently. The area was numb but somehow Peter could still feel the heat of her touch.

She dried his foot, then wrapped it tightly. "Keep this elevated as much as possible," she said. "The swelling has gone down considerably but it won't take much activity to inflame it again."

"I will," he said. "Thank you."

Mrs. Hassler returned along with Susannah. The latter eyed him curiously as the older woman asked, "Feeling better?"

"Yes," he said, but it was true only to a degree. From the corner of his eye he watched Trudy vacate the room. He wondered if she would return.

She did not, but Robert and the rest of the men of the farm did. Their hats were dripping with rainwater and their boots were splashed with mud. While they removed the items at the door, Mrs. Hassler took a pillow from the nearby rocking chair and placed it next to where Peter was sitting.

At least I am not the only one now who is shoeless, he thought sardonically.

"Put your foot here," Mrs. Hassler commanded in that motherly, authoritative tone.

Peter obeyed but politely pressed his case. "I shouldn't be occupying all of your seating," he said. "Especially now that your family is returning."

Caroline entered the room and, along with Susannah, stared at him, as if he were some sort of circus side-show. Mrs. Hassler waved them toward the two vacant chairs across the room. Susannah claimed one. Caroline, however, moved toward the kitchen.

"You aren't occupying all of our seating," Mrs. Hassler replied matter-of-factly. "Only the settee."

"Ja," her husband said. He was called Johannes, and he came to look over Peter for himself. His German accent was much thicker than his wife's. "Don't you fret, now. Da mare is safe und dry."

"Thank you," Peter replied.

"You are most welcome to stay de night as our guests."

Peter appreciated the farmer's kindness, but he knew staying that long wasn't possible. He had work to do back at the church and so did Trudy. Besides, he would not be able to rest easy until he learned that the medical supplies had reached the church safely. *And if Dr. Turner for some reason does* not *arrive with the supplies—*

He didn't allow himself to finish that thought. He didn't want to think about what it would mean if the older physician and his escorts had fallen prey to thieves. Opal would be without medication and Trudy would be beside herself with worry for the old man. He could tell by the way she had talked earlier that she was extremely fond of him.

He remembered then how worried she had been for him when he'd been attacked. *"When I saw him knock you from your horse..."* She had been visibly overcome. No woman, save his mother or his sister, had ever felt that way about him. *I have never let them get close enough to care.*

He pushed that last thought from his mind, for he realized Mr. Hassler was still waiting on an answer. "Thank you for your hospitality," Peter said, "but we really must be on our way as soon as possible. Our friends in Forest Glade are waiting."

The Mennonite man nodded understandingly. "Den we will pray dat de storm will pass quickly."

Peter dared not discourage the man from doing so, especially not in his own home. In commanding German, the farmer called his entire household into the parlor. Caroline returned, along with Trudy. That detached, professional look was still on her face.

"We are going to pray for your journey, sweetness," Mrs. Hassler explained.

Sweetness, that is a fitting name for her, Peter thought. *At least when she isn't arguing with me.*

He clearly remembered her words.

"I will no longer tolerate your sour moods, your bullying, your belittling of my beliefs..."

Had he really given her the impression that he did not believe in God? That he thought less of those who prayed? As for his bullying, his sour moods, he knew for certain he was guilty of that—toward her and toward others, as well. It came with the territory, the circles in which he traveled, he supposed, but he regretted it terribly.

The entire Hassler clan went to their knees, smack in the middle of the parlor floor. She quietly joined them but not without sneaking a glance at him. No doubt she was wondering if he would participate in the exercise of faith.

Feeling wholly conspicuous remaining on the settee, Peter awkwardly swung his leg to the floor.

"You stay where you are," Mrs. Hassler insisted.

"Oh?"

"The Lord does not so much wish for a humble posture, but a humble heart."

Peter returned his foot to the pillow she had given him. The position didn't trouble him now nearly as much as her words. A humble heart? Did he even know what such a thing was? He had always equated humility with weakness, and then he had watched Trudy bathe his feet.

That was not weakness. That had taken incredible strength. A strength he realized he did not possess.

Capturing his attention, Mr. Hassler began to pray. What the man requested exactly Peter did not know. His petition was made in German. The only word Peter understood was *amen*. Evidently confident that God had understood his prayer, the man then stood. So did the rest of his family. The younger women, along with Trudy, quietly left the room.

Amid the rustle of petticoats, Mr. Hassler then said to Peter, "Well, den, tell me about dis woman you seek."

Peter once more explained the story of Daniel's bride. The Mennonite man shook his head sadly. "I will add dis woman to my prayers," he said, "and should she find her way here we shall notify you."

"Thank you," Peter said. "I would greatly appreciate that."

The rain stopped, and within a few moments more, the rumbling clouds quieted completely. Robert looked then to him. "Reckon I'll go hitch the mare," he told Peter.

He nodded.

"Ja. Ja," Mr. Hassler said. "See? De prayer has been answered."

Peter blinked. Had the man prayed for a short storm? *And had the Creator actually listened?*

Hassler looked then at one of his sons. "Ernst, go wid de man. Help him."

"Ja, Papa."

Robert and Ernst had the buckboard ready for travel in a matter of minutes. Thankfully, despite the rain, the ground was not too muddy. Two of the Hasslers' other sons then carried Peter to the back of the wagon.

"You stay off that foot as long as possible," their mother said. "If you don't you won't be much help to your friends in Forest Glade."

"Yes, ma'am," Peter replied. It reminded him of what he had thought when Trudy had injured her hand. He wondered if it was still bothering her. *I should ask*, but he decided now was not the time. Clearly she wasn't in a talkative mood, for after thanking the Hasslers profusely, she climbed inside the driver's box next to Robert. Casting one concerned but silent glance at Peter, she again turned forward.

Robert very calmly picked up the reins and clicked

his tongue, signaling for the horse to move. No one said a word for the rest of the journey.

Mrs. Mackay met them promptly when the wagon pulled in front of the church steps. The sky was dark. The sun had long since sunk below the Alleghenies' ridges. By lantern light Peter could see the look of relief and hopeful expectation on the woman's face.

"Dr. Turner told us you had taken a detour," she said. "Were you able to locate Caroline?"

"No," was all Peter said. He knew how badly everyone had hoped for an affirmative answer, but with none to give he then asked, "How is Charlie's mother?"

"Holding her own," Mrs. Mackay said.

"Did Evan insert the chest tube?" Trudy asked as she eased her way down from the buckboard. No doubt she was in a hurry to escape Peter's presence.

He was eager to escape hers, as well, but for far different reasons than previously—reasons even he himself could not fully comprehend. All he knew for certain was the silence between them, coupled with the thought of her leaving his newspaper, was more uncomfortable than the pain in his ankle. She wasn't being rude to him. Just distant. Sadly he knew that distance was only going to grow.

"He did," Mrs. Mackay said, "but it will be some time before we know if it is actually helping."

"How are the children?" she then asked.

"Well enough," she told her, "but Charlie has been asking for you both."

The "both" cut Peter to the quick, for Mrs. Mackay had looked at him when she had said that. *The little boy has inadvertently linked us together.* As the women hurried into the church, Peter's conscience was again pricked.

They were indeed linked together whether he wanted to admit that or not, and more than just as a former employer to his employee. *She anticipates my movements, follows my thoughts.* He had chosen to visit the Lexington garrison but she had been the one who had the connection that allowed them to secure the supplies they needed. *And another surgeon*, he thought. *Dr. Mackay, as well as Opal will certainly benefit from him.*

As for my endeavors, he then thought, *the only things I accomplished were inconveniencing and insulting a kindhearted Mennonite family, barking at a poor freedman who has more than paid for the notice he wants printed and losing the best assistant I ever had.*

Trudy might have accepted his apology and tended his injury, but he realized their relationship would never again be the same. As saddened as he was by that, he knew he had no time to lament. *Somewhere out there are a mother and child for whom I must take responsibility, and more than likely they are cold and hungry, maybe even suffering sickness like the poor woman Dr. Mackay is presently tending.*

Peter stepped gingerly from the back of the wagon. The ride had made his lame leg stiff, and the sprained ankle was swelling again. Though he desperately wanted to lie, down the mare needed attention first. He hobbled his way toward her. Robert beat him there.

"Let me, Mr. Carpenter. I'll see to her."

The freedman exuded kindness. Peter wondered how he maintained it. Robert had known his share of troubles and disappointments, and his search for his wife had also yielded little fruit. Yet he never displayed the anger or irritability that Peter struggled with every day.

He thanked the man, then lumbered inside. Trudy had already gone to the parsonage to sit with Charlie and the baby. Mackay and Turner were hovering over Charlie's mother. Mrs. Mackay passed by him with a stack of clean cloths.

"How is your ankle?" she asked.

"Well enough," he said. "Don't mind me."

Too busy assisting her husband and the older physician, she took him at his word. In truth his ankle was throbbing and the muscles in his other leg were burning. He needed to soak them again, but he had work to do. Making his way to his desk Peter collapsed into his chair.

Evidently several freedmen had passed through today looking for loved ones. Mrs. Webb had taken down their information. Her writing wasn't as easy to read as Trudy's and she hadn't included the personal details that would make identifying a missing loved one easier.

Peter settled back and did his best to make sense of the notes on his desk. The work was frustratingly long and lonely.

Trudy and the other women had come to the Webbs' cottage to claim a few hours' sleep—at least as much as a fussy baby and a fidgety six-year-old boy would allow. Charlie had been flitting about her ever since she had returned to the church. Trudy could understand why. He was worried for his mother, and with good reason. The procedure Opal had endured, although working to relieve the fluid, so far wasn't actually improving her health. For every ounce that drained, two more seemed to appear. Still, Emily maintained things could be much different in the morning.

"Don't worry," she said. "Dr. Turner and Evan will do everything they can."

Trudy told as much to Charlie. After hearing that the men would keep a close watch over his mother, followed by a Bible story and prayers, he finally drifted off to sleep. That had been three hours ago. Mrs. Webb and Emily had long since found rest, as well, but Trudy and Kate could not.

Although by now it was well after midnight, the two of them were wide-eyed. Kate was content as long as Trudy rocked her, and so for the sake of the others in the house, she continued to do so. Charlie lay on the parlor settee. The flicker of a lone candle brought out the various shades of his hair—dark brown, copper, sometimes almost black. *Just like Peter's.*

Trudy replayed the scenes of the day in her mind. He had wounded her, and for a while she had wanted him to know just how badly. He later apologized. She had accepted it, but oh, how much grace that had taken! She had tended his feet but only after realizing that while his behavior had been unfitting, hers was also.

I cannot be jealous of Caroline. There was never any understanding between us. If he finds his sister-in-law and then chooses to marry her and make a better life for her and her child, then I should be happy.

But to achieve that would take even more grace— and a great deal of distance. Trudy knew she could not wait for the Baltimore train to bring the latter. She would have to begin that journey in her heart while she remained here in Virginia.

Chapter Twelve

Dr. Turner had commanded his Federal escorts to take the night watch, which allowed for much needed rest among the men of the party. The old man then insisted on keeping vigil over Opal so Peter and Dr. Mackay might claim one of the remaining church pews for a few hours' sleep.

Peter appreciated the opportunity but found he was unable to secure more than a small bit of sleep at a time. He simply had too much on his mind to actually rest. Despite the surgeons' efforts, Charlie's mother's condition was not improving.

Twice Peter woke to see the gray-headed physician bent over the woman with a puzzled look on his face. The third time he awoke, Dr. Mackay was with him. Peter wasn't certain but he was fairly sure the Scotsman's head was bowed in prayer.

How do they do it? he wondered. *How do people like them, like the Hasslers, like Trudy continue to see such pain and suffering and still have faith?*

Her words came back to him. *"Just because we didn't*

find who we were looking for today doesn't mean we won't eventually. God is still at work..."

Was it simple naivety or was there something deep inside her, something deep inside them all, something he no longer had that encouraged them to continue on, not grudgingly or out of a sense of obligation but with true hope? Peter knew the stories from Scripture, how the lost were found, swords were turned into plowshares and hearts and bodies were mended with the Great Physician's healing touch.

Scripture also testified that God was the same today as He was yesterday, but Peter had yet to witness that in his own lifetime. Oh, he had known peace and safety and abundance in childhood, *but that was because of my innocence. I did not see all the suffering in the world, because my parents protected me. They protected my sister and my brothers.*

Then the Carpenter children grew to adulthood and they discovered firsthand that the real world wasn't peaceful or safe. *The only abundance is misery and the only true escape from it is death. That is where faith in God comes in,* he told himself. It was believing there was an afterlife, that a better world lay beyond this one.

Sadly, the longer Peter watched the physicians hover over their patient, the more certain he became that Charlie's mother was nearing her time of departure. *What will happen to her children?* It was a question that had been plaguing him for days.

Peter couldn't help but think of how fond he had grown of little Charlie. He wanted to do whatever he could to help the lad, but in actuality, *should* he take on such a responsibility? Did he really even wish to do so? After all, he had a sister-in-law and a niece or nephew to locate.

Still...

What about my parents? he wondered. They might see Opal's children as a blessing in their time of bereavement, following the passing of two of their sons, but it was also possible they might think Peter was seeking to replace the grandchildren they had lost. *Lost.* He was becoming more convinced by the day that he would be unable to locate his brother's wife and child. He lay awake until sunrise thinking about such things.

Daybreak brought not only the return of the women but Zimmer, O'Neil and Jones, as well. The men barely gave Peter time to comb his hair and shave before peppering him with questions.

"How was Lexington?" Zimmer asked.

"How did you know about that?" Peter replied.

Zimmer shrugged. "News travels fast in this valley."

Not fast enough, Peter thought. If it did he would have located his brother's widow by now.

"Is there any word on the supply shipments?" Jones asked. "We are out of cornmeal again."

"My children need more food," O'Neil lamented.

"As do most of the children in this valley," Peter said. He couldn't help but think again of Charlie and his baby sister. As bad as he felt for the men and their families, he didn't have the strength or patience to listen to their complaints now. He hadn't been on his feet for even an hour, yet already his ankle was aching, and his other leg wasn't much better. Reluctantly he knew he would have to confine himself to his desk today.

"Gentlemen, I'm afraid I have no news for you," he told them.

"If you don't, then who will?" Zimmer said.

"Your guess is as good as mine. Perhaps you should go to Larkinsville. You might get further with Lieutenant Glassman than I did." He started to walk away.

"Someone broke into my kitchen last night," Zimmer announced.

Peter froze, then turned back around. "Was anyone hurt?" He asked.

"No, and I can tell you, they didn't run off with anything either, 'cause there wasn't anything to take. Still..."

Peter sighed. "I'm sorry for your trouble, but again, I suggest you press your case at the garrison, if not in Larkinsville then Lexington."

"That's a far way to travel," O'Neil remarked. His compatriots nodded the same.

"What about the soldiers protecting you?" Zimmer then asked.

Peter tried not to take offense at the way the man had said "protecting you," but there was something in Zimmer's tone that he did not like. He decided to ignore it. "Those men are hardly under my command," he said. "You would have to speak with Dr. Turner."

"Then I will," Zimmer said.

"Very well," Peter replied, and at that they parted company.

He went to the pump and collected a bucket full of cold water, intent on soaking his foot while he riffled through the notices on his desk. To his embarrassment, he couldn't lift the pail once it was filled. Thankfully, Reverend Webb was the one who came upon him and not Trudy.

"Allow me," the parson said.

Whether he was growing tired of trying to maintain a facade of strength or he was simply tired, Peter allowed the man to assist him. He went to his makeshift desk and sifted through the latest missing person notices. He also had an article in need of polishing.

That was usually his assistant's job, but after yesterday's resignation, and due to the indelicate nature of the story—the need to continue the cleanup of area battlefields—he was not about to involve her. She had bid him good morning when she had arrived with the children but then quickly busied herself assisting Mrs. Webb. The preacher's wife was doling out small helpings of hominy grits and birch bark tea. Peter noted Zimmer, O'Neil and Jones stayed to partake of the meal, though oddly they did not ask for any servings to take home to their wives.

He stole another glance at Trudy. She looked pale and troubled this morning.

No doubt she is worried about Opal. Instead of abating, the fluid in her lungs was increasing. So was the fever. Peter saw the look that came over Trudy's face when Dr. Mackay asked that she keep the children on the opposite side of the church, away from their mother.

"But why can't we be over there?" Charlie asked after the physician returned to his post.

"Because your mother needs rest," she said. "She must lie very still, very quiet for the time being."

"I can be still and quiet," Charlie insisted.

"I know you can, and that is why I promise to let you have a good long visit with her as soon as Dr. Mackay permits it."

The promise didn't hearten the child. Peter watched his lower lip push forward. As if to voice her own displeasure, the baby began to cry. Trudy offered them both a smile, but it was not as bright as her previous ones.

"Cheer up, my dears," she said. "In the meantime we shall plan ourselves some sort of adventure."

Oh no. Peter didn't know what sort of adventure Trudy was planning today, but he remembered how the last one had gone. There was no way he would let her go out wandering on her own with the boy, especially with Zimmer's report of breaking and entering.

"Charlie," he called. "How would you like to write an article?"

The boy's face lit up at once. "For the newspaper?"

"Yes."

"You mean it?"

"Of course I do. I wouldn't have said it if I didn't. You could tell the people of Baltimore what it is like living in Virginia." *At least some of it,* he thought. Peter hoped the child would never become privy to all the things a postwar society contained. He laid aside his account of Confederate soldiers who still needed to be buried.

Charlie's eyes were as wide as saucers as he looked then to Trudy and asked, "Can we go on an adventure tomorrow?"

Peter hoped she would not think he was stealing the child's attention or affection away from her. He was really only trying to help. He offered her a hesitant smile. She returned it, albeit far too briefly, before looking then to Charlie.

"Of course," she said. "You go have fun with your writing. That way you will have something very exciting to tell your mother when you talk with her."

The boy grinned broadly, then clamored over to Peter's desk, where he promptly climbed onto his lap. That wasn't quite the seating arrangement Peter had planned, but he would honor the boy's wishes, at least for as long as his legs would allow.

"What should I tell everybody?" Charlie asked.

"That's up to you," Peter said, "but I will tell you this. You'll want to lead with a sentence that will capture your reader's attention."

"You mean like…" He pursed his lips, thinking. "'Boy, it's hot today'?"

Peter couldn't help but chuckle at that. It was warm and it was only eight in the morning. What would it be like come noon? "Well," he said, "that's good, but the sun is hot in Baltimore, too."

"Oh. So I should tell 'um something different?"

"Yes, but make certain it's truthful," Peter said. "Never, ever stretch the facts. Always tell the truth."

As he said that, his conscience was pricked. Given his continued thoughts of her, was he really being truthful to himself concerning Trudy?

As usual, Trudy beheld Peter Carpenter's actions with mixed emotions. It would be good for little Charlie to explore his imagination, his dreams of becoming a newspaperman, but the fact that Peter was spending time with the boy was disheartening. For him to put aside his own work to cater to the child, Mr. Carpenter must realize how essential it was to distract Charlie today. That added weight to what she suspected but did not want to believe. Despite the doctors' best efforts, Opal was dying.

Still, Trudy prayed otherwise. *Please, Lord, I know*

You can change her situation. For her sake...for Charlie and Kate's...please...

With the boy in his beloved newspaperman's care and Emily and Evan maintaining a watchful vigil over the mother and baby, Trudy tried to press forward in her duties. She assisted Dr. Turner as he tended a bedraggled family from the backside of Massanutten Mountain.

"You've come quite a long way," Dr. Turner said to the man.

"Yes, sir. Sure do appreciate y'all's help." The father was as thin as a scarecrow and used a crutch in the place of his missing left leg.

How he had traveled as far as he had was beyond Trudy's comprehension. His poor wife, due to lack of nourishment, hadn't enough milk to properly feed her baby, so Dr. Turner encouraged her to begin giving the child broth, in a well-thinned pap, a little earlier than usual.

"Give it to her very slowly," he explained, "and only in very small amounts. She isn't quite ready for heartier food just yet."

While Trudy would hardly call stale bread mixed with broth "hearty food," it was thicker than mother's milk.

"Beg your pardon, sir," the woman said, "but we don't have any broth. Haven't had fowl nor beef for nigh a year."

Dr. Turner blinked. While Trudy knew he and the rest of the men at the Lexington garrison were far from living high on the hog, she could tell Dr. Turner was only now beginning to realize how much the families in some parts of this defeated land were struggling.

It's heart-wrenching, isn't it? she wanted to say. Trudy was feeling the weight of their suffering more each day, so much so that it was becoming difficult to remain hopeful. Standing here now, she couldn't help but wonder for just a moment if this wasn't how it had happened to Peter. Had the day-in and day-out relentless stories of evil and suffering simply eroded his joy for life, and worn down his faith?

She squared her shoulders, determined not to let such a thing happen to her. Dr. Turner was looking at her.

"See what Mrs. Webb can find for them," he said.

"Yes, sir."

Dr. Mackay must have noticed the exchange, because before Trudy could locate Mrs. Webb, he came to her. "I'll see to it," he said. "If you would, go and sit with Opal. Em has gone out for a wee bit of air."

"Of course." She started to turn.

"And Trudy—"

"Yes?"

"Fetch me at once if she appears in pain." He looked as though he expected that.

Trudy's heart squeezed, but she did her best to remain positive. "And if not? If she is awake?"

Dr. Mackay smiled thinly. "Then give her some tea."

Trudy took her place beside Opal's pallet. Baby Kate was sleeping peacefully in the nearby makeshift cradle. Reverend Webb had brought a small drawer over from his house and affixed it to two rocker arms left over from a broken chair that for some reason neither the Confederates or Yankees had claimed for firewood. The contraption worked quite nicely. The baby had been sleeping soundly now for about an hour.

Opal, however, was awake, but her breathing and coloring were not good. Trudy bent near her. "Are you in pain?" she asked.

Opal shook her head.

Trudy wondered if the woman simply didn't wish to be under the effects of the numbing medication, for she then asked, "Where are the children?"

"Kate is right here," Trudy reassured her as she gestured toward the cradle. "And Charlie is writing an article with Mr. Carpenter."

Opal smiled weakly, then drew in a labored breath. It was obvious to Trudy that she was hurting. "Let me fetch Dr. Mackay," Trudy said. "He can give you something to help."

"Not yet… Please…" Her voice was thin but her eyes were determined. "I need to settle my affairs."

Despite the growing heat, a chill washed over Trudy. So Opal had accepted her lot. *Why can't I do the same? If she is going to Heaven then she will no longer suffer.* But the thought of the children without their mother… "I'll fetch the reverend," Trudy said.

"No," Opal said. "I want to speak with you."

With me? Trudy wasn't exactly certain why, but if the woman was more comfortable speaking with another woman then she would surely listen. "How may I help?"

"The children…" Opal drew in another labored breath. Trudy waited patiently for the rest of her words. She wasn't prepared for them when they finally came.

"Will you look after them?"

What? Surely Opal couldn't mean what Trudy thought. *She barely knows me!* Her brain scrambled to find another meaning. *She doesn't like Charlie seeing her this way. Perhaps she wants me to remove them from the church building.* "Of course I'll continue to tend them," Trudy said. "If you prefer, I can look after them in the parsonage. I'm certain Mrs. Webb—"

"No," Opal said. "I mean…after…"

"A-after?"

"After I am gone."

Trudy shook her head. "Opal, you must not talk about—"

"I know it's…a lot to…ask," she said, still undeterred, "but Charlie…loves you so… And there will be…better opportunities…for him in…Baltimore. There is…no future…here. No future…for…either of them."

Tears were threatening in Trudy's eyes. Although she loved Charlie and Kate and would be more than willing to claim them if she could, she knew it was not possible. She couldn't properly raise them on her own! She was, after all, an unmarried woman, and she had just resigned from her only paid employment!

Her mind began to race. Yes, she had a home, one far removed from the stench and pestilence of the battlefield. Yes, her mother would love Charlie and Kate as if they were her own grandchildren. *But shelter and love are not enough. Children need food, clothing, a proper education, and those things cost money.*

Then there was the legality of it all. They were not her flesh and blood. She would have to adopt them, *and it is very unlikely that a judge would approve a single, unemployed, former Confederate sympathizer as the guardian for these two children.*

The court would want someone of proper standing. *They will want a man—if not as primary guardian then at least on paper.*

Trudy thought of her brother, George, but even with his recent oath of loyalty, he would not be viewed favorably by the courts. *And no doubt he is still trying to make peace with the past four years. He would not be suitable. I must help him. It can't be the other way around.*

There was, of course, her brother-in-law, David. He, as an upstanding, loyal citizen, a former Federal soldier and a kindhearted Christian man, was an obvious choice. *But he has already done so much for my family in George's absence, financially, emotionally. Is it really fair to ask him to become the surrogate father to two orphans when he is about to be a first-time father in his own right? Is it fair to Elizabeth?*

I could find an attorney, perhaps even Emily's father, but while the man could serve as legal representative, a guardian on paper, he wouldn't really be able to influence the children's lives on a daily basis.

There was one other obvious choice, but Trudy couldn't even bring herself to go there. *He will see it surely as another scheme, a way to involve myself in his life once again. Besides, he has a family of his own. No*, she told herself. *Out of the question! Absolutely out of the question!*

Opal, however, seemed willing to consider just that. "Perhaps Mr. Carpenter could help… Charlie is fond… of him…and—"

"You must take some tea!" Trudy blurted out, suddenly remembering Dr. Mackay's directive. Flustered couldn't even begin to describe what she was feeling. She was downright disturbed by the woman's talk of her demise, but to add Peter's name into the discussion, and in conjunction with her own!

What exactly was Opal trying to do? Trudy understood her wanting to place her children in a family before she departed this world. *But this will never work! We cannot raise her children! He wouldn't—I couldn't—*

Her heart was pounding. Her hands were trembling. Trudy was so rattled that she practically shoved the cup of tea beneath Opal's nose before she thought better of her actions. She softened her movements at once. "Here now," she whispered, "drink slowly." But she couldn't soften the blow to her own mind.

Had Opal already hinted to Peter about such things? Was that why he had spoken to her so harshly yesterday? Even if the role Opal had in mind for him was only that of a legal guardian on paper, Trudy still did not see how it would work. She had planned to break all contact with him once they returned to Baltimore.

She glanced toward the makeshift writing desk. Charlie was still sitting on Peter's lap, despite the fact that the man was soaking his injured ankle in a bucket of water. With pencil in hand, mouth taut, the little boy was shaping his words. Peter was guiding his actions carefully, not as a fastidious publisher bent on perfection but like a loving father. Trudy's heart squeezed. She could hear it thudding in her ears. She forced herself to return her eyes to Charlie's mother.

Opal had drunk all she wanted. As Trudy set the cup aside and helped her lay her head back to the pillow, she offered her what she hoped was a steady, confident smile. Opal was staring at her, eyes full of hope. Trudy's stomach was in knots. She resisted the urge to once again look in Peter's direction.

She loved this woman's children. She wanted to honor her request. *But I cannot raise them alone, and how can I expect to raise a pair of children with a man who claims responsibility for another family?*

"Opal, I cannot express what your request means to me. The trust you have in me…" Trudy couldn't even finish the sentence. Her chin was beginning to quiver. "I promise we'll talk more about this later, but right now I want you to get some more sleep."

"You will…consider…what I said…won't you?"

"Of course," Trudy replied with much more steadiness of voice than she actually felt inside. "I'll think on it deeply."

For what else could she do? Lives were about to be changed forever, in one way or another. But how much, how closely, her and her former employer's lives would become intertwined, she could not yet say.

Chapter Thirteen

Peter was amazed at how much better his ankle was feeling. *I suppose there is some wisdom in staying off an injury*, he thought, even if it had meant being pinned to his chair by a six-year-old boy. His legs had gone numb. He wasn't sure whether it was the cold water in which he had been soaking his feet, or the fact that Charlie was sitting on his lap.

Probably both, Peter thought.

He had been pleasantly surprised by the child's writing, for Peter hadn't really expected much more than a simple sentence or two that, with some heavy editing, could be printed in the form of a quote. Charlie's spelling was atrocious, but he was sharply intelligent and surprisingly observant. Moreover, he had a knack for expressing his observations in an engaging way. In the end he had produced what amounted to a decent little column about foraging for food.

He told of his adventure with Miss Martin, although, at Peter's encouragement, he left out her name and the details about cutting her hand with the knife. The fact that they were digging for lily tubers was enough. Any

Baltimorean would be appalled that children, even the children of rebels, were now forced to dig roots to supplement their meager suppers.

If this doesn't stir the public conscience, promote the need for full-scale, organized relief, then I don't know what will. "You have done very well," he told the boy.

Charlie looked up at him and grinned. His shift in position brought an ache to a part of Peter's leg that apparently was not quite yet numb. "When will it be in the newspaper?" he asked.

"In a few days. First I will have to wire it to Baltimore."

"Then what?"

The boy was clearly eager to learn. Peter admired that. He eased him back to his original spot. "Well, then one of my employees will proof it," he said.

"Proof it?"

"Look for mistakes."

At that Charlie frowned slightly. He studied the paper in front of him. It was covered in scratches. "I thought we fixed 'um already."

"We did," Peter explained, "but sometimes telegraph operators make mistakes when they transcribe the wire."

"Oh. Then what happens?"

"After your article is proofed?"

The boy nodded.

"Then one of my other employees will determine the best location to place the article."

"The front page?" Charlie said hopefully.

"Well," Peter said slowly, "that is usually reserved for breaking news…battles…arrests…changes in law…"

His face fell. "Oh."

"But don't worry," Peter encouraged him. "Your story will still be placed in a very good spot."

The smile returned. "And then?"

For the sake of bypassing a few questions, Peter skipped the remaining editorial steps. "Well, then my pressmen will lay the type."

"The letters, right?"

"Yes. The little words and marks of punctuation that will get covered in ink."

"Miss Trudy told me all about that."

"She did, did she?"

Charlie nodded. "She said she takes the proofs to you and then you decide if you want to make changes."

"That's correct," Peter said, or at least it had been. He couldn't help but wonder who would cover that duty now.

"Then my story will get printed," Charlie said proudly.

Peter tousled the boy's dark hair, thankful to him for bringing his thoughts back into the proper focus. "Yes. Then the people in Baltimore will open their newspapers and read the words of Charles T. Jackson."

The boy was now grinning from ear to ear, and Peter couldn't help but offer him a smile in return. In some ways he felt like he was looking at a younger version of himself. He remembered very well how it felt when he had first gotten started, when he had read his own name in print for the first time.

That was so many years ago, he thought. He had started as a pressman at *The Baltimore Sun*. His father had gotten him his job. Peter had worked his way up through the ranks, pinched and scraped up enough money to eventually buy a worn-out, old-style flatbed press. With long days and even longer nights he churned out a one-page publication, then a two-page, then three and so on.

He loved what he did, the path he had chosen, but admittedly it could be a lonely profession, especially when what he printed often made enemies on both sides of the political aisle. Sometimes, especially lately, he couldn't help but wonder what it would be like to share the burdens and the joys of life with someone. Someone who understood him. Someone who was as committed to the truth as he.

The memory of Trudy's hand in his came to mind. It had fit so perfectly, just like the name he had used when he had done it. *I called her Tru.*

Charlie then slid from his lap. "Where are you going?" Peter asked.

"I'm gonna go tell Ma about my article."

"Oh...uh...wait."

"Why?"

The surgeons had wanted Opal to rest, but at this point wasn't it more important for the child to be with his mother? *He needs time to say goodbye,* Peter reasoned, but he was torn. What Charlie really needed was to know the truth about his mother's condition. *But when should he be told and who should tell him?*

"I want to come with you," he said, which of course he did. Trudy was not here to take Charlie. She was outside, doing what, he did not know. *One of us should be with him.* "But I can't very well meet a lady in my bare wet feet."

Charlie looked down at the bucket. "Reckon not," he said.

"Fetch me a towel, will you?"

The boy scampered away. Peter couldn't help but

notice he went immediately to Trudy, for she had just stepped through the church door. The baby was settled in a fabric sling tied about her chest. A lock of red hair was clinging to her cheek. Peter noticed it was extra curly today as he watched her brush it back behind her ear. She looked like a field hand, a very tired but still beautiful one.

While Charlie was completing his request, Peter quickly shook the water from his feet, doing his best to keep the droplets contained to the bucket and not the church floor. His toes were nearly blue. Peter quickly rolled down the cuffs of his trousers, lest once again the woman behold him in all of his ignobleness. He tucked his still bare feet as best as he could beneath his chair, for she was the one now approaching with the towel.

"Has the well water helped?" she asked. Her tone was warm and caring but far from the eager-to-please, acquiescent manner she had displayed to him upon first coming into the newspaper office. No doubt this was the compassion she had shown at the military hospital to the patients there. *I've become just another wounded man to her,* he thought, and he realized he rather missed the way she used to look at him—like he was something grand and noble.

"It has," he said. He reached for the towel, his fingers inadvertently brushing hers. Had his hands gone numb, as well? Why the tingling sensation? "Charlie wishes to visit his mother," he said. "Is she awake?"

She glanced over her shoulder, looked toward the physicians' area, and then turned back. "She is, I believe, but…" A look of anxiety filled her face. She knew as well as he that Charlie needed to be told, but it was obvious to Peter that she dreaded doing so. He wanted to spare her that if he could.

"I'll sit with him while he visits if you like," he offered. "You look as though you could use some fresh air."

She blinked. "I was just outside."

"But you were working. Were you not?"

She patted the baby's back lightly through the fabric and nodded. "I was gathering wood for the fire. Boiling water. One of the soldiers who arrived this morning has lice."

He remembered back to his thoughts of her when she had first arrived in Virginia. He'd called her naive, believing she knew nothing of what awaited her here. Well, she knew now—and he was sorry that she did.

Missing supplies, mysterious attackers, hunger, lice and soon-to-be orphans... A lady her age should be concerning herself with wedding dresses and setting up a household, he thought. If she had stayed back in Baltimore she might be doing just that. *But if she had, then where would I be? In the church cemetery with a bullet through my heart?*

"You've been working very hard," he said. "You should take a moment for yourself. Go for a short walk. You know, just somewhere close by. Do something to clear your mind."

She looked rather startled at that. Peter wondered what nerve he had touched. He hoped she didn't think he was insinuating that she might be thinking of him. Although a part of him hoped she had.

The look then softened to a polite, albeit somewhat reticent, smile. "Thank you," she said. "Perhaps I will."

"Good." Charlie was tugging restlessly at his hand. "Don't worry about us. We will be just fine."

He said the words with a little more surety than he actually felt.

* * *

"Do something to clear your mind," he had said.

Mr. Carpenter had no idea just how much was actually on her mind when he had offered to sit with Charlie and Opal. It wasn't that she didn't wish to tend the boy or his mother. She did, but after Opal's request that Trudy care for her children, she did not know what to say—to either of them. That was the reason when she saw Charlie working with him she had decided to go outside.

While Kate had cooed from a blanket beneath a shade tree, Trudy had worked efficiently. Gathering firewood and boiling clothes had kept her occupied, but they had not brought her any closer to a decision. She simply did not want to accept the fact that Opal was dying.

Lord, I want You to heal Opal. I want her and her children to live and be happy...but it looks as though You are going to take her home to be with You. Help me come to terms with that. Help Charlie...

With Kate now sleeping in the sling across Trudy's chest, she walked out of the churchyard. Trudy had learned to carry a baby this way by watching her friend Rebekah Nash tend her youngest niece. Rebekah had apparently learned it from her cook, a former slave named Hannah.

She halted. *Wait a minute. Isn't Robert's missing wife named Hannah?* For a moment she did her best to remember but then moved on. Her thoughts were simply too muddled to focus on a new subject. She already had too much on her mind.

A mockingbird was singing his repertoire from one of the red cedar trees along the road. Trudy traveled in the direction of the sound until the bird darted across her path, then disappeared into a thick tangle of brush just opposite the crossroads. It was there that her walk ended.

She did not wish to stray too far from the church—both so she could be close at hand if she was needed, and also so her friends would be able to hear *her* if she called. She'd heard about the break-in at Mr. Zimmer's home.

Trudy shifted the baby ever so slightly in the sling and gazed down upon her sweet little face. Her mouth was working, as though she was dreaming of delicious milk. Trudy couldn't help but smile.

Not a care in the world, she thought. In contrast, she was feeling the weight of her troubles immensely. Hot, tired and feeling very overwhelmed, she slid to the base of a cedar tree.

I've been asked to claim her and her brother. The wonderment in the idea of an instant family, of children who were so easy to love, was tempered by doubt. Was this the right thing to do? Was this what God wanted *her* to do?

Trudy heaved a sigh. How she wished her sister Elizabeth was here, or rather, again, that David had come as he had planned. He would know what to do about Charlie and Kate. Surely he would have telegraphed Elizabeth about their predicament, and Trudy and her sister would have discussed what might be done.

The thought crossed her mind that perhaps she should still wire her mother, sister and brother-in-law, tell them of the situation. *But doing so will mean traveling to Larkinsville, and no one is going to allow me to do so own my own.* She could hear Dr. Mackay's words now. *"No, lass. 'Tis far too dangerous."*

The mockingbird had returned. He was now singing happily from the branches above her head. Trudy paid him no mind. A few weeks ago she would have become lost in the melody, but now she had the responsibility of children to hold her attention.

Her mind continued to churn. *I could ask Dr. Turner if he might spare an escort or two to travel with me.* But two men had already been sent out on patrol because of Mr. Zimmer's complaints. She didn't like the idea of further depleting the protection for her friends. Her thoughts inadvertently went to a third option. Peter would be traveling to Larkinsville in another day or two to wire work to the paper. She *could* ask him to send a message to her family.

No, she told herself. *I will not involve him.* It wasn't that she was bent on carrying a grudge over the incident at the Hassler farm, *but I must distance myself. I must sever all ties if I am to ever recover my heart.*

She still wondered if she could realistically do that. Even after resigning her position, separating from the man himself entirely would not be easy to do. Elizabeth planned to still work for the paper, sketching on a part-time basis even after the baby was born. David, of course, would continue to work there full-time. Peter Carpenter would always be a topic of conversation in her family home. There was no escaping it.

Trudy sighed heavily as she pushed her stubborn stray curls back from her face. *And what of Charlie? He is fascinated by the presses, not to mention the publisher himself. If I claim Charlie as my own, then what is he*

*to think if I deny him the opportunity to ever interact
with Peter? He already knows we live in the same town.*

She knew she had to make a decision, and soon. She
couldn't wait for her family's insight. She wasn't even
sure she had time for them to answer. Opal was growing worse by the hour. *She deserves an answer*, yet as
much as Trudy wanted to bring a measure of peace to
the woman, she still had no answer to give her.

Again she sighed. *Lord, I don't know what to do.
I love these children, but the idea of raising them on
my own... You know my knack for running ahead, for
scheming. Don't let me do something contrary to Your
will, but don't let me forgo an opportunity to help someone else just because I'm afraid.*

The baby was beginning to stir. Trudy caressed her
cheek lightly, hoping to soothe her before she awakened fully. As much as she enjoyed Kate's company,
right now she needed a few more moments of quiet to
be able to think, to pray.

She wasn't granted them, though.

A cry stole her attention. Trudy immediately looked
in the direction of the church, only to see Charlie escaping from Peter's grasp. When the boy spied her, he
bolted in her direction. She immediately assumed the
worst.

Heart in her throat, Trudy wrapped her arms safely
around the still sleeping Kate and hurried toward him.
The boy was in tears. He flung himself headfirst at her.

"Oh my dear boy..." Trudy whispered as she stroked
his hair. "My dear, dear boy..."

"Mr. Carpenter says Ma is going to Heaven soon!"

Soon? Waves of differing emotions crashed over her.
She felt relief that Opal was still alive, heartbreak for

the child in discovering the gravity of the situation and anger toward the man who had revealed the truth to Charlie in obviously such an indelicate way.

The last threatened to pull her under completely. While Charlie buried his head in the folds of her skirt, Trudy looked beyond him to see her former employer making his way toward them. *How could you?* she wanted to say. *This isn't one of your headlines! And he isn't a naive young woman blinded by infatuation. He didn't need to be set straight with blunt talk! You should have let me or Mrs. Webb tell him!*

She bit back the tirade only because she didn't want to argue in front of Charlie, but she glared at Mr. Carpenter, hoping her eyes alone could convey her thoughts.

Evidently they did. "He asked me," he said in that detached, matter-of-fact way of his. "So I told him the truth."

His words only served to make her angrier. She wanted to rail at him. *Of course you would! What about his feelings? What about showing a little sympathy?* It wasn't that Trudy wanted him to lie to the boy. She didn't know what she wanted—at least not from him. Why did the sight of him inject such confusion, such turmoil into her thoughts?

Her head was pounding, her thoughts swirling. The only thing that was clear to her in that moment was that Charlie was in great pain and she was determined to alleviate it in any way she could. Kneeling to the ground, she folded the boy completely in her arms. Kate was beginning to stir. "Oh Charlie, I am so sorry this is happening. I know this is breaking your heart in two."

"If Ma goes to Heaven, what's gonna happen to me and Kate?"

The moment had come. There was no longer any time to wonder what was right. This wasn't the way she'd imagined she'd gain a family, but she would accept what had been handed her. "I'll take care of you," Trudy said.

He looked up at her questioningly. Tears streaked his face.

"Your mother has asked me to look after you and your sister," Trudy told him, "and I will. You have my word on that."

From the corner of her eye she saw Mr. Carpenter shift his weight from one leg to the other. He was leaning heavily on his cane. She ignored him. Charlie was still looking to her.

"I know you are afraid," she said. "I know you feel very sad. I do, too, but remember, God loves your mother and He loves you and Kate."

The words sounded empty even to her. How did one convince a hurting child of the Creator's love when He chose not to heal a beloved mother? Even Kate was crying now.

Mrs. Webb joined them. Either she'd heard what had happened or she could very well guess. Her look was full of sympathy, especially for Charlie. "Come, my love," she said to him. "Let me take you and Kate back to the church. Your mama wants to talk with you again." The preacher's wife claimed the baby, then slowly, tenderly peeled Charlie from Trudy's side.

Tears were rolling down Trudy's face as she watched them walk away. Charlie was still crying.

"I was only trying to help," she heard Peter say.

She turned her attention to him. His expression was sincere, but even so, Trudy had to swallow back the words that he had once spoken to her. *"I don't want your help!"* Yet she knew deep down that she was lying to herself. She *did* want his help. She wanted to fling herself into his arms, just like Charlie had done with her. She wanted to cry until someone bigger, stronger and wiser than herself promised everything would be alright.

He did not promise that. "Are you sure about this?" he asked. "About taking on such a responsibility?"

Her back and shoulders were aching. The July sun was beating down upon her, making her feel almost nauseous. Trudy knew if she did not walk away from him now she would either sink to the ground in defeat or fall into his arms.

Neither is an appropriate response. I have to remain strong. The man standing in front of me is not the one who will take care of me. Lord, I don't know what the future holds, but You do. Give me the courage to trust You.

She drew in a deep breath and squared her aching shoulders. "If you will excuse me," she said making quite the effort to keep her voice even, "I must go and see Opal."

With an awkward shift of his feet, Peter quietly stepped out of her way.

Chapter Fourteen

Peter had never felt lower or more lonely in his entire life, not even when he had received word of his brothers' deaths in battle. Watching Charlie, tears in his eyes, be led away by Mrs. Webb, and subsequently seeing Trudy turn from him looking very much the same, cut him to the core.

He *had* only been trying to help both of them, but things had not gone as he had intended. Charlie had been babbling on about his article, including every detail and step Peter had explained concerning publication. His poor mother had been listening intently to a point, but what strength she had mustered for the visit quickly drained. Coupled with the mind-numbing effects of the morphine, she soon closed her eyes.

Her six-year-old son was insulted. "Ma!" Charlie said loudly. "I didn't finish telling you my story!"

Opal tried to rouse herself. She muttered a soft "I'm sorry," but then within a few moments her eyelids had once again drifted shut.

"Ma!"

"That's enough, young man," Peter said, encouraging

the boy to his feet. "Your mother needs to sleep. You can finish telling her about your article later."

He succeeded in getting Charlie away from Opal's pallet, but just barely. The boy dragged his feet, nearly causing Peter to trip over his own twice. "She's always sleeping now," the boy lamented.

At this point Peter had managed to herd him to the front door. "That is because she is very sick," he said.

Charlie looked up at him with those inquisitive brown eyes. "How sick?" he asked.

Peter cleared his throat, telling himself the child might as well know. *At least then he will have time to prepare for the inevitable,* he thought, *and it will spare Trudy the unpleasantness of breaking such news herself.* "Come outside and sit on the steps with me," he had told the boy.

Charlie obeyed but not without his expression darkening. He was intelligent enough to know that whatever Peter had to say wasn't good. "Is my ma going to Heaven?" he asked.

Peter'd had barely enough time to lower himself to the steps and put his arm around the child. "I am afraid so, my boy."

He had expected a flood of tears, but remarkably the only emotion Charlie displayed was a twitch of his jaw. *I should have realized it was shock,* Peter told himself.

"When is she going?" the boy then asked.

Far be it from Peter to give the child a fixed time. "I don't know precisely," he said, "but it will be soon."

Reality began to sink in. The twitching jaw tightened into a scowl. "You're lying," Charlie said.

Peter squeezed the boy's shoulder gently. "I assure you, I am not. I'm sorry."

The scowl hardened further. So did the boy's voice. It became like steel. "You're lying! You say to always tell the truth but I know you're lying!"

"Charlie—" Peter moved to embrace him fully. The boy shoved him back, then bolted to his feet.

"No!" he shouted.

Peter did his best to scramble to his own feet. He only ended up crashing into the railing while Charlie struck out across the churchyard. The child was quick as lightning. "Charlie, wait—"

"Liar!" he screamed. By then he had spied Trudy.

Peter's legs might have been deficient, but his eyesight was as sharp as an eagle's. Even from the distance that separated them, he could tell she assumed the worst. She came running toward them. The look on her face as Charlie flung herself into her arms pierced Peter's soul. She felt the child's pain deeply, excruciatingly. *And then she silently blamed me for being the cause of it.*

Her scathing look had cut him to the core. She had obviously assumed he had been blunt and uncaring with the boy, as he had been with her once before. *But what possible benefit could I find in breaking a poor child's heart?*

Still, his defense that he was only trying to help sounded empty and insincere even to him. He knew that he *had* only made things worse. Charlie was in tears and she was angry with him—again. He hated the thought of Trudy being so—especially when she'd misunderstood his intentions.

Standing there at the edge of the churchyard, the sunlight beating harshly down upon his head, Peter considered his next move. Did he turn around and go back inside the building, offer what assistance he could to her and the boy? Did he try to further dissuade her from taking custody of the children, as she had proclaimed?

He knew she hadn't liked him questioning her decision. He could tell that by the way she had lifted her chin, but he *was* concerned for her. *Does she have any realization how difficult it is going to be raising not only one child but two? On her own?*

Granted, she wouldn't be staying here in Virginia, but still, life in Baltimore was far from ideal. Peter had no doubt she would care for Charlie and Kate to the best of her abilities. She would love them unconditionally. *But a child needs a father, and by taking on this obligation, she is very likely eliminating any chance she has of ever securing a husband.*

Because of the war, there was a shortage of eligible bachelors. *And those men who have survived will not be eager to take on another man's children—not in this economy. I should know,* he thought. *I am one of them— and I have gainful employment. She now has none and her likelihood of securing any is as good as nil. She'll be competing with returning veterans, not to mention thousands of freed slaves.*

Peter raked his fingers through his hair. *Stubborn, naive woman,* but he didn't want to see her get in over her head. If she was determined on this course then he knew he needed to do something to assist her—at the very least convince her to return to her position at the paper. The question was—would she allow him to help her?

Despite the turmoil caused by Mr. Carpenter's harsh delivery, Charlie had calmed after speaking to his mother. Opal was now resting more comfortably, and the assurance that she was going to Heaven soon, and that Charlie would still be well cared for in her absence, had consoled the child enough that he had been willing to go off in the temporary care of Mrs. Webb while Trudy settled things with his mother.

"Thank you," Opal had whispered, "for taking care of the children. I know they will be in good hands."

Trudy still trembled at the thought of caring for not only one, but *two* little children on her own, but she did not allow Opal to see her fear. "I will love your children as if they were my own," she promised.

It was then that Opal delivered a startling revelation. "Kate isn't truly mine," she said.

"What?" Trudy's pulse quickened. Her mouth went dry. If Kate wasn't Opal's child, then whose was she? *What have I gotten myself into?*

Opal's face twisted in pain. "What I mean is…she is now but…she wasn't born my…flesh and blood. She's…Agnes's daughter."

"Who's Agnes?"

"My friend."

Trudy's brain scrambled. She remembered Charlie mentioning something about a Miss Agnes once, sometime in their conversation concerning from where babies originate. *No wonder he had questions… Oh Lord, this is too much to process. Do I now need to locate this woman? Why has she given up her child?*

"How then did you come to care for Kate?" Trudy asked, trying hard to keep the anxiety from her voice.

"Agnes died…giving birth," Opal explained. "She had come to live with…me and Charlie when…her husband died. We had been friends since…childhood. She had…no other family."

Trudy's heart slowed but only slightly. Tears again were threatening in her eyes. Would there ever be a story in this valley with a happy ending? *Or are the effects of war, famine and pestilence to reign here forever?*

"I should have told you…before," Opal said, "but… I was afraid you…might not…want them both. I didn't want…to see them…separated."

To tell the truth, the thought had crossed Trudy's mind for the briefest of seconds. *But how can I turn down an innocent baby, choose one child over another, especially in circumstances such as these? Of course they must stay together!* "I will care for them both," Trudy said, "and I will love them equally. You have my word."

Opal offered her a weak but genuine smile. "God… bless…you."

Trudy squeezed the woman's frail hand. Despite the warmth of the day, Opal's fingers were cold. With great effort the woman went on to explain that back at what remained of her home were letters from Kate's father to her mother.

"Will you…get…them?" she asked. "So Kate…will one day…have something of…her own?"

"I will," Trudy promised, "and I will do the same for Charlie."

"I'm afraid there isn't much of…an inheritance. His father's sword… A tintype taken on our wedding day…" Opal drew in a shallow breath. "My husband died before he could be pardoned. Our land is forfeit. The Federals just…haven't gotten around to…claiming it yet."

Emotions were tearing through her—pain, sadness,

anger, a sense of futility, a determination to see justice done and a family preserved. *God help me...* Trudy prayed. *Help me...* "Nevertheless," she insisted, "he will not forget you, nor his father. I will make certain of that."

Again Opal smiled. She started to tell Trudy how to find the house, but Trudy stopped her. "Wait," she said. "Let me fetch paper and a pen. I want to take this down properly."

By now Mr. Carpenter had returned to his desk. He must have heard Trudy's words for as she approached he handed her the items she needed. Previously he'd worn that haughty, arrogant, know-it-all expression. She knew he didn't think she could handle the charge she had been given. She was determined to prove him wrong.

Now, though, his eyes revealed compassionate sympathy, enough to make Trudy's throat tight. She dared not look at him long. "Thank you," she said, taking the writing implements from him. Once more she felt that familiar jolt when their fingers brushed, but ignoring it, she quickly returned to Opal.

Much to Peter's surprise, Charlie's mother lived through the evening and into the following day. It was Sunday and Reverend Webb planned to hold his usual service. The meeting, however, was anything but *usual* at least as far as Peter was concerned.

He had long ago given up the ritual of corporate worship, for he found the exercise artificial and all too predictable to be of any personal benefit. Peter's fellow congregants in Baltimore, parading about in their silks and satins, stove pipe hats and leather gloves, made an impressive show socially on the society pages, but some of those same people who supposedly prayed devoutly the first day of the week could be found on the scandal sheets the other six.

Over the years he had seen it all. *Bribing Federal officials for business contracts, failure to pay the former slaves who continued to work for them as servants, giving false testimony in court, drunkenness, adultery...*

At this service, however, there was not a stove pipe hat or a silk dress to be found. The tattered families who had passed in and out of the building all week long were the only congregants present, and they didn't claim pews, only a collection of chairs, benches and, in some cases, blankets upon the floor. Peter had helped Reverend Webb arrange the seating earlier that morning.

"This way Opal can be part of our meeting," the man had said.

Perhaps it was that simple lack of formality, or the fact that Peter knew firsthand that the reverend was a man who practiced what he preached, but for the first time since he'd started his own press, Peter found himself listening to a sermon and, not only that, actually *pondering* how the Bible passage might pertain to his own life.

Reverend Webb had chosen the book of Ecclesiastes. *Not necessarily an uplifting portion of Scripture*, Peter thought, *but fitting for the times.*

"'To everything there is a season, and a time to every purpose under the heaven,'" the preacher read.

Peter had learned from Mrs. Webb, who was seated beside him, that this was Opal's favorite passage, or at least the one to which she had clung most fervently these past four years, as she tried to make sense of this terrible world.

"'A time to be born, and a time to die…'"

Peter glanced across the expanse to where Opal lay. Charlie was beside her. Trudy was next to him with the baby nestled in her lap. Kate was chewing on her fingers as the reverend continued to read. "'A time to kill, and a time to heal; a time to break down, and a time to build up…'"

Build up, Peter thought. Thankfully he and Charlie had been able to make their peace, at least as much as was possible under the circumstances. Peter had told the boy he was sorry for having to give him such dreadful news but that he was proud of the child for the way he was now accepting the situation.

"You are well on your way to becoming a man," he had told Charlie, and as a gesture of proof, Peter extended his hand.

Charlie had grasped it, albeit somewhat hesitantly. The tears had dried and now, except for the brief time when Mrs. Webb had called him away for food or rest, Charlie was keeping a constant, quiet vigil beside his mother.

Trudy, at her own insistence, had remained at her post the entire time. *She looks so tired*, Peter thought. Her cheeks were thinning because of their meager rations. Dark circles dimmed her eyes. The poor woman seemed to have aged ten years in one week's time, yet there was a beauty about her beyond physical qualities.

"'A time to keep silence, and a time to speak…'"

Humph, Peter muttered to himself upon hearing that phrase. He had wanted repeatedly to go to her, offer what assistance he could, but he sensed now was not the time to speak to her. She wished to keep her watch alone.

"'A time to love, and a time to hate; a time of war, and a time of peace.'"

Peter sighed to himself. *Four years of war. Will there ever truly be a peace?*

He inadvertently looked once again at Trudy. Her attention was fixed solely on Reverend Webb. If nothing more, Peter wanted to make peace with her. Not that they were locked in battle, but they did disagree. Oddly enough, the distance caused by that served to make her all the more alluring. Peter found himself drawn to her in a way he could not explain, and did not want to admit.

Perhaps it is just a sense of responsibility. I am more aware of the world than she. All he knew was he could not allow her to bear the burden of raising Opal's children on her own.

Reverend Webb had finished chapter three and had moved into Ecclesiastes 4. "'Two are better than one, because they have a good reward for their labor. For if they fall, the one will lift up his fellow…'"

At that, Peter couldn't help but grin. The image of her, pitchfork in hand, red hair flying, had come to mind. His grin quickly faded, though, not only because he knew it was an inappropriate reaction to a solemn Scripture reading, but also because he realized that now she was the one in danger of falling. *Not literally but emotionally.*

He could see it in her face. He knew the weight she now carried, the responsibility. He also had a pretty good idea of the questions circulating through her mind. *How will I manage this? Where is God in all of this mess?*

Peter could not bear to see her fresh, fragile face old before her time. *Or worse, her sweet and hopeful temperament turned sour and cynical like mine.*

The reverend's words repeated in Peter's mind. *"'Two are better than one...a reward for their labor...'" If I was to form some sort of partnership with her concerning the children, at least financially speaking, that would certainly ease her load.*

He chewed on that thought throughout the rest of the service. When it ended, he approached her. "May I speak with you privately for a moment?" Peter asked. "It concerns the welfare of the children."

Her eyebrow arched. "If you've come to talk me out of caring for them, you might as well save your breath," she told him.

Succinctly put, he thought. "I haven't," he promised. "I want to help."

She blinked in surprise, then glanced about the room. Chairs were being relocated, blankets folded. The aid stations that had cluttered the sanctuary all week were being reerected.

This is hardly the place to have this discussion, he thought. "Would you come outside with me?"

"I..." When she again glanced about, Peter knew that she would rather be helping her friends than speaking to him. He supposed he couldn't blame her. He wasn't exactly encouraging when he'd first learned what she intended to do.

"I promise I won't take much of your time," he said.

Reluctantly she followed him outside. "I don't see how you can help," she said as they descended the steps.

"I have a few ideas..."

"What ideas?"

He waited until he reached level ground, specifically the shade of the oak tree, before answering. He didn't want to be interrupted and he didn't want to be overheard, either.

"I'd like you to consider returning to the paper," he said.

Her face was stoic. When she didn't say anything he added, "I'll give you a raise and you won't have to take on more hours."

All she did was blink.

"You'll need the extra time and income in order to look after the children."

Her shoulders rose and then fell with a sigh. Evidently she saw his point, but she was clearly torn on how to respond to his offer. Biting her lower lip, she looked down at the ground. When she still hadn't said anything after a considerable length of silence, he then added, "I want to help Charlie and Kate, but I confess it is more than that."

Her head came up. A questioning look filled her face.

"You are a good worker," he said. "We make a good team. Frankly, I don't want to lose you. You are far too valuable."

Her expression softened so that for a moment he thought she was going to smile. He realized he *wanted* to see her smile, but she stopped just short of doing so. "Thank you for saying that," she said. "I appreciate your offer to assist…"

He could hear the unspoken qualification. "But…?"

"You will need the income you are offering me in order to care for your own family."

"I assure I—"

"I must see to Charlie and Kate in my own way."

An unmistakable pang of disappointment struck his chest. Peter told himself she was being foolish, stubborn. Evidently she intended to prove to him she could handle this on her own.

He wanted to ask why, but he didn't want his inquisitiveness to be mistaken for begging. He wanted her back at the paper, yes, *because she is a hard worker, and those children are going to need my help.* If, however, she did not want his help, if she was naive enough to believe she could find employment on her own somewhere else, he would let her try.

"Very well," he said. "You know where to find me should you change your mind."

"I do," she said, but the way she lifted her chin when she turned and walked away told him that she had no intention of ever changing her mind.

Chapter Fifteen

By sunset Opal had slipped into deep sleep, never to be awakened again this side of Heaven. Trudy had sat with her for most of the day, as had Charlie. Accepting the situation as well as any young child could, he told his mother the rest of his newspaper story and then of the articles he planned to write one day for his own press.

Trudy listened with mixed emotions. She was grateful for the boy's dreams, his hope in the future, but deeply saddened that the lad felt compelled to give his mother a full report, knowing she would not be here to witness the fruition of his ambitions for herself.

Why God? Trudy silently asked. *I've seen you answer so many prayers in the past. Why won't you answer this one? You know that I'm a poor substitute for this boy's mother.*

When the last rays of light had disappeared from the western sky, Opal's breathing became shallow and intermittent. Knowing Trudy wanted to stay until the end, Dr. Mackay signaled to Mrs. Webb. The reverend's wife came to fetch Charlie.

"Here, love," she said in that gentle way of hers, "it's best that you come away with me now."

He understood exactly why. Trudy's heart wretched as the boy kissed his mother goodbye but did not leave with Mrs. Webb. He wanted Peter. Again she watched with mixed emotions. She was relieved that Charlie and he had mended their strained relationship but saddened that she could not seem to follow suit.

He offered to help me, but she knew deep down she could not accept his assistance. It wasn't a matter of pride. She wasn't vain enough to let his rebuff of her romantic interest make her spurn his assistance for the children. *It is a matter of doing what is right. He wishes to right all the wrongs of the world, but we are not a problem for him to solve. His responsibilities lie elsewhere. And my feelings will never subside unless we make a clean break.*

Despite her determination not to pine, she knew she was doing exactly that. He couldn't touch her, even in the most ordinary way, without sending shivers down her spine or a flush to her cheeks. He couldn't walk into or exit a room without her noticing.

Just like now...

Trudy watched her former employer scoop the boy up into his arms and carry him outside. How the man had the strength, given his lame leg and recently injured ankle, she did not know, but the scene was so tender it made her eyes cloud. Charlie's head was buried in Peter's left shoulder. Only the top of his chocolate-brown hair was visible as the pair departed.

Kate let out a wail. Trudy moved to claim her from the cradle but Mrs. Webb reached it first. "I'll take her to the parsonage and give her something to eat," she said.

"Thank you."

Opal struggled for another breath. Mind heavy, heart full, Trudy did her best to pray. *Please God...please, the children need her. Don't let it end this way...*

An hour later she was still pleading the same when Dr. Mackay put his stethoscope into his ears and listened to Opal's chest. He then looked up at Trudy. His eyes were full of compassion. They told Trudy what she already knew but did not want to accept.

Methodically, she let go of Opal's hand, placed it on the woman's chest. Dr. Mackay did the same with the other. Emily gently touched Trudy's shoulder.

"I'll see to her, love," Emily said. "Why don't you get some sleep."

Trudy appreciated Emily's offer, but sleep? How could she do that? *There are children to tend, a funeral for which to prepare them.* She struggled for her own breath.

Reverend Webb was standing to the left of Dr. Mackay. "I have a suggestion," he then said, almost as if he had read Trudy's mind. "Although I'll admit it is rather unorthodox."

She looked up at him, as did the others.

"What is that?" Dr. Turner asked.

"We have already told Charlie that his mother is going to Heaven," the reverend said. "Why confuse him with a wake?"

Trudy wasn't following. Apparently neither was Emily.

"You mean bury Opal tonight?" Emily asked.

Reverend Webb nodded.

"There aren't likely to be any friends or family to attend a viewing," Dr. Turner said.

"Aye," Dr. Mackay agreed, "and given climate conditions…"

Mercifully, he did not finish the sentence. At times he reminded Trudy of Peter with his appalling bluntness—though she couldn't dispute his logic. Cleanliness and decency demanded quick action. And she did think well of the idea of sparing Charlie the confusion of a burial. "Would you still have a graveside service tomorrow?" she asked Reverend Webb.

He shook his head. "I think just a few hymns here in the church, a passage of Scripture, an emphasis on going home."

Home. She knew he meant home with God, but the word still sent a shiver down her spine. *Charlie and Kate's home will now be with me.* She shook away the thought. She couldn't ponder the future right now. She could barely comprehend the present. Emily was asking her a question.

"I'm sorry," Trudy said. "W-what did you say?"

Emily smiled sympathetically. "I said, that given Charlie's young age, I thought the reverend's plan a wise one, but that it depends on your decision. You are now, after all, responsible for the children."

Trudy swallowed back a lump in her throat. *Yes, I am,* she thought, *but that doesn't mean that I know what is best for them.* She wanted to spare Charlie additional pain and of course confusion, but this wasn't how things were normally done. *Funerals are for saying goodbye…aren't they?*

She bit her lip, looked at her friends, but realized no one was going to make this decision for her, not even the reverend. *Charlie did say goodbye*, she then told herself. *He's been saying goodbye for the last two days. Why prolong the agony?* "Yes," she said, with more decisiveness then she actually felt. "I think we should do as the reverend suggested."

The preacher nodded, and then silently looked to the other men.

"I'll fetch the shovel," Dr. Mackay said.

"I'll help your wife," Dr. Turner said, "and then I'll join you."

The four of them looked to Trudy. Again Emily renewed her promise. "I'll see to her, love. Why don't you go and look in on the children?"

Trudy knew she should, but why did she suddenly feel so numb at the thought of doing so? *I haven't even cried. What is wrong with me?* Forcing herself to her feet, she slowly moved toward the door.

Peter had never held a child before tonight, not even his sister's children when they had been born. On both occasions he had simply peered into the cradle, witnessed they'd had two arms, two legs and the appropriate fingers and toes, and pronounced that they were fine-looking.

He'd had no interest in cuddling or cooing, nor carrying them about the house and proclaiming himself a proud uncle. He was in the news business and the birth of a child hardly fit that bill. It was ordinary, routine. Necessary, yes, for the continuation of society, but hardly life-altering, at least not for him. Tonight, however, Peter had to admit, his life *had* been altered, not by birth but by death.

In Charlie's hour of grief he had not wanted Mrs.

Webb, or even Trudy. He had wanted me. What exactly a worn-down, cynical newspaperman could do to comfort him, Peter did not know. *Maybe it is simply a male presence in a time of uncertainty*, but whatever it was, Peter was determined to give him what he could. He'd carried the boy to the parsonage.

For lack of knowing what else to do, Peter had followed an example from his own childhood. He remembered once when he was very young, four or five perhaps, that after having been awakened by a nightmare, his father had come to him. Carrying Peter to the parlor, the man had simply sat down in his reading chair near the fire and held him against his chest until sleep again claimed them both. Peter now did the same with Charlie.

It was much too warm for a fire, but the light from a nearby candle offered a similar glow. Neither he nor Charlie spoke a word, but every now and then Peter heard a slight sniffle. Whenever he did he tightened his arms around the boy.

God in Heaven, he silently prayed. *If You really are concerned with the everyday affairs of men, then I ask You to comfort this boy...or give me the wisdom to know how to do so.* He hadn't lifted a prayer in years. He had come to believe God did as He wished and there was no changing His mind, but tonight Peter felt desperate, if not for divine intervention for himself then for this child and his sister.

And for the woman who's responsibility they have now become. The world was a cruel and dangerous place and Peter wanted to believe that someone stronger and more capable than himself would watch over them all.

She needs help, God, Peter said, as Charlie's head lay atop his heart. *I know I have little to offer, but show me what to do.*

The rustle of petticoats turned his attention toward the hall. He was expecting Trudy. Instead, Mrs. Webb was standing in the doorway. He swallowed back his disappointment as she then asked, "How is he?"

Peter brushed Charlie's hair back from his eyes. The boy had fallen asleep clinging to his vest. "Asleep," Peter mouthed, not wanting not to wake him.

Evidently Mrs. Webb had been in the house for some time, although he hadn't heard her. *She must have come through the back door and into the kitchen*, he thought, for she then told him, "I've given little Kate something to eat and laid her down. She should sleep at least for a few hours."

Peter nodded.

The preacher's wife quietly came forward. "I'll take him for you."

He appreciated the offer, but he wanted to look after the boy a little longer. "I can manage," he said. Carefully he maneuvered his way to the edge of the chair. Balancing Charlie in one arm, Peter pushed to his feet with the other. The child stirred only slightly. One hand still gripped his vest, and the other now dangled in midair.

"There's a trundle in the back bedroom," Mrs. Webb said. She picked up the candle from the table, showed him the way.

His leg was stiff and his ankle again tender, but Peter somehow carefully placed Charlie in the trundle bed. After lightly brushing the hair from the boy's eyes again, he then turned to his sister. She, with her arms at her ears, lay asleep in a nearby drawer. Peter studied her for a moment.

Poor little girl, he thought. *What is to become of her? What man will guide her life?*

Mrs. Webb's voice invaded his thoughts. "You look as though you could use a bit of rest," she said. "I'll take care of the children."

Peter glanced again at Charlie. He didn't want to leave him lest he wake and wonder where Peter had gone, but he did wish to look in on Opal, and on Trudy. "When he wakes, tell him I'll be back shortly."

Mrs. Webb nodded, and with that Peter moved slowly, carefully back through the house. He realized he needed to fetch his cane, which he had left back at his desk, or his legs would not last until morning. Gingerly he maneuvered down the back porch steps. He was halfway across the yard when he noticed lantern lights in the cemetery.

His chest tightened. He could guess what had happened, and if the activity there wasn't enough to confirm Peter's suspicions, the muffled sounds of a woman's tears was. As he neared the oak tree that stood between the parsonage and the church, he found Trudy. She was leaning against the trunk, her head buried in her hands.

Peter's footsteps were heavy on the ground, and hearing his approach, she bolted upright. The moon was only at a crescent, but even by its scant light he could see the tears streaming down her face. She had been trying her best to be brave, to remain strong for the children's sake, but tonight she had reached her breaking point.

Poor little thing, he couldn't help but think. *What is to become of her?*

He didn't know if what had worked for Charlie would for her, but he found himself desperately wanting to hold her. Silently he reached for her. Much to his surprise, she allowed herself to be held. As Peter closed his arms around her a muffled cry met his chest. It pierced his soul.

God, help her...

He stroked her hair. Her tears were soaking his shirt-front but he didn't mind. His legs were aching but he would hold her as long as she needed. He realized he wanted her to need *him*.

"I p-prayed," she stammered. "I p-prayed so hard..."

"This is why I didn't want you to come here," he said.

He'd have done better for both their sakes if he had kept his mouth shut. She immediately lifted her head, moved out of his embrace. "Forgive me for inconveniencing you."

Peter's arms now hung heavily at his sides. He recognized how his words had sounded. "I didn't mean it that way," he said. "Honestly..."

Tears still stained her cheeks but the look of vulnerability was gone. Her jaw had hardened. She was again trying to be brave.

Still, Peter continued, "I only meant that from my experience, God doesn't always answer prayers in the way we want. I didn't want to see you get hurt. I didn't want you to lose faith. I...*want to help*." That determined expression remained on her face. *We are more alike than I have realized*, he thought.

"Didn't you once say that you already had enough responsibility?" she said. "That you had no need for more?"

Why did I have to put it that way? He was an edu-cated, articulate reporter and editor. He was skilled in publishing sound articles. Why couldn't he effectively communicate with this woman? And why did he have the sudden desire to draw her back into his arms and kiss her as if that would set everything in the world right?

Peter cleared his throat, then changed the subject entirely. "I'm sorry about Opal," he said.

With that, her look softened. She nodded, then after a moment or two of awkward silence told him of the reverend's plan for a simple funeral.

"I think that's very wise," Peter said. "You made the right decision."

She closed her eyes as if soaking in those words. Peter could tell she was starved for assurance. He wanted to give it to her. "Things will be alright," he said. "I'll help you with the children."

Her eyes flew open. "What about Caroline?" she asked.

He drew a calculated breath. *I never intended to have any children in my life. And now it isn't one child. It is three.* Still, he stepped closer. "We will figure all that out when I find her," he said.

In the distance he could hear the sound of the pickax working the hard red clay ground. Trudy heard it, as well. As she cast a glance in the direction of the ceme-tery, tears again trickled down her cheeks. Peter reached out and touched her face lightly. It was so soft. "Don't cry, Tru."

"*Please* don't call me that," she said.

He again dropped his arm. "Alright," he said.

The crickets were chirping. She was staring at him. He was staring at her. Neither dared to move.

"I promised Opal that I would go to her house," Trudy then said. "She has letters, photographs, things that she wants—" she caught herself "—things she *wanted* the children to have."

"I'll take you," he promised.

"Thank you. I would appreciate that. Besides the personal items that Opal requested, I'm not certain I would know what to collect."

Peter nodded slowly. "We will figure that out, too. Together. When does Reverend Webb plan to hold the service?"

"First thing in the morning."

"We could leave after that," Peter said. "I had intended to go to Larkinsville anyway." He then added, "Dr. Turner will be traveling with us."

"Oh?"

"A missive came from Lexington this evening ordering him and his escorts to return to the garrison. Evidently there have been thefts happening in that area, as well, and the soldiers are needed."

She sighed heavily, rubbed her hand across her forehead. Peter again felt the incredible urge to draw her close, to taste her lips. He swallowed it back. She had already pulled away from him once, and was making it clear that she would accept only limited help from him.

"Where are Charlie and Kate?" she asked.

"Sleeping. Mrs. Webb is with them."

"I should go to them." She slipped past him, the edge of her dress brushing against his lame leg. By now both legs were killing him but something else was happening inside. Something Peter had never expected.

I can't change the world but perhaps I can change the lives of a few.

He had told himself for years that he was not a family man. That he did not wish to be the father of children. He was changing. Was it simply circumstantial or was God working directly in his life? Was He preparing him for the role of raising Daniel's child, and possibly Opal's children, as well?

All he knew was whatever his involvement with the latter, he wanted Trudy Martin beside him, as more than as an employee or even a legal partner. *Am I in love with her?* He honestly did not know. He understood attraction, desire, and he certainly felt both for her. But this was different. It was all of that and more.

He watched as she walked toward the Webbs' cottage. Her back was ramrod straight. Her head was held high. She might have wept in his arms but she was determined not to remain there.

Peter's chest further tightened as he realized his musings were moot. *Whatever I may now want, it's obvious she wants nothing to do with me.*

As Trudy laid her hand on the Webbs' backdoor latch, she took one last look toward the oak tree. Peter was still standing there. She could just make out his tall, broad form in the faint moonlight. She could tell he was watching her.

A week ago, him paying her that much attention would have made her heart pound. Now Trudy felt only sadness—deep, immense, mind-numbing sadness. She looked just beyond him. The glow of lanterns could be seen from the cemetery. Oh, she had cried, and done so in his arms, but once the tears were spent, only the emptiness remained.

Tomorrow would be the funeral—and then the trip to Opal's home. Trudy felt as if a millstone had been tied around her chest, and with every passing moment it was pressing harder against her lungs. *God*, she breathed more in frustration than in faith, *what am I supposed to do?*

A twig snapped. Trudy realized Peter had taken a few steps toward her, *no doubt wondering why I am still standing here on the porch*. She lifted the latch and stepped inside the house. She then closed the door behind her and leaned heavily against it.

Trudy still felt the desperate need to cling to him, draw what strength he would give. For just a few seconds she had felt that in his arms was where she belonged, and she wanted to capture that feeling again.

But that is not the place meant for me, she reminded herself. He had said he wanted to help her and no doubt he did, for he had taken to Charlie so. *But any fanciful idea I have of joining forces with him, raising Charlie and Kate together in not only a legal partnership but a loving household, is absurd. He already has a family for whom he must care.*

No, Trudy told herself, *I am not numb after all*. She only wanted to be.

Mrs. Hassler had been correct when she had said Trudy was in love with him. She *was* in love despite his arrogance, his gruffness, his responsibility toward and care for another woman. But his heart was not hers to claim.

She hadn't time, however, to shed further tears, for

down the hall Trudy could hear the sound of baby Kate. She herself was crying. Trudy hurried to fetch her, lest she wake poor Charlie.

Chapter Sixteen

It was a short service, just a few hymns and a Scripture reading from the book of Revelation with an emphasis that there were no tears, no sickness, no hunger in Heaven.

"Families are reunited with long departed love ones," Reverend Webb said.

That made Charlie smile. "Then one day I'll see Ma and Pa together?" Peter overheard him ask Trudy.

"Yes," she whispered back. "They will be waiting for you."

Peter had boldly chosen a seat next to her. Although she had initially seemed somewhat uncomfortable about his choice, she quickly set those qualms aside for Charlie's sake. The boy had climbed immediately between the two of them.

When Reverend Webb offered the final prayer, Charlie asked Peter if he would help him write an article about Heaven. As much as Peter wanted to help the boy, he shifted uneasily in his seat. That was one subject he wasn't quite sure he was qualified to write—not because he doubted its existence but because his discussion of the matter would likely reveal other doubts. He didn't want to make the boy question his own faith.

Peter's main problem was what it had always been. Where was God when life was falling apart? *Off "preparing a place" for us?* he wondered. *We would all do better with a little more intervention in the here and now.*

"I am afraid I must go to Larkinsville today," he told Charlie.

"Can I go with you?" the boy immediately asked.

Given the mission that he and Trudy were about to undertake, as well as the length of the journey, Peter didn't think it wise to take him. "Not this time."

"But I want to go with you."

Trudy reached for Charlie in the same instant that Peter moved to put his arm around the child's shoulder. When their hands bumped she at once drew back. Peter's lingered awkwardly before settling on the child. "And I would like that very much, but Miss Trudy and I have business to attend and it is better that you remain here."

"But I thought you were going to be my new Pa."

The bottom dropped out of Peter's stomach—partly from the boy's assumption and partly because of the look on Trudy's face. It was one of absolute horror.

How far I have fallen, he thought sadly, *and thanks to my own actions? My brashness and cynicism have made me repulsive in her eyes.*

Charlie was still looking at him, waiting for an answer. Peter was at a complete loss for words. Once again she came to his rescue.

"Charlie," Trudy said softly. "Mr. Carpenter and I are following your mother's last wishes. She asked that we go to your old house and bring back special things for you and Kate."

"Pa's sword?" the boy asked, a hint of pride in his young voice.

"Yes," she replied, "along with a tintype from the day they were married."

"What will you get for Kate?" he then asked. "Ma doesn't have no jewelry."

Peter silently admired how Trudy had skillfully steered Charlie's attention away from its previous focus. "No need to fret over that," she said. "I'll find what is best for her, but in the meantime it is important that you stay here and help Mrs. Webb look after the baby."

"That's right," Peter then added. "You are Kate's older brother. She needs you."

The boy looked back at him. A hint of fear had returned to his eyes. "You will come back, won't you?"

Peter's chest tightened. *Father, mother...everyone closest to him is now gone.* He lovingly squeezed the boy's shoulder. "We will indeed," he said. "You have my word."

Trudy offered Charlie a smile just as Mrs. Webb came to claim him.

"You'd best be off," she said, "if you want to return by sunset."

"Indeed," Peter thought, for even with the presence of Federal escorts, he did not want Trudy traveling after dark.

A few minutes later, after she had finished hugging and kissing the children goodbye, they climbed into the wagon. Without the presence of a child between them now, the awkwardness returned.

"Dr. Turner was correct in assuming there would be few people to pay their final respects to Opal," she commented as she eyed the small band of blue-uniformed men in front of and behind them.

Besides those already at the church at the time of the woman's death, only Mrs. Zimmer had showed, although Peter suspected she had come more for rations than for Opal's sake. He said as much, and then wished he hadn't. It sounded hard-hearted. After Charlie's comment about him becoming his new Pa, Peter was having terrible trouble knowing what to say to Trudy. She had left so much room between them on the bench seat that Peter worried she might fall out of the wagon.

"No doubt Mrs. Zimmer is in need of extra rations," Trudy said.

"No more than anyone else around here," he quipped. *What is wrong with me?*

"She is letting out her dresses," Trudy said matter-of-factly.

Peter blinked. "Shouldn't she be taking them in?" After all, her husband needed to start doing so with his shirts. They were hanging more loosely upon him with each passing day.

The look Trudy gave him told him he should be smart enough to figure out why Mrs. Zimmer would be doing so.

"Oh," Peter then said. *She's expecting a child.* "Just out of curiosity, how did you happen to notice she was altering her dresses?" he asked.

"I noticed the fabric was slightly darker at her side seams," she said.

"Astute observation." He had meant that as a compliment but she didn't seem to take it as such.

"I noticed it because I have a work dress of the exact same cloth at home," she said. "The fabric caught my eye."

"I wasn't doubting that," he said. "I've long known that you have an eye for detail and that is a great benefit in our business." *Our business?* Had he really just said that? She'd already made it perfectly clear that she did not wish to be part of his business any longer.

If I don't shut my mouth, either I'm going to offend her further or she is going to think me begging. So he stayed quiet. As the wagon jolted along, Peter silently eyed the trees. They were now at their heaviest, their limbs hanging low across the road.

"Did Mrs. Zimmer say if there has been any more trouble at her house?" Trudy then asked.

"Trouble?" he repeated, his mind still on their previous exchange.

"Thievery."

"No," Peter said. "I suspect whoever did such in the first place has long moved on. Once a thief sees there is nothing worthwhile to steal, he goes on his way."

"I wonder in what condition we will find Opal's home."

In truth, Peter had wondered the same, but he didn't tell her that. He didn't want to give her anything else over which to worry.

He was rather tetchy with her today, but then, she supposed no more so than she was with him. She didn't mean to be, but the events of the past few days, coupled with the responsibilities of the future, weighed heavily upon her.

Trudy had managed to get through the simple service this morning thanks in part to the fact that Charlie seemed comforted by the idea that his mother was reunited with his father up in Glory. But any tranquility she'd found was shattered by the comment he'd made about Peter becoming his new Pa. Charlie's obvious fear that they would abandon him was heart-wrenching. It was all she could do to let go of him.

"We will both be back soon," Mr. Carpenter again promised.

He seemed intent that there would be some sort of partnership. And maybe it was time for her to give the idea more consideration. Trudy knew deep down that more than likely, she was going to have to return to her position at the paper, at least for a while. *At least until I can find some other employment.*

After all, it wasn't fair to her mother or the rest of her family to return to Baltimore with two children in her charge, with no means of supporting them. *Perhaps Peter would be willing to allow Charlie to work there as well as an errand boy. Charlie is so interested in the newspaper business. Not to mention, he is so fond of Peter that being near him would help ease the transition to a new life in a new place.*

But she also knew what Peter was like at the office. Forceful, short-tempered and extremely blunt. Trudy didn't want Charlie to see that side of him. *He will only get hurt.*

She sighed heavily. She didn't want to think about any of that right now. All she wanted was to find what items Opal had wanted to give to her children and then return to church.

The wagon bumped along. With conversation awkwardly lagging between her and the man beside her, Trudy engaged Dr. Turner, who was riding to her right. Although out of his way, Dr. Turner and his escorts promised to first ride to Larkinsville with them so they could press the young lieutenant there to send soldiers back to Forest Glade. The older physician and his escorts would then return to their garrison. Trudy hadn't liked leaving the Mackays and the Webbs without a soldier's presence, especially with the children there, as well, even though Dr. Mackay insisted they would be fine.

Peter planned to visit the telegraph office to wire Charlie's article and other matters back to the paper before stopping in to see the lieutenant.

"It will give Dr. Turner time to convince the man that we need his help," Peter had said. "Then the new soldiers can escort us to Opal's farm."

At the turnoff to the garrison, he halted the wagon. Dr. Turner pulled his horse to a stop and dismounted. He shook hands with Peter then returned to Trudy's side of the wagon.

"Well, my dear," he said, removing his kepi and holding it gallantly to his side. "I suppose this is farewell."

She had a sudden inclination to burst into tears, as if she feared she would never see him again. Trudy told herself that was ridiculous, but still her eyes clouded when the old gentleman kissed her hand.

"Give my regards to your sister and to young Mr. Wainwright."

"I will," Trudy said, "and please give mine to your wife. Please tell her how grateful I am for your kindness."

He grinned. "She'll be grateful to hear that. Glad to know the army hasn't turned me into a crotchety old man." He then turned serious. "God be with you," he said.

"And with you." Mounting his horse, he signaled

to his men. A cloud of dust kicked up as they trotted down the road.

"Good man," Peter said.

"Y-yes," Trudy replied. He must have heard the hitch in her voice.

"Are you alright?" he asked. "Is your hand bothering you?"

My hand? With all that had happened as of late, Trudy had nearly forgotten about her injury. The pain from it was little compared to that of her heart, which seemed to compound each day. "I'm just having trouble saying goodbye," she said.

"That comes with age," he said. As if the ten years he had over her were the wisdom of a century. "Life is uncertain. The friendships we forge one day dissolve the next."

As low as she felt, she couldn't help but beg to differ. Peter Carpenter simply had a knack for bringing out her argumentative side. "I hardly think my friendship with Dr. Turner is now dissolved," she said.

"That isn't what I meant," he said. He gave the reins a snap. "What I meant was that we must make the most of the time we have here, while we have it. What was it Reverend Webb said yesterday? 'To everything there is a season'?"

She was surprised by his quoting of Scripture, but it did little to lift her heavy heart. *This season has been one of disappointment, pain and immense responsibility.*

"When was the last time you slept?" he then asked.

"What?"

"You heard me. And I don't mean an hour snatched here or there. I mean proper sleep. More than that, when was the last time you had a moment to yourself? And I don't mean a walk with Charlie or rocking Kate to sleep."

She shook her head as if his suggestion that she should be lollygagging about was preposterous. "I cannot sleep. There is work to be done. I have to care for the children."

"My point exactly," he said. "You are exhausted and it shows."

Fear crept upon her. *It shows? How? Am I mishandling the way I am caring for them?* She had never been a mother before. "I want nothing more than to do right by them."

"I know you do," Peter said. "I know you love them. I see how much you care about everything, how hard you work." His voice had softened. "But that is the problem."

"Problem?"

"You are trying to carry too much on your own." He paused, looked at her. "You know I want to help."

"Y-yes."

"Then why won't you allow me to do so?"

Reverend Webb's Bible verses crossed her mind: *"Two are better than one..." What exactly are you proposing?* Trudy wanted to ask, but instead she bit her tongue. He wasn't proposing, at least not like that. *He never will.*

"Tru?" The sound of her name on his lips was torture. "Why won't you let me help you?"

"Because I still care for you!" she wanted to say. *"And because you care for someone else!"* "Because you must find Caroline and her child. Because they are your responsibility, not me."

"*You are* my responsibility," he said, "and I want you to come back to the paper. As for the rest of it all, we will figure it out in time."

Figure it out? What was there to figure out? He might be able to claim three children, but he could not claim two women. Even if Caroline chose not to marry him he could carry a torch. *Just like David would have done if Elizabeth had been able to marry his brother, Jeremiah. He would have loved her silently, from a distance, but he would have loved her no less.*

Her stomach was in knots. *Am I destined to do the same? What else can I do?*

They were pulling into Larkinsville. The telegraph office was just ahead. The temptation to wire David and Elizabeth, to beg them to come to her rescue, was strong, but Trudy refused to give in to it. This was her life, and she needed to be in command of it.

Sighing deeply, she looked at Peter. "If your offer to remain at the paper still stands, then I will accept, but only until I can find work elsewhere, until you can hire a replacement."

"A replacement?" His tone suggested he'd been hurt by what she'd just said. Why? Given all the tension between them in the past, didn't he want to offer only temporary assistance? *Or has he grown so fond of the children that he can't bear the thought of not seeing them?* She did not have the chance to ask him to explain further, as he then climbed down from the wagon.

"You can stay here," he said, his customary all-business look on his face. "I don't need you."

At those words, Trudy's heart wrenched. He irritated her. He unsettled her. But he also had a way of making her feel that she could do anything, be anything, accomplish anything the world threw her way. She felt that whenever he complimented her concerning the children. She had felt that the night he had held her.

He was gruff and arrogant at times, but beneath that facade was an honest, good and caring man. He certainly didn't need her. He had a family of his own, but she needed him. She just couldn't ever let him know that.

Her rejection stung, but Peter was not about to let her see that, especially when there was work to be done. Charlie's column, along with other articles Peter had written, needed to be sent to Baltimore. After that, Peter planned to visit Lieutenant Glassman to hopefully collect additional guards and to see if Glassman had received any word from the garrison commander in Lexington concerning the mysterious man whom Peter had deposited there several days ago.

The officer had promised to send word of any developments, for he, like Peter, had suspected the attacker was part of a thieving ring in the area.

I am not about to wire David Wainwright and tell him to send another shipment of supplies until I know for certain they can be protected.

Dr. Turner's opinion of the local garrison officer came to mind. "Glassman is young and inexperienced, but I do believe he is an honest man."

Peter respected the gray-headed physician, but he was hard-pressed to share his opinion, especially when, upon opening the telegraph office door he came face-to-face with the carpetbagger who'd been lording about Glassman's office the day Peter came to see him. *And whom I met again the day I just happened to be transporting my assailant to Lexington.*

"Mr. Carpenter." Johnson smiled thinly as he lifted his stove pipe hat. "It seems our paths continue to cross."

"So it seems," Peter replied.

"Sending wires to Baltimore?"

"Simple matters of business," Peter replied. He knew in his gut this man was responsible for the trouble in the area, but he still he couldn't prove it. *And until I can, I will keep my mouth shut and my eyes open.* "And if you will excuse me…"

"Of course… Of course," the man said. "A good day to you, then."

Peter nodded in return, but as he walked through the office door, he realized Johnson's present path would lead him directly to Trudy. The hair on the back of his neck stood on end. He didn't think the man would cause trouble here in the middle of the street, but still Peter did not wish to leave her unattended.

He spun back around.

Johnson had spied her. He lifted his hat. *Keep walking*, Peter silently willed as he closed the distance between them. *You don't need to speak to her.*

For a second or two Peter found he was thankful for the tension between him and Trudy. She offered Johnson a polite smile but nothing more. Clearly she wasn't in the mood for making pleasantries, either.

Johnson continued past. Reaching the wagon, Peter offered her his hand. "It turns out that I need you after all," he said.

She gave him a curious look, but apparently it wasn't related to his change of mind. "Wasn't that the man—"

"—from the road," he finished as she grasped his hand and slowly stepped to the ground. Peter continued to eye the scene. Three storefronts down he spied Zimmer's friend, Tom O'Neil. He was coming in this direction. Johnson slowed his pace. The two men exchanged brief words, and as they passed, Johnson slipped something into O'Neil's hand. Peter struggled to see. A note? Money?

Johnson then continued in the opposite direction. O'Neil was now coming toward them. At the last moment before reaching them, he turned in to the tavern.

"Did you see that?" Trudy asked.

"I did." Did O'Neil not wish to be noticed by them or was the man simply out for a drink? Peter was tempted to go after O'Neil but didn't want to take Trudy into such a place, and at this point he certainly wasn't going to leave her unattended.

"Come on," he told her. Realizing he was still holding her hand, he released it promptly. "Let's send our wires and then head for the garrison."

After all, there were still escorts to be claimed, a sister-in-law and a child to find and a mother's last wish to be fulfilled. Any personal disappointment Peter felt at Trudy's limited term of employment he must push aside for her sake and for the good of those back in Forest Glade.

They sent their wires and returned to the wagon. The bench seat shifted as Peter climbed into the driver's box. Trudy pressed her left hand hard against the wood lest she be tossed into him. Her stitches pulled. She grimaced.

Thankfully he hadn't noticed, for Peter's expression was just as tight. He had been on edge ever since the encounter with Mr. Johnson. Her employer was convinced that the man was involved someway in the missing supply shipments, perhaps even the attack. She wondered if he was worried some harm would befall them both today.

He said not another word until they reached the garrison. Under the watchful eye of a blue-uniformed guard, Peter pulled the wagon to a stop and told her, "Wait here."

She did, but not without constantly surveying the grounds. Had Dr. Turner been able to secure an escort for them? Would there be some word on the missing supplies, or on the man who had attacked Peter? *Will we make it back to Charlie and Kate before nightfall?*

She watched then as Mr. Johnson rode through the front gate. After handing his reins to a waiting private, he slid from his well-groomed horse and strode toward the officers' mess. He didn't notice Trudy, but Peter saw him.

He was stepping from the lieutenant's office just as Johnson was going inside the opposite building. Peter watched him for a moment, then came toward the wagon. He was frowning. "Did he speak to you?" he asked.

"No. He didn't seem to notice me at all."

He climbed into the wagon. This time Trudy leaned upon her opposite hand so as not to feel the pain of her stiches.

"Glassman says the escort detail isn't yet prepared to leave," he said.

"But he is providing one?" she asked just to be sure.

"Yes," Peter said, "although grudgingly. He still maintains he hasn't enough troops to keep order and provide protection everywhere."

"What are we to do in the meantime?"

The frown deepened. "We haven't enough daylight left to wait here and then still gather the items from Opal's home. I told him where we are going. Glassman swore he would have the escorts meet us there."

Trudy nodded. "Thank you. I don't want to be away from Charlie any longer than necessary. I don't want him to worry."

"I know that, and neither do I," he said. "Which is exactly why I told Glassman what I did." The frown softened, almost to the point of a smile. "Don't worry. Everything will be alright. We haven't that far to travel, and while I may not be able to win a footrace, I'm armed and I am quite skilled at hitting targets."

He was trying to inject a little humor into the tense situation. It didn't have the desired effect. Her fear wasn't for herself or even him. It was for Charlie and Kate. *If something were to happen to us...*

As they pulled from the garrison, the late afternoon sun was shining through the trees, slanting shafts of gold to the valley floor. Trudy wanted to enjoy the beauty but could not. The scenery was marred by the times. *God protect us all...* she silently prayed. *And send the escorts quickly.*

Finally, they had reached the last turn to Opal's home. Unlike the Hasslers, who had begun to rebuild, the landscape here was marred by the charred remains of barn. The house was still standing, but barely a shutter remained. The roofline was sagging. A broken second-floor windowpane had been stuffed with a rag. One window on the first floor had a gaping hole.

Trudy couldn't help but remember what Mr. Zimmer

had said about his own house being burglarized. Has someone been here? An uneasy feeling moved through her, and for a moment Trudy was tempted to slide a little closer to Peter for protection. She resisted. Her warring thoughts of clinging to him for support and standing on her own two feet were quieted only by the sobering thought that she was about to enter a home a family no longer occupied.

"I feel like an interloper," she said.

"You are acting on Opal's last wish," he said matter-of-factly.

Peter brought the buckboard to a stop in front of the porch and lifted the brake. Trudy slid from the wagon.

Leaning now against his cane, Peter navigated the buckling steps. Trudy silently followed him to the threshold. A spider was making a web across the frame. She shivered as Peter knocked the silky strands away with his stick, then pushed open the door. It creaked mournfully.

The moment they stepped inside, a pair of squirrels scurried across their path. Jolted, Trudy clutched Peter's arm, hid behind his back. He chuckled softly, no doubt amused by her foolishness, as the critters raced up the banister.

Watching them flee, she could feel herself blushing. *I tell him I will raise those children on my own and here I am jumping in fright at the sight of a few squirrels.*

Mercifully he said nothing about her inconsistent behavior. Trudy had released his arm but still maintained close proximity. What at one time was surely a cozy family parlor now resembled something from a Gothic novel. Faded draperies hung lopsided at the window. The furniture, what little remained, was mismatched and broken. More spider webs hung in the corners. Ashes littered the hearth.

"Someone has been here," Peter said as he poked at the kindling remains.

Trudy shivered. "Recently?"

"After Opal and Charlie."

She glanced about, half expecting to find some Heathcliff-type character emerging from the shadows. No one was there. In truth, the place looked so desolate that it was difficult to imagine anyone choosing to stay there at all. The only indications that this had once been a loving home and not a setting ripped from the pages of *Wuthering Heights* lay on the mantel. Two small framed photographs marked the days of the past. The first was a solider, thin-looking but proud and dressed in full Confederate regalia.

Charlie's father.

Peter picked it up first and eyed the picture with an expression of sadness. He then handed it to her. She wondered if he was thinking of the little boy now in her charge or his brother Daniel. Whichever, she knew he felt pain. His Adam's apple bobbed as he then said, "There is supposed to be a sword, correct?"

"Yes."

"I'll look for it." He started to walk away. His footsteps were heavy on the floorboards. Just before he passed into the foyer he called, "Stay here and alert me at once if anything seems amiss."

She swallowed back her growing anxiety. She wondered if the sword was the only thing for which he was looking. Was he seeking more indicators of the squatter or squatters who had stayed here? Trudy wasn't skilled enough to know how fresh the ashes in the fireplace actually were. A day? A few days? A few hours?

Did he think someone was still lurking about the property? She remembered vividly the last time he had met an intruder.

"Please be careful," she told him.

He glanced back at her. The corner of his mouth lifted with the barest hint of a smile, likely prompted by the memory of her wielding a pitchfork on his behalf. In spite of herself, her heart was stirred by his handsome grin. She returned her attention to the mantel and picked up the wedding picture. It had clearly been taken before the war. Charlie's father's face was fuller and he was dressed in civilian clothes. Opal looked young and healthy. While not a fashion to grace the pages of *Godey's Lady's Book*, her simple, most likely home-sewn wedding dress was beautiful. Trudy drew in a ragged breath, struggling to hold back tears. Peter was ascending the staircase. His footsteps grew fainter the farther he went.

In the center of the mantel was a small rough-hewn box. Trudy lifted the lid. It was full of letters, just as Opal had said it would be. The ones on the top of the pile were addressed either to Mr. and Mrs. C. T. Jackson or to Opal herself. After taking the box in hand, Trudy sank to the floor.

At first she perused the letters lightly, intending to read each more carefully after she was certain she'd located what she'd been told to collect. Some of the letters addressed to Opal were signed by Agnes.

Coming upon those, Trudy drew in another breath.

Kate's birth mother. These she read very carefully. The letters spoke at first of happy, prosperous times, the good price wheat would fetch and the fabric bought for a dress to wear to the church-sponsored taffy pull. Then came the storm clouds. Childhood friends were enlisting. Illness had taken over her family.

The boards above Trudy's head groaned under the weight of Peter's uneven steps. The sound of a thud made her jump, but when she listened again and still heard his steps, Trudy figured he'd simply bumped into something. She went back to her letters, reading hungrily the tale of a handsome, nonnative Virginia soldier. *Kate's father.*

> He is part of General Ewell's division… His eyes are dark and serious but my heart melts at his smile…

Trudy silently quipped to herself that she could be reading a description of Peter's effect on her. As Trudy read further, Agnes delivered another startlingly similar detail. "His name is Daniel. He comes from Baltimore."

Gracious! she thought, *what are the odds that Kate's father would bear the same name as Peter's brother and be from Balti—* She quickly unfolded the next letter. This one was different. It was not in the handwriting of the previous ones. The penmanship was smudged and the paper creased and worn as though it had been read and reread many times.

"My dearest Agnes…" it began.

> I know I never call you by your given name. It

just doesn't seem to suit you, but a soldier must find some way of keeping amused when he is far from the woman he loves...

Feeling more and more like an intruder, Trudy continued to read.

The word in camp is that we will leave Winchester. There are too many Yankees around and we cannot keep ourselves well supplied and in fighting condition this far north of Richmond. So never you fear, my dear Agnes Caroline Sewell. We will soon pass your way again.

Trudy's breath hitched. *"My dear Agnes Caroline"? Caroline? Was it really? Daniel?* Heart pounding, she had an immediate instinct to call out for Peter, but given the disappointment he'd experienced at the Hassler farm, she wanted to be certain first.

She pulled out the next letter, then the next. There was no more reference to Agnes. It was now *"dearest Caroline"* and *"forever yours, Daniel."* Trudy's hands were trembling. The next letter she read left no doubt.

And you can be certain, my dear Mrs. Carpenter, the lovely, though altogether too brief moments we shared will carry me through battle...

Trudy's jaw dropped as the pieces fell into place. *He called her by her middle name. That's why no one around here knew who Peter was searching for!* Kate's mother was Peter's Caroline. The baby, Peter's niece, had been right before his eyes all along!

Then it hit her. *Peter's niece!* Legally Kate belonged to him and despite Opal's wishes, Trudy had no rightful claim to the child. Profound sadness rolled through her, along with uncertainty and fear. *What about Charlie? What does this mean for him? He thinks of Kate as his sister. How can he be separated from her, especially when he has no other family? Opal wanted the children to stay together.*

She pressed her hands to her face as her thoughts continued to race. Knowing Peter's fondness for the boy and his growing declarations of his determination to be of assistance, surely he would offer to take both of the children. *But where does that leave me?*

She had been overwhelmed by the responsibility Opal had laid upon her, but she loved the children and she didn't want to give them up. *Not even to him.*

The floorboards in the foyer were creaking softly. Had Peter come downstairs? In her distraction, she hadn't heard his footsteps on the staircase at all. For a moment Trudy was seriously tempted to shove the letters back into the box and keep their contents from her employer, but she knew it would be wrong to do so. *Kate is part of his family,* she told herself, *and I am not. Oh, God...please help me do what is right.*

He was behind her now for the chill of cold steel touched her neck. Obviously he had located the sword. She drew in a breath, knowing the longer she waited, the harder it would be. "Peter, there is something that I must tell you."

"There is much I want to be told," a man's voice said.

Trudy quickly turned. It wasn't her employer leaning over her. It was Jack Zimmer. Charlie's inheritance, his father's sword, was pointed at her throat.

Chapter Seventeen

"Don't move."

The initial shock and confusion of finding Jack Zimmer standing over her with a sword had turned to petrifying fear. Trudy's heart was racing, pounding in her ears so loudly that it sounded as if the entire Federal cavalry were thundering to her rescue. If only that was the case! But Lieutenant Glassman had insisted his soldiers were not yet prepared. Peter had told her.

Her heart lurched. *Peter! Where is he?* Had Zimmer found him first? Had he opted for a sword instead of a pitchfork? She eyed the blade before her. It held no crimson stain but had the man simply wiped it clean since using it last?

Oh God, please...

Sweat was trickling down her back and her stomach was churning so violently she was certain she was going to be sick. "W-why are you doing this?" she asked. "Wh-where is P-Peter?"

Zimmer pressed the point of the sword to Trudy's neck as if intent on running her though. Ignoring his earlier command, she instinctively moved back.

"I told you not to move," he said. Then he reversed himself. "Get up! Stand against the wall."

Trudy obeyed, scanning around her for something in reach with which to defend herself. There was nothing, though, and Zimmer soon had her pinned.

"When is the next shipment of supplies to arrive?" he demanded to know.

"Wh-what?"

"Don't be coy with me. I know you were at the telegraph office."

Trudy's mind raced. How did he know that? Had Johnson, the man Peter suspected, sent word from Larkinsville? Or Tom O'Neil? She didn't want to believe that the very neighbors she had been assisting all week were bent on doing her harm, yet here was Mr. Zimmer with a sword pointed at her throat.

"The world is a dangerous place, Miss Martin," Peter had once warned her, and she knew now for certain it was true. The intensity in Zimmer's eyes told her he would stop at nothing to get what he wanted. She had never been more frightened in her life.

"I know you got word," he said.

"No," Trudy insisted. "We didn't. I promise you. We only wired in a set of articles. We received no news." She then realized the less she told this man was probably better. He clearly wasn't of sound mind, and there was no telling what might set him off. But at the same time, staying silent seemed a poor idea, as well. If the lieutenant was sending escorts, like he had promised, then Trudy wanted to keep Zimmer talking until they arrived.

Or Peter. Please God! Pease let him be alright! "Mr.

Zimmer, please… I understand that your family situation is desperate."

The sword dropped from his hand. As it clattered to the floor he grabbed her shoulders and pressed her hard against the wall. "Don't speak about my family situation! You know nothing of it!"

"I know your wife is surely expecting a child. I know you are desperate to feed them both, but please, Mr. Zimmer…*please*. If you are caught by the authorities and sentenced to jail, who will help your wife, your child then?"

His fingers were digging into her flesh. "Just tell me when the next shipment will arrive!"

"I promise you, I don't know!"

He shook her. "You lie!"

"I-I'm n-not! Honestly…"

"I need that money to keep my farm."

"Wh-what money? We didn't bring any money. All the funds we raised went to buy food…medicine."

"I'm going to get it," he said. "You are going to tell me what I need to know or else *he* will. I will make him!"

Him? So was Peter lying incapacitated but still alive somewhere in this house? Was him falling the thump she had earlier heard? "W-what do you p-plan to do?" she asked.

He sneered but did not say. Trudy's heart beat even faster. *Is he now going to use me as a hostage to make Peter tell him whatever he thinks we know? It will not work—we have no information! Oh God, please! Please make him believe me.* "Mr. Zimmer, there is no pending shipment. At least, not yet."

"Then you'll tell me when it will come," he insisted. "Tom and I will see to that."

Tom? Tom O'Neil? Then he was part of this, as well. Who else? Lieutenant Glassman? The soldiers he was supposed to be sending? Overwhelming fear threatened to make her swoon, but Trudy was determined not to give in, no matter what Zimmer and O'Neil, or anyone else for that matter, had planned for her.

As the man began dragging her toward the foyer, Trudy did her best to push away from him, but he was far too strong. She then tried to tangle his feet, trip him. Twisting sharply, she forced him to turn. His back was now to the foyer entry. All of the sudden Trudy saw an arm, heard a thwack. Zimmer staggered, and with a second hit to the head he fell to the floor.

Trudy looked from the man at her feet to the one standing in the doorway. Peter was clutching his derringer in his hand, held so as to use the grip as a bludgeon. Sweat was beading on his forehead.

"I didn't want to shoot him," he said, "but I would have if necessary. Are you alright?"

Alright? Thrilled he was alive and immensely grateful she was free, Trudy flung herself into his arms and covered his neck and stubbled cheek with kisses. She realized only all too late what she was doing and immediately stepped back.

Peter's dark brown eyes were wide with shock.

Peter felt as though he were in a daze. He had expected Trudy to be grateful for his assistance, but that appreciation went far beyond his expectations. Apparently it had gone far beyond hers, as well. She looked like she was in shock.

"Tom O'Neil is lying upstairs on the bed," he said matter-of-factly, ignoring her actions as if what had just happened was purely confined to his imagination. Had it been?

"T-then he w-was the thud t-that I heard?" she asked.

"You didn't think it was me, did you?" He offered her a grin. She didn't seem to notice it. A bewildered expression now filled her face.

"I... I didn't think anything of it, at first. I was... reading the letters," she said.

Letters? Alright. He'd take this route but only because after what had just happened, he didn't know what else to say. "Did you find what you were looking for?" he asked.

Her face was now as red as a sunset. *As red as the Virginia soil...* "Yes...and... I..." She moved to the spot on the floor where the box lay. The letters were scattered all about. "Y-you'll have to read them."

He followed after her, but looking away from her for long enough to read anything at this point was the last thing on his mind. "Just tell me," he said.

She took step back from him. Was she still in a fog because of what Zimmer had done? Had she been out of her mind when she had kissed him? Peter's confusion and frustration were mounting. He had been on the verge of declaring himself, but now...

From the parlor threshold, Zimmer was groaning. Peter promptly went to the draperies, yanked one down. "Help me," he said to her.

Guessing his intent, Trudy immediately came forward and began tearing the cloth into strips. Together they quickly and quietly bound Zimmer's hands and feet. The man muttered something unintelligible but remained unconscious.

"What about Mr. O'Neil?" she then asked.

"I've already seen to him."

Finished now with the ugly task, Trudy backed away. Peter told himself her kisses had most definitely been a sign of shock, for now that it was wearing off, she was looking more frightened by the moment. "I don't understand any of this," she said. "These men came to us for help."

"Maybe so," he said, "but it was part of a well-ordered scheme."

"How so?"

"Tom O'Neil was in Larkinsville today. You and I both saw him speak to Johnson."

"Yes, and Johnson gave him something."

Peter nodded. "I didn't know what it was until I searched his pockets just now."

"What did you find?"

"Money. More than what an honest man in these parts would have." He pulled the pile of greenbacks from his pocket, showed her.

"You think they are responsible for our missing supplies?"

"I do. Food and medication fetch high prices around here. I think O'Neil and Zimmer were Johnson's informants. More than likely they discovered the time of our first shipment and then reported it so Johnson might draw away the Federal escorts, allowing them to steal it undetected."

"But who would have told them?"

"Likely someone in complete innocence who was eager to help hungry men."

"The reverend?"

"Perhaps. I don't know. In actuality, it doesn't matter. The future shipments will be kept in strict confidence now. I dare say we have all learned from mistakes."

"Indeed," she said. She absentmindedly touched her cheek. Both were still crimson. "Do you think O'Neil rode to find us after his encounter with Johnson?" she asked. "How could he know where we were headed?"

"I don't think so. More likely, they were using this as their hideout, and our traveling here today was just a case of bad timing. I think O'Neil came to alert Zimmer, to tell him that he had seen us at the telegraph office. They probably planned to overtake us on the road."

"Instead we came straight to them…" She visibly shuddered at the thought. "Thank the Lord that Charlie wasn't with us."

"Yes."

"Zimmer mentioned something about wanting to keep his farm," she then said, "but why would he need to rob to make that happen? Couldn't he apply for a pardon?"

"Perhaps he had done something in the war for which he thought he couldn't be pardoned, or perhaps Johnson lied to him and told him the only way he could keep his land was to buy it back after it was confiscated."

She sighed heavily.

"I don't know for certain, of course, but with a little further digging, now that I know whom to look for, it shouldn't take long to discover the truth."

She nodded affirmatively. The conversation was flowing better than previously. He wanted it to continue that way but he also wanted to get to the bottom of what she had done, why she had kissed him. The sound of approaching riders, however, kept him from doing so.

Peter recognized the steady hoofbeats and thump of canteens as the mark of Federal cavalry. She did, as well. The look of fear returned.

"Stay here," Peter warned, as he again drew out his derringer. He moved to the door, eyed the approaching soldiers through the broken glass. The men looked perfectly at ease. Sliding lazily from their horses, they appeared to be an honest escort detail with no knowledge of any skulduggery hereabouts.

Peter slid the derringer into his frock coat pocket but kept his hand upon the steel just in case. A middle-aged corporal was the first to step through the door.

"Lieutenant Glassman said you were in need of an escort," he said.

The man's name was Anderson and even though the scar across his chin proclaimed him a likely battle veteran, the corporal's eyes widened at the sight of Zimmer lying bound at his feet.

"There is another one just like him in the upstairs bedroom," Peter said.

The man looked taken aback until Peter explained who he was and what had happened, as far as he knew.

"Was the young lady harmed?" Corporal Anderson asked.

"Physically? No. At least, she didn't appear to be."

"Then I'd like to speak with her."

Four other soldiers were now at the door, and Zimmer was beginning to stir. Corporal Anderson ordered two of his men to guard Zimmer. The other two went upstairs to watch over O'Neil.

"If his eyes are open then bring him down," Ander-

son said. The corporal then turned for the parlor. Peter
edged ahead of him.

Trudy was standing in the center of the room, looking as pale and skittish. She had retrieved the letters
and was clutching them and the small box to her chest
when he and Anderson stepped into the room.

"The corporal wants to ask you a few questions,"
Peter told her.

The man removed his kepi and stood at a respectful distance. Even so, she was visibly trembling. Peter
moved beside her, slipped his arm protectively about
her waist. The look she gave him told Peter she welcomed his assurance.

"It's alright," he whispered. "He won't hurt you. I'm
here."

"Mr. Carpenter has already informed me of what
took place, miss," Anderson said, "but I would still like
to hear your story."

"Of c-course," she said. Her voice was wavering but
she dutifully explained.

She told Anderson about reading the letters. Then
she told him Zimmer had crept up upon her and pressed
the sword to her neck. Peter was horrified. He stole a
glance at the back of her neck. Her hair was pinned
into a bun but for a few stray curls which had escaped.
There were no telltale signs of injury on her neck, but
when he looked then at the area about her collar he noticed a small, superficial cut.

She touched it with a trembling hand as she told Anderson, "He looked as though he would run me through.
Then he forced me against the wall."

Peter was outraged, and he tightened his arm about
her. It was a good thing he hadn't witnessed that or

he would have very likely shot the man on sight. She told the corporal what Zimmer had said about the relief shipments.

"He claimed he needed the money to keep his farm."

Peter then explained what he had seen between Johnson and O'Neil in Larkinsville and his theory surrounding those men. How well Corporal Anderson knew Johnson, Peter did not know, but the soldier seemed to agree with Peter's notion.

"My men and I will take your assailants back to the garrison and get to the bottom of this. I'll leave Private Wood and Private Redman, who is presently guarding the horses, here to escort you back to Forest Glade."

"Thank you," Peter said.

Anderson nodded to Trudy, then replaced his kepi. Peter walked him to the foyer, where Anderson subsequently gave orders for O'Neil and Zimmer to be carried out.

"You can expect to hear from me or one of my superiors on this matter," Anderson said.

"Thank you, Corporal," Peter said as he extended his hand, "and please give my regards to Lieutenant Glassman."

Peter waited at the door until the cavalry detail rode away. He then told the remaining soldiers that it would be a few more minutes before he and Trudy were ready to return to Forest Glade. The men simply nodded. They seemed content to wait.

Peter went back to Trudy. She was still standing in the center of the room, still clutching the letters. "I am so sorry," he said. "I never should have left you alone."

She shook her head. "It wasn't your fault," she said. "Besides, you came when I needed you."

"Like you did for me." He offered her another smile, but she simply looked down at the letters in hand. "So what did you discover?" he asked.

She drew in a ragged breath, looking so anxious that he hastened to reassure her. "If you don't want to discuss it now then it can wait."

"N-no," she said. "I n-need to tell you."

"Very well."

"Remember when I told you that Kate wasn't Opal's natural child?"

"Yes." He had to wait several seconds for the rest.

"She's Caroline's."

"What?"

She sorted through the stack of papers she was presently holding. After choosing a particular letter, she handed it to him. "Opal's friend, the one Charlie referred to as Miss Agnes... Her full given name was Agnes Caroline Sewell. *She* married your brother..."

"And then?" Peter asked.

"She...died in childbirth."

He had guessed as much, but even so, Peter was stunned. Trudy pointed to a particular paragraph, but he was having trouble focusing. *My brother's wife is gone*, he thought. *God, have mercy...*

Then he looked at the woman standing beside him. She laid her hand comfortingly upon his arm. Tears rimmed her long eyelashes. "Peter, I am so sorry," she said softly. "I know how much you cared for her."

Something in her voice told him she meant more than just familial condolences. *How much I cared for her?* "What do you mean by that?"

She immediately dropped her hand and took a slow

step back. The color was once again creeping into her face. "She was important to you. You had to find her."

"Yes," Peter replied. "Because she was my brother's wife. Because there was a child. My parents' grand-child. *My* niece. And she deserved—" he caught himself "—she *deserves* a better life than what she'll have now in postwar Virginia."

Then it hit him. Trudy's sister, Elizabeth, had once been engaged to David Wainwright's brother. David had once silently pined for the woman his brother was going to marry.

"Trudy, did you think I was secretly in love with Caroline?"

"I... *Aren't you?*"

His jaw dropped. "How could I pine for a woman I have never even met?" As his mind drifted back to previous conversations, he realized then how she might have arrived at such a conclusion. *I told her I would never marry. I told her I had other responsibilities... Was that why she pulled away, because she thought my heart was already taken? Is there a chance she is still in love with me?*

There was only one way to find out. As Peter stepped closer, she lowered her eyes. "Look at me," he said, in the gentlest voice a cynical newspaperman could muster. "Do you still think I am an arrogant manhandler who belittles your beliefs?"

She slowly raised her face. "Yes."

Peter felt the air leave his lungs. It wasn't quite the answer he'd been hoping for.

"But I have always believed there is more to your character than that."

"You do?" His heart beat a little faster.

"Yes. You are changing. I can see it. And…I understand now why you thought me naive."

"I don't think that anymore," he said. "In fact, I think what you have is worth keeping."

"What is worth keeping?" She asked.

"Hope," he said. "Faith. The children need that. You need that. *I* need that. And you were right. God does involve Himself in our everyday affairs. How else can you explain Kate? How else do you explain Opal wanting you to gather the letters that would reveal the full story?"

Was that a flicker of a smile? He was aching to touch her but held back. "Do you still find me infuriating?"

She flushed. "Only at times…"

At that, he chuckled. Then he asked what he most wanted to know. "Do you think my physical infirmity in any way disqualifies me from being an effective father for those children?"

"Those?" she said.

"Opal wanted them to remain together."

"Yes," Trudy agreed. "Then you will take them both?"

"Not so fast," he said. "We will get to that in a moment. You didn't answer my question."

Her brow furrowed slightly. "About your leg?"

"Yes."

"No, it does not disqualify you at all. You have proven yourself capable of being a strong defender more than once. I know the children will be safe with you."

He could see it then in her eyes, at long last, and his joy, his pride swelled so that he felt as though he would burst. He couldn't help himself. "Now, one last question, and I must remind you how highly I value an honest, straightforward answer." He cleared his throat and then studied her momentarily as if this were an office interview. "Do you love me?" he asked.

The color in her face increased. Her green eyes widened. He knew then he couldn't keep this mock interrogation going any longer. "I am asking because *I love you* and I want to *marry you*. I want us to raise Kate and Charlie *together*."

"Y-you c-can't be serious?"

Peter was having a difficult time keep up the stern employer facade. "Oh, I assure you I am most definitely serious," he said.

The look of disbelief on her face, however, remained.

"I suppose I shall have to convince you properly," he said. With that he closed the remaining space between them. Slowly, gently he cupped her face, pressed his lips to hers. This time neither of them drew back.

Chapter Eighteen

The evening sun had dipped below the Alleghenies so that by the time the wagon started back for Forest Glade, the sky was awash in purple, pink and gold. Yet it was hardly the setting for the ending of an idyllic novel.

The Federal soldiers trotted a few paces ahead, scanning the surroundings for any indication of mischief, and the hero and heroine were both physically and emotionally spent. His recently injured ankle was swelling again and her stitched hand was aching from clenching it tightly. The road was rutted and rocky and every now and then it threw them off balance. Still, Trudy nestled contentedly against Peter's arm.

"What exactly changed you?" she asked him.

"Humph," he said. "Well, I suppose it was the fact that you no longer wanted me."

She raised her head, looked at him incredulously. Obviously he would never lose his penchant for brutal honesty—but then again, she hoped he wouldn't. That was part of what she had come to love about him. "Then it is to my credit that I made you think such," she quipped.

He chuckled heartily. "Indeed. That was fortunate." He paused. "No, not *fortunate*. That isn't the right word."

"Oh?" She had an idea of where this might be going and she was right.

"Which leads me to the answer to the question I believe you were actually asking…"

"Faith?"

He nodded. Turning his eyes back to the darkening road, he then said, "My belief in God, in Christ, was always there. Although at times, especially of late, it lay latent."

"Because of the things you had seen of the world? The war?"

He nodded once more. "You start looking at the circumstances around you, the evil, the continual suffering, and you begin to believe either there is no God, or if there is, then He doesn't care about us."

"Daniel's death hit you terribly hard, didn't it?"

"Yes. So did Matthew's, and all the others, all of the faceless names I printed in the casualty lists. I kept thinking—" he glanced at her again "—I could have been an officer had it not been for my club foot."

"Is that why you don't want people calling you 'sir'?" she asked.

He sighed. "That's it exactly. I felt I failed to do my duty, by my country, by my family…"

"But you didn't fail," Trudy insisted. "You've done everything you can to make things better. The stories you have published. The former slaves, like Robert, who you are trying to help. Coming here to care for starving Confederates… You have done your duty to your family, as well. You found your brother's child."

"*You* found her," he said, "with God's help."

"Two are better than one?" she asked, quoting Ecclesiastes.

He smiled at her. Although it was a tired smile, it was also genuine and heartfelt. "And what was that next part? 'A threefold cord is not quickly broken'?"

"Yes."

"You know it wasn't until the other night when I was with Charlie that I realized my utter need for Divine intervention."

"How so?" she asked.

"I was holding him, like I remember my father doing with me, and I realized no matter how much I wanted to, no matter how hard I tried, I couldn't keep him safe, or protect him from life's disappointments. All I could do was put my trust in someone who could."

His jaw tightened with emotion. Trudy had never seen this side of Peter before, this vulnerability. It was endearing.

"I'm sorry," he said. "You must think me very weak."

"On the contrary," she said. "I think it shows great strength."

His eyebrow arched.

"It takes great strength, great trust to place oneself in the hands of someone more powerful than you."

"You amaze me," he said.

She blushed at his compliment. "And you lifted my hope when I needed it most," she said.

All seriousness passed as he then grinned at her. It was almost roguish, but Trudy found it incredibly handsome. "You mean when I asked you to marry me?"

"Yes," she said in a mockingly playful tone. "That was it exactly."

Leaning over, Peter kissed the top of her head. Trudy felt the warmth of his touch all the way down to her toes. "I love you," she said. "I don't think I told you that earlier."

"Thank you," he said. "I *was* wondering…"

With a shared laugh, and a feeling of complete security in God's sovereignty, Trudy snuggled happily, contentedly against her fiancé for the remainder of their journey.

It was dark by the time they pulled into the churchyard. Privates Redman and Wood, along with Robert, were kind enough to see to the horses while Peter edged his way from the driver's box. His ankles, his legs were aching, but still he turned to clasp Trudy by the waist and assist her to the ground.

Mrs. Mackay, who'd met them on the porch, was the first to comment on the change. "Well, the two of you seem to be in fine spirits," she said with a grin.

Peter couldn't help but offer one back, even though he had to limp his way up the stairs with the assistance of his bride to be. Dr. Mackay met them, as well.

"Looks like a pail of cold water and rest are in order," he said.

Peter nodded, but all in good time. "We have much to tell you." He had meant concerning Zimmer and O'Neil, but the couple took his words to mean something else entirely. Even the Scotsman was now grinning.

"But first," Trudy said, "where is Charlie?"

"I'm here!" a boisterous voice called, and the boy came bounding toward them. He ran headlong into them both since Peter and Trudy were standing side by side. "Did you bring Pa's sword?" he asked.

Ugh. That sword. Though it was of obvious senti-
mental value, Peter was definitely going to hold it in
safekeeping for a while, at least until Charlie was much
older. In fact, he had asked Robert to take it tonight.
There had already been enough excitement for one day.

"We did," Peter said, "and I will show it to you later.
I promise."

Charlie's lip pushed forward in a slight pout, but
then he looked at Trudy. "Did you bring something
for Kate?"

"Yes, I did. Some very special letters."

"Are there any special letters for me?"

Trudy bent and kissed the top of his head. "I brought
tintypes of your mother and father for you."

As Dr. Mackay and his wife slipped back inside the
church, Peter couldn't help but think that it was a pity
Kate would have no likeness of her own mother when
she grew older. *But there are plenty of images of her
father, especially on my parents' mantel.* He smiled to
himself then, thinking of how joyfully his mother and
father would receive these two young children.

Trudy looked at him and smiled, conscious of the secret they shared between them. On their journey they
had discussed when to tell Charlie the news of their en-
gagement and his pending move to Baltimore. He appeared to already be anticipating such.

"Am I going to live with you?" he asked Trudy. Then
he turned to Peter. "Or you?"

The adults exchanged glances. Peter seemed to be
waiting for her consent. Trudy nodded.

"Well," he said to Charlie as he leaned forward upon
his cane, "it just so happens…both."

Charlie blinked, then looked back at Trudy.

"Mr. Carpenter has asked me to become his wife," she said. "He wants to take care of me, you and Kate."

"In the same house?"

"Yes," Trudy said.

Charlie turned again to Peter. "So you *will* be my new pa?"

"Yes."

The boy chewed his lip for a moment, thinking on the matter. "Will you take me to see your newspaper?"

Peter smothered a grin. If that was the criterion on which Charlie was going to base his decision, then this edition had already been put to bed. "Of course I will," he said.

At that, Charlie flung himself against Peter's legs and squeezed them tightly.

"I knew it!" Emily said when Trudy told her the details the following morning as they collected fresh water from the pump. "I knew he was going to give in eventually. I saw how he looked at you, but for some reason he just kept fighting it."

"You mean like Evan did with you?"

Emily grinned. "Those two are cut from the same cloth," she said, "stubborn, independent, prideful—"

"—but utterly handsome and, deep down, honorable, good men?"

"Exactly."

They giggled.

"When is the wedding to take place?" Emily then asked.

"As soon as we return to Baltimore. Although Peter has asked Reverend Webb if he will come and conduct the ceremony. I don't believe Reverend Perry will mind."

"Not at all," Emily said, "and if I know our preacher as well as I think I do, he will probably be the first to come forward to help organize further relief for Reverend Webb's community."

"That was probably Peter's intent," Trudy said.

They shared another laugh as they returned to the church. They delivered their pails of drinking water to Mrs. Webb's station.

"Look," the preacher's wife said with a smile.

Trudy's soon-to-be husband had confined himself to his desk today, this time with Charlie *and* Kate on his lap. Her heart swelled at the sight. The boy was busy filling a sheet of writing paper. The baby was steadily trying to eat hers.

"Don't you think she is a little young for the newspaper business?" Trudy teased as she claimed the soggy, crumpled paper from Kate's chubby hands and then took her into her arms.

"One is never too young to start learning," Peter said, giving Charlie's dark hair a tousle.

The sound of riders approaching caught Trudy's attention. She moved to the doorway, looked out. She had learned to recognize rank from her time in the military hospital. "It's a lieutenant," she said, "and several escorts."

Peter urged Charlie from his lap and then came to where she stood. "It's Glassman," he said.

Trudy watched the young lieutenant dismount and walk toward the church steps. He greeted Peter and nodded politely at Trudy.

"What brings you here, Lieutenant?" Peter asked.

The officer removed his kepi, then his gloves. There were sweat stains on his blue wool coat. It had been a long, hot ride. "News, for one," he said, "and an apology."

"An apology?" Peter said.

"Yes. For not scrutinizing Johnson more closely," he said. "Word arrived this morning from my fellow officer down in Lexington. The man you deposited in his care…"

"You mean my unknown assailant?"

Glassman nodded. "He started talking."

"Oh?" Peter said.

"You were right. Johnson was more interested in lining his own pockets than growing the local economy."

Trudy glanced at her betrothed. She could tell by the look on his face that he took no pleasure in having been proved right this time. People had suffered.

Lieutenant Glassman continued, "He employed Zimmer, O'Neil, Jones and Oliver—that's your assailant's name—along with two men from my own garrison to steal supplies."

"And the land?" Peter asked. "Zimmer's farm?"

"Again, it was as you suspected. Johnson intended to purchase the men's farms when they were officially confiscated. The properties lie back-to-back and together make a considerable spread that is well-watered, for the Shenandoah runs straight through them both. I don't think Johnson ever intended to allow the men to buy back the property, no matter how much morphine they stole."

"What about Mrs. Zimmer?" Trudy asked. "She was here yesterday morning but no one has seen her since."

"I spoke with her personally this morning," Glassman said as he slapped his riding gloves against his leg.

Dust scattered. "Apparently she knew nothing about any of this and as for her husband…well, he won't hang, but he will be spending a good deal of time locked away."

Oh dear, Trudy thought. "Does she know this?"

"She does, and she has asked for permission to travel to Savannah to rejoin her family. I'm going to send her."

"That's good of you," Peter said.

The lieutenant shrugged. "It is the least I can do. After all, I have a responsibility to the people of this valley. Peace won't be maintained if we don't solve the problems caused by this war."

"Well said." And in the space of a heartbeat Peter added, "May I quote you on that?"

Glassman chuckled. "You may, for what it's worth…"

"Lieutenant," Trudy then said, "we have fresh, cold water. Won't you and your men come inside and rest a bit?"

"Thank you, ma'am." He motioned to the other soldiers. "Oh," he then said as he reached into the right pocket of his frock coat. "I was at the telegraph office this morning. I took the liberty of picking up your wires. Thought I'd save you a trip into town."

"Thank you," Peter said. While he opened the missives, Trudy ushered the soldiers inside. Dr. Mackay took to chatting with the lieutenant while Mrs. Webb doled out water for his men.

"Tru?" she heard Peter call.

Shifting Kate, she turned and met Peter at the threshold. He was limping again. "You should rest," she encouraged him.

"I will," he said, "but take a look at this. I don't think this message is exactly what it seems."

He handed her the telegram. It was from David.

"Prayers answered," it read. *"Bundle of blessing arrive Wednesday. Sam to bring details."*

"I know you said Elizabeth is with child," Peter said, "but a delivery so soon? That can't be correct."

"It's not," Trudy confirmed. She chewed on the words of the message for a few seconds. *Bundle of blessing?* What could David mean? Then it hit her. "It's a shipment of supplies!"

"What? I told him not to send anything else until I wired that it was safe to do so."

"Evidently he thought we couldn't wait that long. Hence the coded message. Apparently Sam Ward, a friend of ours, is personally overseeing the trip and bringing a detail of soldiers."

Peter laughed heartily, happily. Obviously this was one time he was glad an employee had disobeyed his directives. "Apparently soldiers aren't the only thing Sam is bringing."

"What do you mean?"

He held up another telegram. Kate reached for it but failed to claim it as Peter pulled it back. "This one is from Councilman Henry Nash."

"My friend Rebekah's husband?"

"It seems his wife saw the notice in my paper concerning Robert. They employ a cook who fits the description Robert provided."

Trudy's heart beat faster. "You mean Hannah?"

"So he thinks. Mr. Ward will come with a letter from the woman as well as a train ticket to Baltimore should Robert choose to claim it."

She felt as though she was going to burst with joy. "Oh, God, thank You! Thank You! And Wednesday?"

she said, remembering David's missive. "That is to-morrow!"

"Indeed. We must organize a party to ride to Mount Jackson to meet the train."

She could see he had the bit between his teeth. She couldn't blame him. So did she.

"I'll tell Lieutenant Glassman," Peter said. "Then I'll find Robert."

"*I'll* find Robert," Trudy insisted. "You must rest. After all, Henry and Rebekah are two of my dearest friends. I must share their news."

He grinned at her. Then, glancing about to make certain no one was looking, he placed a quick kiss on her lips. Kate reached for his face when they parted as if she, too, wished for one. Peter obliged her, then said to Trudy, "Make certain that you invite the Nash family to our wedding."

Epilogue

Baltimore, Maryland
April 1866

The scene was more chaotic than a newsroom when a story was breaking. Peter stood with his back against the wall and took in the view. His wife and five of her closest friends, along with several of their additional friends, were clustered about a large oak table in the Maryland Institute Hall. Toddlers were teetering about the room, and some children younger than that were crawling about their mother's skirts.

Peter spied Charlie just to Trudy's right. He was lying on his belly, scribbling furiously on the large sheet of paper in front of him. Noting Peter, he waved excitedly, pushed to his feet and came running.

"I'm making a sign," he announced.

"You are?" Peter scooped him up into his arms. The event Charlie was planning to advertise, the one the women were organizing here tonight, was a Relief Fair. Trudy, along with Emily Mackay, had patterned the event after a very successful wartime effort here in Baltimore that had raised thousands of dollars for Federal hospitals and prisoner-of-war camps. Peter remembered it well. He had sent David and Elizabeth, along with several other members of his staff, to cover the story.

This fair was different, though, in that it was exclusively designed for Southern relief. The money raised would be distributed throughout the former Confederate states, with a considerable portion going to the Shenandoah Valley. The idea had certainly pleased Trudy's brother, George. The former prisoner of war was finally home.

Though this event was sponsored by the Ladies Southern Relief Association, it was hardly limited to women. Beginning with Peter, Trudy had enlisted the service of practically every man she could. He and Charlie, of course, were in charge of publication. Henry Nash had convinced the city to offer this meeting hall. Sam Ward, a history teacher and the husband of Trudy's friend Julia, was lining up guest lecturers, and David Wainwright and Dr. Mackay were soliciting donations from their former military contacts. Peter had been pleasantly surprised at just how many Federal soldiers were willing to give aid to their former enemies.

God does answer prayer, he thought. *My wife has certainly shown me that.*

Trudy had even managed to enlist one man who had thus far avoided matrimony but looked now to be steadily proceeding toward it. Edward Stanton, a one-armed former Confederate officer who had remarkable skill in carpentry, was crafting the fair booths. He'd been in a close working relationship with Trudy's only remaining unmarried friend, Sally Hastings. Sally had been conveniently placed in charge of decorating the booths that Edward was crafting.

Peter chuckled to himself. *She's still scheming*, he thought.

"What's so funny?" Charlie asked.

"Nothing all that important. Where's your baby sister?"

"Over there with Andrew." Peter followed the general wave of Charlie's hand to find Kate, now almost a year and a half, stacking a set of wooden blocks with Dr. Mackay's son. "I'm watching them," Charlie said.

"You are? Well, good for you. I'd best let you get back to them." The boy slid from his perch and scampered away.

Peter looked again at his wife. Trudy was assessing assignments like a seasoned editor and he took great pleasure in watching her work.

"What about the flowers?" she asked Rebekah Nash.

"Ready to go," the woman replied.

"Good, but are you certain you have enough help? I don't want you under any strain."

The councilman's wife laughed demurely. "You sound like Henry. I assure you, I am fine. The baby isn't due for another month and Hannah and Robert have me well looked after."

Listening, Peter smiled. Robert Smith had at long last been reunited with his beloved wife and his nearly grown daughter, Sadie. All three were employed by the Nash family.

Satisfied, Trudy moved on. "Baked items?"

"I've more than enough for two tables," Julia Ward replied.

"We could always set up another station," Elizabeth offered. Her three-month-old daughter, Noelle, lay asleep on her lap.

Trudy considered the idea for a moment. "What do you think, Em?" she asked.

Mrs. Mackay studied the hall diagram in front of her. "I think there is enough room. Just to be certain, though, I'll check with Edward."

"Good," Trudy said. "Sally, that will mean another booth to decorate. Have you enough bunting?"

"If not, I can make more."

"Wonderful. Thank you."

Peter observed then that as Trudy looked at her notes, she was stifling a yawn. *Alright, Tru, it's time to call it a night. You will wear yourself down.*

As if reading his thoughts, she laid aside the list she had been holding. "Well, that looks to be everything for now. We can cover the rest at our next meeting. Thank you all so very much for coming."

As the ladies began to scatter, Peter approached the table.

"You're here," Trudy said with a wide smile. "I thought you would still be at press."

"We finished early."

Kate came tottering over, hands in the air. "Up, Pa!" she insisted. Peter did not hesitate. The little girl grinned as she threw her arms around his neck. "Love," she said.

"And I love you too, little one," Peter said as he rubbed Kate's back. He then looked back at his wife. "Soon there will be another one to hold."

Trudy immediately flushed, her face turning as red as her sunset hair. As she glanced frantically about, Peter couldn't help but grin. She was especially beautiful when she was flustered. "How did you know that?" she whispered. "I wasn't going to tell you until after the fair."

"Oh yes," he said, "I know. You held off on breaking the story because you knew I'd hound you about getting enough rest."

Her smile said she was guilty as charged. "I suppose turnabout is fair play," she then said. "I have certainly said that to you plenty of times."

"Indeed you have, and as for how did I know? Well, let's examine the facts... You've eaten almost no breakfast for the past two weeks and you're spending much more time in the water closet then usual..."

She flushed even further. "Oh Peter, hush. Those aren't exactly newsworthy details."

"They are to me."

The smile she gave him then practically took away his breath. "I am so glad you think so," she said.

Realizing they were now alone, except for the children, Peter drew his wife close and kissed her. If someone had told him a year ago he'd be a happily married man with a family, he never would have believed them. God, however, had other plans. Peter Carpenter had been surprised by love.

* * * * *

Dear Reader,

Thank you so much for choosing *Handpicked Family*, my final book with Love Inspired Historical. Writing this Civil War series has been a wonderful journey, one I could not have completed without the help and support of many people. I am so thankful to my family for their prayers and loving encouragement, and also my church family and friends for their enthusiasm. I am especially appreciative of my extraordinary editor Elizabeth Mazer, who was willing to take a chance on me, all of my readers who picked up one of my books, and Wanda Lee and Melinda, my faithful pen pals, whose kind letters always arrived just when I needed an encouraging word! Most of all I am grateful to the God of Heaven and Earth who holds each of us in the palm of His hand.

Writing may require solitude but it is hardly a solitary process. Each of you has played a crucial role in the crafting of my stories and in my daily life. For that I will forever be thankful! May your lives be blessed as much as you have blessed mine!

I hope you enjoyed Peter and Trudy's adventure. For information on any of my future writing endeavors, please follow me on Twitter @_SFarrington.

Until we meet again,
Shannon Farrington

We hope you enjoyed this story from
Love Inspired® Historical.

Love Inspired® Historical is coming to
an end but be sure to discover more
inspirational stories to warm your heart
from **Love Inspired®** and
Love Inspired® Suspense!

Love Inspired stories show that
faith, forgiveness and hope have the power
to lift spirits and change lives—always.

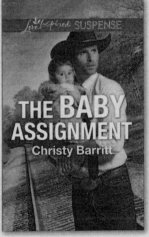

Look for six new romances every month
from **Love Inspired®** and
Love Inspired® Suspense!

Get 4 FREE REWARDS!

We'll send you 2 FREE Books plus 2 FREE Mystery Gifts.

Counting on the Cowboy
Shannon Taylor Vannatter

Reunited by a Secret Child
Leigh Bale

Love Inspired® books feature contemporary inspirational romances with Christian characters facing the challenges of life and love.

FREE
Value Over **$20**

Her family's future in the balance, can Clara Fisher find a way to save her home?

Read on for a sneak preview of
HIS NEW AMISH FAMILY *by* Patricia Davids,
the next book in **THE AMISH BACHELORS** *miniseries,*
available in July 2018 from Love Inspired.

Paul Bowman leaned forward in his seat to get a good look at the farm as they drove up. Both the barn and the house were painted white and appeared in good condition. He made a quick mental appraisal of the equipment he saw, then jotted down numbers in a small notebook he kept in his pocket.

"What is she doing here?" The anger in his client Ralph's voice shocked Paul.

He followed Ralph's line of sight and spied an Amish woman sitting on a suitcase on the front porch of the house. She wore a simple pale blue dress with an apron of matching material and a black cape thrown back over her shoulders. Her wide-brimmed black traveling bonnet hid her hair. She looked hot, dusty and tired. She held a girl of about three or four on her lap. The child clung tightly to her mother. A boy a few years older leaned against the door behind her holding a large calico cat.

"Who is she?" Paul asked.

"That is my annoying cousin, Clara Fisher." Ralph opened his car door and got out. Paul did the same.

The woman glared at both men. "Why are there padlocks on the doors, Ralph? Eli never locked his home."

"They are there to keep unwanted visitors out. What are you doing here?" Ralph demanded.

"I live here. May I have the keys, please? My children and I are weary."

Ralph's eyebrows snapped together in a fierce frown. "What do you mean you live here?"

"What part did you fail to understand, Ralph? I… live…here," she said slowly.

Ralph's face darkened with anger. Paul had to turn away to keep from laughing.

She might look small, but she was clearly a woman to be reckoned with. She reminded him of an angry mama cat all fluffed up and spitting-mad. He rubbed a hand across his mouth to hide a grin. His movement caught her attention, and she pinned her deep blue gaze on him. "Who are you?"

He stopped smiling. "My name is Paul Bowman. I'm an auctioneer. Mr. Hobson has hired me to get this property ready for sale."

Don't miss
HIS NEW AMISH FAMILY by Patricia Davids,
available July 2018 wherever
Love Inspired® books and ebooks are sold.

www.LoveInspired.com

LIEXP0618

Looking for inspiration in tales
of hope, faith and heartfelt romance?

Check out **Love Inspired**® and
Love Inspired® **Suspense** books!

New books available every month!

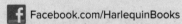

CONNECT WITH US AT:

Harlequin.com/Community

f Facebook.com/HarlequinBooks

🐦 Twitter.com/HarlequinBooks

📷 Instagram.com/HarlequinBooks

📌 Pinterest.com/HarlequinBooks

ReaderService.com

Love Inspired®

LIGENRE2018

Inspirational Romance to Warm Your Heart and Soul

Join our social communities to connect with other readers who share your love!

Sign up for the Love Inspired newsletter at **www.LoveInspired.com** to be the first to find out about upcoming titles, special promotions and exclusive content.

CONNECT WITH US AT:

Harlequin.com/Community

 Facebook.com/LoveInspiredBooks

 Twitter.com/LoveInspiredBks

LISOCIAL2017